ABOUT T. .. AUTHOR

Carol Westron is a successful short story writer turned novelist. Fascinated by psychology and history, Carol writes crime novels set both in contemporary and Victorian times. Her books are predominantly set in the South of England, where she now lives.

Author's note: No cats were harmed during the writing of this book.

The
Terminal
Velocity
of Cats

Carol Westron

To Nina
a great writer & friend
love
    Carol
    xx

pentangle
press

ISBN 978 1 48499 104 6

Book design by The Art of Communication www.artofcomms.co.uk
First published in the UK 2013 by Pentangle Press www.pentanglepress.com

To my family with love and gratitude.

To my husband, Peter; daughter, Jo; sons, Paul and Alan;
daughter-in-laws, Claire and Lyndsey;
and my grandsons, Jack, Adam, Oliver and Henry.

Thanks for always being there with your love and support
and laughter. You never fail to remind me
of what truly matters in life.

Acknowledgements

Thanks to The Art of Communication for spending the time, trouble and talent that created the cover I had been dreaming of and for laying out the book.

An enormous thank you to my son, Paul Westron, for all the information about archaeology and for the inspirational first line for this book. Thanks also to Paul for the conversation that helped create the title.

Especial thanks for their on-going help to my partners in crime in Pentangle Press, Christine Hammacott and Wendy Metcalfe, superb writers, true friends and great colleagues. To Eileen Robertson, another good friend, fine writer, and the only person who totally gets my sense of humour. To Jane Finnis, good drinking buddy, dear writing friend, ever willing supporter, and creator of my favourite ever detective, Aurelia Marcella.

Thanks for years of support and friendship to Catherine King, Della Galton and all the Dunford Novelists. To Lizzie Hayes of Mystery People, a steadfast advocate of crime and mystery fiction, and to my fellow Deadly Dames: Joan Moules, Nicola Slade, Charlie Cochrane and Eileen Robertson. To Barbara Large, creator of The Winchester Annual Writers' Festival where I have gained so much inspiration, and to Sally Spedding, whose workshops have been the highlight of my writing year and whose friendship has so often supported me. To Richard and Helen Salsbury for years of writing friendship and fun, and my sister-in-law, Loree Westron, who loves words as much as I do. To all my good friends at the Society of Women Writers and Journalists. To Keir Cheetham and the members of Penultimate and Havant Writers.

Last but not least, thank you to Tails the cat for his patience in several photo sessions, with gratitude that he neither bit nor scratched me, even though the provocation was immense.

Chapter 1

"In what other job do you get to drive round all day with a dead man's toenails in your van?" As she spoke, Mia had a nasty thought. She cast a quick glance at her police mobile in its hands-free stand. It was one thing to swear to yourself when your plans had been over-turned, quite another to forget to turn off your phone so your senior officer could listen to every word. It was okay, instinct had served her well, and she'd keyed off.

She'd spent the morning in a sordid squat, collecting evidence of a drug overdose. The coroner would require proof of long-term drug abuse, so she had to give the corpse a final pedicure.

She turned her van and headed towards Bridge Road. There was a CID team waiting for her opinion on a pit of bones, discovered on a building site. She was the only archaeologist in her Scene of Crimes team and was often asked to check out suspicious bones, which, fortunately, usually turned out to be animal remains or a historic burial. It depended on her whether the detectives swung into a full-scale investigation or declared it a false alarm and moved on to other jobs. Either way, money was being wasted until she arrived, so there was no time to stop off and lodge the evidence from her last case.

As she parked behind the empty police vehicles, Mia thought Bridge Road looked dismally uninviting. It had been raining all day and, even with the van's heater going full blast, she felt chilled through. The road appeared deserted. She scanned the area and planned her route to the crime scene before she unlocked her door. Being watchful was part of the job but nowadays she'd moved into hyper-vigilance. Ledleigh had always been a quiet, south-coast town and the recent murders of three young women had traumatised the whole community. Police officer or civilian, no woman felt safe.

She grabbed her SOCO bag, jumped out of the van, clicked the central locking and sped down a narrow alleyway between the houses.

The back gardens were a tangle of undergrowth, dying back for winter, but the end garden was alive with colour and movement as the cops went about their business. The contractors' digger had been in action and the ground was muddy and trenched.

DI Oliver Sutton came to meet her. He looked harassed. He'd only been in the district a couple of weeks and she'd never worked with him but she'd seen him around the Station. She knew he was fair, although at the moment his hair was dark with rain. It was a point in his favour that he shifted the scowl from his face to greet her. "Constable Trent? Thanks for coming. We've got a situation here that needs your skills."

Two plus points, not many senior officers said 'thank you.' "What have we got, sir?"

"Building work started here today. The archaeologist employed on watching brief spotted what he claims are two human bones amongst a lot of pet ones, so he called us in."

"And the construction guys are kicking off so you need an expert to give you the go ahead? With any luck it'll be historical. This area was the site of a 14th Century plague pit." She pointed towards the scrubland that divided the coast from the gardens of Bridge Road.

"The Black Death?" queried Sutton.

That surprised her; most cops knew nothing about history and cared less. "Yes, I helped excavate it, about twelve years ago."

She examined the tray of bones he'd indicated. "Two vertebrae and a rib bone." Definitely human. They were in good condition and it seemed unlikely they were part of an ancient burial.

She suited up and entered the tent that shielded the remains. Her first gentle excavations revealed only small

10

mammal bones but the texture of the soil warned of recent decomposition of a much larger creature. "DI Sutton, come here please."

"What have you got?" asked Sutton.

"I've got a skull with modern dentistry. Which means you've got a Scene of Crime."

She saw his face grow tense. "Is it just the one body?"

"Only one human that I've found so far. And, at a rough estimate, six or seven cats."

He stared at her. "What is this? Tell me it's not some sort of weird, ritual killing?"

"I don't know." Both her careers had left her certain of only one thing: there were no limits to the evil people could do to one another. "If it's anything major it'll get passed to DCI Craig."

"He's got enough on his hands already."

That was undeniable. Ledleigh didn't boast a Serious Crimes Team of its own, so the senior officer in CID was working with the team brought in to investigate the three murders.

"I want to know what we're dealing with before I yell for reinforcements," continued Sutton. "That's why I asked for you."

"I'll get working. But I ought to warn you, I'm due off duty so I'm on over-time." The current situation meant all the SOCOs in the county were working flat out.

"So watch my back when it comes to the money men? Thanks for the heads up."

"No problem." Mia thought she must be getting soft. This guy was a DI before he was thirty; that made him tough and clever. Unless he had influential relatives. In either case, he didn't need her looking out for him. "I'll need more SOCOs."

He nodded agreement. "I'll phone your Office Manager."

"Chantelle's on call out this afternoon."

"Oh, right." Evidently he'd already encountered

11

Chantelle. "She's a bit difficult, isn't she?"

"You could say that." Although those who had to work with her every day would put it somewhat stronger. "It would be useful if Inspector Mayfield could spare Adam as well. We need to process the scene before the rain washes everything away." A vigorous downpour rocked the tent. "I'll move the skull as soon as I've finished my photos."

"Won't the pathologist want to see it in situ?"

"There's no hope of that. The diggers have undermined the stability of the ground."

"Okay. You sort here and I'll check the other gardens for signs of soil disturbance."

"You know what to look for?"

He pulled a wry face. "Yeah."

Mia realised he'd done the shallow grave hunt before. She'd walked it many times herself and knew there was no more soul-curdling, dismal job in the world.

She worked solidly at cleaning up the scene and taking soil samples, photographing and recording as she went. The consistency of the soil took her back to the mass graves she'd excavated. Western archaeologists were often called to the sites of massacres. It paid well but no-one could cope with more than three months at a time. The memory stiffened her neck and shoulders and she shrugged to loosen up.

Twenty minutes later an uniformed constable peered into the tent. "You ready to have lights put in yet? The DI told me to get it sorted."

Another bonus point for Sutton. He didn't believe the CSI television myth that SOCOs worked best by torchlight. It was early afternoon but the dismal weather made it dark inside the tent. "That's great, but suit up and make sure you stay on the boards."

"Could you check out something for me?" Sutton spoke from outside the tent but, from his tone, she knew this was more than a casual request.

She went to join him and swore as a deluge from the tent flap hit the back of her neck. Sutton waited while she stripped off her coverall and pulled up the hood of her waterproof jacket.

"What's the problem, sir?"

"It's over here, next door." Again she caught the tension in his voice.

He led her across the garden and over the remains of what must have been a substantial brick wall. The contractors hadn't got to this garden yet, so it was still a jungle with its rampage of untended plants. This house appeared in better condition than its neighbour and had an ornate conservatory that looked ludicrous tacked on to an urban, terraced house.

"I'm sure there's some sort of shallow pit, bigger than the one you've been working on."

"Yeah, you're right." There was a large area with a different pattern of plant growth than the surrounding ground.

"Your mates have arrived," said Sutton.

"That's good." She was glad to see Adam was with Chantelle. They made a strange pair, both dressed in black SOCO uniforms with CSI in white upon the sleeves. Adam in his mid-twenties, tall, black and lightly built; Chantelle close to forty, small and blonde. She wore more make up than was appropriate for the job, but no-one would mention it. Chantelle was too fond of making harassment complaints. "I'll go and sort them out."

She briefed them and left them to work on the original pit of bones.

When she returned a new tent was in place.

"I'll put in a test pit and go down deep and narrow to see what I can find."

The soil felt different in this pit and she was less convinced it was a burial ground. There was no reason she could define, just years of experience whispering in her ear. Soon she got her answer and called softly, "DI Sutton, could you come in here please?"

He was there within seconds. "What have you got?"

"A few small bones."

"Human or cat?"

"These are fish bones."

"What the hell?" Sutton's voice rose in frustration.

"I've hit concrete at five foot down, so I'd guess it's the remains of a fishpond."

She saw his face tighten. "Thank you. I'm sorry to have wasted your time."

"Now we've started, I need to check a bit further just to make sure."

"I'm aware of that." His controlled rage was scarier than if he'd shouted. "It's my fault. The builders have probably got plans of this site. I should have talked to them myself instead of relying on those losers." He nodded towards two of his detective constables.

Mia didn't know what to say. She felt as angry as he did about the waste of SOCO resources when they were needed for a major murder case.

He left and she recorded the scene and bagged and tagged the fish bones.

When she emerged from the tent, Sutton was in the original garden, talking to the guy in charge of the construction site. Sutton was tall but the other man was larger in every way. She strolled across to stand next to the DI and find out what the builder had to say.

"Yeah, I remember who lived in the end house. Old girl with hundreds of bloody cats. Funny old thing, she was. Always givin' sweets to us kids. Me mum used to belt us and tell us not to take stuff off strangers. Not that I fancied 'em, even the sweets seemed to smell of cats. And as for the old girl herself…" He made a fanning gesture with his hand which wafted his tobacco and beer laden breath towards them. Mia wished she'd kept her distance.

"This is Dennis Plummer," said Sutton. "He used to

live along the road when he was a kid. He says there was a fishpond in that garden."

"We weren't allowed near it. The old bloke who lived there was a miserable old git. It got like a challenge to catch things and throw 'em in for the fish to eat. Real ferocious them fish were. Me cousin found a bird with a broken leg, they didn't half go for that."

Mia controlled her disgust and said, "Probably Koi carp. They can turn carnivorous."

"So who are you, darlin'?" Dennis gave her a leering once-over. "And, more important, what you doin' tonight?"

"This officer is in charge of the forensic side of our investigation." Sutton intervened. "Do you remember the name of the old lady? Mr Plummer, pay attention please!"

Reclaimed from the mental striptease he was blatantly performing, the builder tore his gaze away from Mia. "Nah. It was a long time ago."

"How long ago are we talking about?" asked Sutton.

"What?"

"How long since the old lady lived here?"

"Well, what I'm talkin' about was thirty-five years ago. I was twelve when Mum moved us nearer the centre of town. She never liked bein' too far from the decent sized shops. But the old girl was here right up 'til the last five years. She was the last one to leave. Me cousin could tell you more about it. He convinced her to move out." He looked over his shoulder and bellowed, "Mike, what was the old girl who lived here called?"

There was a brief silence, then one of the men said, "Lucy Logan," and turned away.

"Don't mind him," said Dennis. "He's kinda shy. Yeah, I remember now, Loony Lucy that's what me and me mates called her."

"Do you know where she went after she left here?" Sutton's voice was pleasant, which annoyed Mia. She was thinking how much she'd like to concrete Dennis Plummer

15

into the foundations of the new building destined for this site.

"No idea. Nowhere would want her, not with all them cats. Chances are she topped the cats, then herself. That's it, case closed. Now can we get back to work?"

"How did you know they were cat bones?" demanded Sutton.

"I dig up enough pets' cemeteries in back gardens. I could be a flippin' expert witness on pet bones. And fish ponds. Me and the boys were havin' a laugh at you lot wastin' your time buggerin' round with that one." He leered at Mia. "Mind, it was a bonus, gettin' you over here to work at close quarters."

Anger skewered through her. This bastard thought it was funny to waste their time. She met his hot gaze, then deliberately disengaged from visual conflict. Instead she looked him over, coldly and analytically. He was around the mid-forties and his shaven head sported less stubble than his unshaven jowl. He had powerful muscles, apart from his beer gut. Despite the icy rain he wasn't wearing a coat, and his shirtsleeves were rolled up revealing a tattoo on his left forearm, with the name Helen woven into the intricate swirls.

Clearly unsettled by Mia's scrutiny, his florid face became a darker red. "What d'yer reckon, Babe? You fancy taking me on as a CSI?"

"The next time I analyse a rubbish dump, I'll think of you."

"That's all for now, Mr Plummer," said Sutton hastily. "It's a pity, when you were watching us waste our time, you didn't consider the implications for you getting your site back. If you and your men give names and addresses to the sergeant over there, you can go."

He turned his back on the builder and walked away from his protests. Mia kept pace with him. "Wanker," he muttered.

"Pardon?"

"Dennis the bloody Menace."

"I thought you were getting on with him okay."

He stared at her. "That's called diplomacy. Otherwise

16

known as not antagonising arseholes until you've got something to charge them with. And, hitting on female police officers isn't illegal."

Mia wondered how he'd read her mind. "Sorry. I shouldn't have stirred him up."

"No problem. It was worth it to see his face. Do you think he's right about it being the old girl who lived there? If she couldn't bear to be parted from her cats, she could have killed them and then herself."

"And buried herself?"

"Of course not. But there may be someone close enough to her to have done that."

"I had a better look at the skull before we got side-tracked. I think the victim was male.

"You sure?"

"Reasonably. Male skulls have more pronounced brow ridges. And they're a lot thicker, the bones I mean."

"Point taken. You got any more subtle insults, concealed as facts, you want to share?"

She grinned back at him and carried on her list, "So far I've found a…"

What the hell?" exclaimed Sutton.

She broke off and followed his gaze across the garden to where a macabre figure was galloping towards the original SOCO tent. She was bent almost double and dressed in layer upon layer of torn and filthy clothes. She brandished a stout walking stick and was screeching something, but it was hard to make out the words.

Mia toiled after Sutton as he sprinted to intercept the old woman. He reached her just outside the tent entrance and his first words were so correct they came out as ludicrous, "I'm sorry, Madam, but I cannot allow you to go in there."

The woman stared past him into the tent. A blob of spittle dribbled down her chin. "Defiler! Desecrater of the sacred burial ground." She raised the stick and brought it down full force.

Chapter 2

Sutton got his arm up and shielded the blow, but he lost his footing and went sprawling.

The stick rose again.

Mia lunged forward and grabbed the upraised arm. She struggled, turning her face away to avoid the spray of spittle and the repulsive smell. She was vaguely aware of Sutton clambering to his feet and of Adam darting from the tent.

"It's okay, Mia, we've got her." She released her grip and stepped back, feeling sick.

Cops came running but Sutton said curtly, "Show's over. You two stay here and the rest get back to work."

Mia stared at the old woman. Now her rage had drained she looked frail and ancient; her breath creaked and, under the grime, her face was greyish-blue.

Sutton spoke to the two uniformed officers, "Take her back to the Station. And lose those handcuffs! I'm sure that guy over there's a reporter. Ask the police doctor to look at her. She may need a Social Worker as an advocate."

The policewoman gave him a sour look, clearly resentful of being forced to convey the old woman in her patrol car.

"Yes constable?"

"Sir." The policewoman hustled her charge away.

Sutton turned to Mia. "Thanks for the rescue. Are you okay?"

"Fine. What about you?"

"I'll live, though I'll have one hell of a bruise on my elbow."

"If that guy's a reporter, you'd better clean up before he takes a photo," said Adam. He rummaged in his rucksack and produced a pack of wet wipes. "Never leave home without them."

"Is that part of the SOCO kit?" asked Sutton.

18

"No, it's part of the proud father kit. My son dribbles as much as that old girl, but at six months it's not so vile."

"Thanks for that." Sutton's look of revulsion matched the way Mia felt.

"You need a mirror." Chantelle appeared from the tent and produced a folding mirror from her bag. She held it out but Sutton made no attempt to take it. She laughed as he bent to try and look in it, then she took the wet wipes and cleaned his face, standing on tiptoe to reach.

Mia scrubbed at her own face and watched sourly as Chantelle's slender fingers went deftly about her job. She wondered how Chantelle managed to keep her hands immaculate.

"That's better." Chantelle stepped back and surveyed Sutton, her head on one side.

"Thank you." He smiled down at her.

"This newspaper guy wants a quote, sir." Detective Sergeant Dave Bycroft approached, followed by the reporter.

Mia saw Sutton's lips tighten. "You know that's the Press Office's job."

Bycroft shrugged. "Thought you might want to make your mark. You being the new kid on the block. Chances are we'll have a lot of them flocking here as soon as word gets round. This week, anything that happens in Ledleigh's major news."

The reporter was already within earshot. He was a middle-aged, cheerful-looking guy, who Mia had often encountered at crimescenes. "Welcome to Ledleigh, Inspector. I'm Mike Reardon of the Ledleigh and District News. Could you tell me if you plan to charge Miss Logan?"

"I certainly don't wish to deal harshly with such an elderly lady."

"And what's the story about this body?"

"You know that information will be channelled through our media spokesperson. But perhaps you could tell me what you know about Miss Logan?"

"What's the game? You tell me nothing and I help you out?"

Sutton met his challenge with a smile. "It's a good idea to keep the new kid on the block happy, especially when he's an unknown quantity."

Reardon chuckled. "Okay, I can tell you about old Lucy. She lived in that house, always had done, right from a kid and she's close to ninety now. First with her parents, then, after they died, by herself, apart from seven million cats."

"How many do you mean by seven million?" asked Mia, fearing the worst. Adam and Chantelle had gone back to work but she lingered.

The reporter shrugged. "Hard to tell. There were between six and ten that were relatively tame, and dozens more wild ones she used to feed. We did a feature on her when these houses were targeted for development."

"Why was that?" asked Sutton. "I mean what angle was there for you?"

The reporter grinned. "Lucy's Last Stand. Cat Woman Fights the Developers. We got some lovely headlines out of that. They offered her a small fortune to get out, but she stayed here after everyone else had gone."

"All the other houses were empty?"

"That's right. Made a wonderful story. Of course we had to touch up the pictures of the house. Most readers don't have much sympathy with an old girl who chooses to live in filth."

"How did they eventually get her out?"

"No idea. One day she was here, the next she'd given up. Moved into a bungalow across town."

"Do you know why?"

"No. We're not interested once the story's dead. I don't know why you're asking me. Your sergeant's local, he could have told you about Lucy." He nodded towards Bycroft.

"Sometimes it's worth hearing an outside version. Thanks for your help." Sutton spoke to an uniformed officer.

"See Mr Reardon off the site. DS Bycroft, you stay here."

Sutton didn't speak until the reporter was out of hearing, but while he was waiting he stared at the sergeant, his blue eyes like flint. At last he said, "You've pushed your luck too far. If you know anything else about that old woman I suggest you start talking."

"No sir, I don't know more than you've already heard."

Mia slipped quietly into the SOCO tent. If she watched Bycroft hauled over the coals it would be resented by the sergeant and his mates in CID. However, once out of sight, she didn't move far from the doorway. She was curious to hear how Sutton dealt with it.

"In that case, sergeant, you can listen to me. In the past two weeks I've had nothing but insolence from you. Today you've taken several steps too far. I want everything you can find out about the former residents of this terrace, in writing, before you go off duty tonight."

Mia heard Bycroft mutter, "Sir," and move away. Aware of her status as eavesdropper, she shot across the tent and pointed out a bone fragment Chantelle had missed.

A moment later Sutton looked inside the tent. "You've got reinforcements arriving."

Mia came out to greet the middle-aged SOCO who was approaching stolidly over the slippery ground. "Hi Geoff. This is DI Sutton. Thanks for coming."

"Trev said it sounded like you'd need all the manpower you could get."

"We do." Trevor Mayfield, their office manager, had come through as usual. "I need you to process the next door garden. As far as we can tell it's an old fishpond, but we've got a buried body in this garden, so we've got to make sure."

"Right." The good thing about Geoff was that he never argued; the bad thing was he worked at his own pace.

"I've got two detective constables that can give him a hand," said Sutton.

Mia smiled. She was glad he didn't plan to let the

troublemakers get away with it. "Tell them I'll be over to check on them," she said. As Crime Scene Manager she outranked the DCs.

"I'll do that." Sutton strode purposefully away.

"Excuse me, officer." The quiet voice startled her. She whirled around and bumped into the builder Dennis Plummer had shouted to. "Sorry, didn't mean to frighten you."

"That's okay."

"I'm Mike Plummer, Dennis' cousin." He was a tall, well-muscled guy, with a quiet manner and low, unemphatic voice. "Sorry I didn't come over before. I hate it when Denn gets loud like that. And sorry about that fishpond business. He's got a funny sense of humour."

She thought there was no reason Mike should have played along but she didn't need aggro with this builder as well. "You could just record the word 'sorry' and play it on a loop," she suggested, smiling to take the sting out of her words.

His answering smile was as reticent as his voice. "Yeah, with Denny, that's a good idea. He fancies girls in uniform. Thinks he's in heaven with you policewomen about."

Not just a loud-mouthed bastard but pervy too; no surprises there.

"Your cousin said you were friendly with the old lady who lived here?"

He shrugged. "I felt sorry for her. I must go." Sutton approached and Mike Plummer hurried back to his fellow builders who were leaving the site.

"What was he after?" asked Sutton.

"Apologising for his cousin."

"Right." It was clear Sutton had run out of patience with the contractors. "You hadn't finished briefing me about what you'd found in the first garden when that crazy old woman turned up."

"Ignoring the cats, we've got bones consistent with one human body. The construction activity scattered them but

I've uncovered enough major bones to indicate the victim was elderly. There's notable calcification of several joints. There's damage to the right side of the skull but I can't tell whether it's pre or post-mortem. It's for the pathologist to decide whether that caused or contributed to his death,"

"We'll get onto the local dentists. Hopefully they'll give us an ID."

"There's a couple of fillings and several missing teeth. What's strange is there's no sign of any clothes."

"Perhaps the material's rotted away."

"It shouldn't have, not totally, and anything metal should have survived. It's hard to be exact with decomposition, so don't count on this, but I'd be surprised if the body had been there for much over ten years."

"Thanks. I'll keep that in mind. Will you talk to Tim Lewis with me? Knowing about archaeology, you may pick up on something I'd miss."

As they approached, Mia thought Tim Lewis looked pale and nervous. She felt sorry for him. She remembered the stress of watching briefs at building sites, torn between dread of missing valuable archaeology and fear of the hostile work force.

His first words confirmed this, "The contractors are furious. They've been waiting for years to get planning permission and now, on the first day, this happens."

"That's their problem," said Sutton brusquely.

The boy gulped, as if trying to swallow his prominent Adam's apple.

"You called it right, Tim." Mia gave a reassuring smile. Sutton had asked for her input so he could take the questioning at the right pace for this shocked boy. Although Tim's reaction did seem extreme. Most archaeologists have little problem in coping with fleshless bones.

"They made a late start, didn't they?" said Sutton. "I'd have thought they'd be onto it first thing."

"They had problems with the digger. They were really

mad about it. Mike kept saying this dig was cursed and now, of course, they're certain it's true."

Mia struggled to keep a straight face. Did they think this was Tutankhamen's tomb?

"What happened when they got the digger going?" asked Sutton.

"They dug up most of this garden. Then Dennis said they'd hit a pets' cemetery, but I spotted what I knew was human bone. For a moment I couldn't believe it, then I was sure, but I thought it would be an ancient burial."

"Thank you. We'll need you to make a formal statement. We'll be in touch," said Sutton.

He was so curt that Mia felt forced into gushing thanks, "You did a really good job. Thanks for being so conscientious."

"Thank you." He looked absurdly like a puppy that had been kicked by one master and patted by another. "I wonder... would you have a drink with me sometime?"

Great, just what she needed, being chatted up by a kid while a glowering DI listened in.

"Sometime perhaps, when things aren't so hectic."

"Thank you. Please call me any time you're free." He handed her his card.

Sutton waited until the boy had moved away, then said, "Don't disappear. I want a SOCO with me when I look over the old woman's house."

"Yes sir." Mia had worked under temperamental SIOs before but never one whose mood changed as swiftly as this.

The house was a standard two-up-two-down with the lavatory outside the back door. Sutton led Mia and two uniformed officers into a dreary old-fashioned interior that smelled of damp and, after all the years, still held the lingering odour of cats. No signs of violence were obvious, but Mia was grateful for the protection of her SOCO suit and gloves.

The stairs to the top floor were rickety, the banister gone and several boards missing. Sutton said to the younger, more agile constable, "Nip up and check the bedrooms." He looked at Mia. "Do you mind going up?"

"Sure." So what was that about? Was Sutton scared of heights? Or cockroaches and rats? She wasn't too keen on rodents herself, but she followed the constable upstairs.

Ten minutes later she came down again. "Nothing obvious."

"I didn't think there'd be a spot labelled 'The Murder Happened Here'."

"We don't even know it's murder."

"True." His phone rang.

As he answered it, Mia hung around, uncertain if he still needed her. She was tempted to head back to the tent but he seemed in the mood for aggro and she didn't want to be summoned out again. She heard him say, "What do you mean you've lost her?" and abandoned any thought of slipping away.

As Sutton listened to the caller his expression turned from bad-tempered to downright grim. "What's up with you? Can't you out-pace a ninety-year-old? Yeah, I'll get people out looking. It's not as if we've anything else to do." He keyed off.

"What's happened?" asked Mia, although she thought she could guess.

"Believe it or not, they've lost the old girl."

"How?"

"The oldest trick in the book. She asked for the lavatory, so they stopped at a shopping centre."

"The Margrave Centre? The toilets are on the first floor, along a corridor. Surely the female officer went with her?"

"Fancy you thinking of that. Apparently not. She waited at the end of the corridor, while her colleague nipped off to buy a lottery ticket."

That was unbelievably stupid. "But how did she get away?"

"She put on a cleaner's uniform that was hanging up,

25

went out carrying a bucket and floor mop, and nipped down the service stairs. She left the cleaning things and overall by the fire door and headed out of it."

"What now?" Mia felt a sneaking admiration for the old woman.

"Now we hunt for her. And we check out her bungalow. I'll lead that myself."

"If you don't need me I'll get back to sorting bones."

"Yeah. Thanks for your help."

In the tent, the pile of bones had grown. "Still only enough for one human body," said Adam, "But the cat count's up to at least nine. You'd better check them over, you're the bone expert and I've had enough of living cats today."

These last embittered words were clearly directed at Chantelle. Against her better judgement, Mia asked, "What's wrong?"

"Chantelle brought her cat into work again and Trevor hasn't got the guts to stop her."

Mia knew this was harsh but true. Trevor was a decent guy and a good office manager but Chantelle's complaints about sexual discrimination had got him on the run.

Chantelle pouted. "I can't help it. I'm trying to get a new cat-sitter. I can't leave poor little Pixie alone. The last girl used to do it after school but she was too unreliable. She actually took him out on the balcony! He could have fallen and we're six floors up."

"I heard somewhere that cats achieve terminal velo…"

"Adam, that's not a good idea," interrupted Mia. She too had taken part in the Gross Science Quiz, in which teams of SOCOs had taken each other on for a local kids' charity. That meant she knew that cats achieved terminal velocity when dropped from the seventh floor. Chantelle had not been present and Mia did not need the aggro of Chantelle complaining to Human Resources yet again.

Choking back a giggle as Adam mouthed, 'Splat cat!', she changed the subject. "All hell's breaking loose out there.

Uniformed managed to lose that old girl and the DI's furious."

"He's gorgeous though, isn't he?" giggled Chantelle. "Really fanciable."

"And ten years younger than you," muttered Adam, but fortunately Chantelle didn't hear.

Work went on in silence until DS Bycroft peered into the tent. "How's it going?"

"Nine cats and one human," said Adam.

"That's really weird."

"You in charge out there?"

"Yeah. Sutton's gone off to look for the old girl."

"Probably wants to make sure she stays captured next time," commented Adam.

Bycroft scowled. "With any luck he'll get sick of us and transfer back up North."

Mia kept her head down but she watched Bycroft from the corner of her eyes. He was around forty, dark-haired and solid. In past dealings with him Mia hadn't found him the best cop in the world, but he was far from being the worst.

"You were the blue-eyed girl round here this afternoon," he said.

She looked up and shrugged. "The DI wanted forensic advice."

"Cocky bastard isn't he?"

CID could fight their own civil war. She grinned. "You all are. It goes with the territory."

He laughed, then said, "Best get on, or the Boy Wonder will be on my case again. Hey, I've just realised, we've got Cat Woman and the Boy Wonder, all we need is Batman turning up."

As Bycroft left, Mia glanced at her watch. No way was she going to finish until late evening. She got out her mobile. "Jason? It's Mia. Sorry, I can't make it. I've got to work... Yeah, it's a pity. I was looking forward to it. I'll ring you soon." She keyed off and met Chantelle's nosy look with a bland smile.

"I didn't know you had a boyfriend, Mia?"

"There's lots of things you don't know about me." And plenty she had no intention of sharing with Chantelle, including the fact that Jason was an old friend from Uni and their platonic date was to have dinner and attend a talk on Saxon burials.

Thinking of the dinner she was going to miss reminded Mia she'd forgotten to eat lunch. She stripped off her SOCO suit and gloves and went to eat her sandwiches in the peace and safety of her locked van.

As she ate, she monitored her radio, there was plenty of routine stuff but nothing on the triple murder enquiry. In a way, no news was good news. It meant no more deaths had been discovered. Mia had helped process the dumpsites; different lay-bys just outside town. The primary crimescene, the place where they'd been raped, tortured and strangled was still unknown. After death, the three women had been submerged in disinfectant, which had compromised a lot of evidence.

Lunch finished, Mia's survey of her surroundings was more thorough than usual. She couldn't banish the thought that all the victims were in their late thirties, just a few years older than herself. Carefully she checked out the parked vehicles. Behind her van were the two others used by Adam, Chantelle and Geoff. In front there were two patrol cars, Dave Bycroft's family saloon and a MPV she thought belonged to Oliver Sutton.

That was strange. Why was Sutton's car still here? Commonsense told her he'd probably grabbed a lift. Nevertheless she walked past his car en route to the crimescene.

"Mia." The quiet voice made her jump. "Mia." Spoken in the same controlled tone.

She realised it came from one of the narrow alleyways that ran between each four terraced houses.

Something in the voice made her turn slowly and carefully, as if afraid of triggering a bomb.

Chapter 3

Sutton was standing in the alley. Just beyond him was the old cat lady, wielding a piece of painted wood, spiked with nails.

"It's her. Your conspirator. She who desecrated my babies' grave." The old woman's voice was unexpectedly deep and resonant. She took a threatening step towards Mia.

"No," said Sutton. "Listen to me, Lucy." He waited until the smouldering stare returned to him. "We won't hurt your babies. Mia is treating them very respectfully, aren't you Mia?"

"Very respectfully," echoed Mia. She fixed a reassuring smile on her face and hoped it looked less phoney than it felt.

"But, if you carry on with this, you won't be able to reclaim them," said Sutton.

Mia flinched as the old woman's grip tightened on the wood.

Sutton's voice was sharp with tension, "Put that down, Lucy. Come on. Be sensible…" He trailed to a halt.

"If you do as Oliver says, I'll get a beautiful carved box and gather all your babies together so you can have them at your new home," promised Mia.

"I'd like that. It's a long journey, every day, coming to visit them."

"Every day?"

"Every day, to mourn my precious ones." Anger kindled again. "And then you came and desecrated their resting place."

"Not us. The builders," protested Mia.

"You are all desecraters of a sacred burial site."

Okay, if the old girl wanted to discuss desecration so be it. "Do you know how that human body got buried there?"

A sly smile twisted the woman's mouth. "At first I thought it was an obscenity. Then I understood it was right." Her voice rose triumphantly, "It was a sacrifice of the destroyer that the innocent might go to their reward."

Mia stared at her. "You know who's buried there, don't you?"

There was a long silence. The old woman's eyes met hers, cunning and gloating.

"Mia." Sutton's voice was hoarse.

"What's wrong?"

"My arm. I'm sorry. It's killing me."

Mia realised he was bleach white and swaying on his feet. Anger crashed through her. This woman was holding them hostage with nothing but her age, her lunacy and a piece of nail-studded stair support. "Right Lucy, this is your last chance. I've had enough. Put that wood down now."

The old woman stared at her. Then, to Mia's amazement, she let the spiked wood drop. Its clatter echoed around the alleyway. Mia approached, still wary of the heavy walking stick. Sutton pulled himself together and walked with her.

"This time I'm afraid you're going to be handcuffed." He pulled the cuffs from his pocket and handed them to Mia. "Would you do the honours? In front will be fine, that way she can lean on her stick."

Gingerly Mia obeyed. It was a while since she'd done anything like this. Her street experience had been brief because they'd wanted her back in Scene of Crimes.

Sutton got out his mobile. "DS Bycroft? DI Sutton here. Send officers round to where the cars are parked to take charge of the prisoner we've recaptured." He leaned back against a house wall, eyes shut, mouth blue-shaded.

"Do you think your arm's broken?" asked Mia. At least that explained why he'd been so bad-tempered since the injury occurred.

"Don't know. Thanks for another rescue." Sutton pushed himself upright as four cops, led by Bycroft, arrived at the run.

"What's she doing back here?" demanded the sergeant.

"Checking on her bloody cats of course," snapped

Sutton. "Detail someone to take her to the Station and this time make sure she gets there. The rest of you get back to work. And call off the search. We've wasted enough time and manpower as it is."

The abrasive tone had a swift effect. Within two minutes the street was clear, apart from Sutton and Mia.

"That's not the way to make friends," she remarked. "Although it worked pretty well on influencing people."

"I've given up hope of making friends round here. You and that other SOCO are the only ones who've been friendly."

Mia considered pointing out Chantelle was flirting, which was different from being friendly, when Sutton continued, "He seems a nice guy."

"What?"

"Adam. Seems a decent sort."

"Oh I see. Yes, he is."

She waited for Sutton to map out the next move but he seemed uncertain where to go or how.

"Give me your keys. I'll drive you to hospital."

"I can't afford the time."

"You can't afford not to. If you neglect it you could end up permanently crippled."

He passed over his keys and they got into his car. He fumbled his seat belt and she had to lean over from the driver's seat to help. As she drove, she asked, "Shouldn't you let Dave Bycroft know where you're heading?"

"And give him and his pals something else to snigger about? No thanks!"

Mia wondered how he was going to keep his injury secret if his arm was broken.

He misinterpreted her silence. "It's true, you know. I'm not being paranoid."

"I know. Bycroft wanted the DI job you got."

"If he wants it that badly, he can chase it the same as the rest of us."

31

"His chances are limited. He can't move away because of uprooting his family."

"In that case he doesn't want promotion badly enough."

Tough, ambitious and ruthless; instinct told her that Oliver Sutton was all of those.

"The Appointments Board understand about commitment, you know, Mia. They take how much you want it into the mix." He shut his eyes, closing the conversation.

After a few minutes Mia asked, "Had you been in that alley very long?"

"It felt like forever. When I first spotted her it didn't occur to me I couldn't take her with my arm like this. I had this nightmare fear everyone would leave and we'd be standing there all night, just me and Dracula's grandma." He shuddered.

"It's okay, sir." She hesitated over the last word, which seemed absurdly formal.

"Oliver," he corrected.

"That's not a good idea."

"Why not? You called me Oliver when you were talking to the old girl."

"I was trying to reassure her."

He offered her an unsteady smile. "Well I could do with some reassurance now." Then swiftly, as if ashamed of his descent into pathos, "You can leave me at A&E and take the car back to work. No point in us both wasting the afternoon."

When Mia left Sutton she headed back to the Station. A quick call to Adam had established they'd be packing up soon and it wasn't worth her coming back to the site. She'd arranged for one of them to drive her van back and told him where to find the spare keys in her SOCO kit. Back in the office, she set to collating evidence.

An hour later her office door opened and Oliver Sutton entered. His hand was tucked into his jacket pocket, supporting his bad arm.

"That was quick."

"They heard I was a cop and fast-tracked me."

Are you okay?"

"Yeah. It's my elbow... a damaged nerve. Painful but shouldn't give me long-term grief."

"That's good. Are you going on sick leave?"

"No. We're too shorthanded... Mia, I need a favour." His manner was a shade too casual.

"What sort of favour?"

"I was hoping you'd transfer to CID."

"What?" Mia stared at Sutton, convinced one of them had gone mad.

"Just a temporary secondment. The DCI told me I needed a driver and I told him I wanted you. If you're up for it he'll do his best to square it with your DI."

"That's crazy. I'm not a detective."

"Maybe not but you're a lot brighter than most of the dozy devils they've landed me with."

"Thanks for that." He certainly had a wonderful way with words.

"I'm sorry. I know I've got no right to ask this but I do need you. Apart from a driver, I need someone to watch my back. I guess I'm too knackered to say things properly."

Mia suspected it was that technique again. The apology with a touch of vulnerability. 'Only you, only you can save me.' And the problem was it worked. But one thing rankled. "I haven't got much choice. If DCI Craig wants me to move across I'll have to do it."

"I swear I didn't mean to set you up. I'll tell him I've changed my mind."

"No, it's okay." As long as Oliver Sutton didn't think he could command her.

"Thank you." He favoured her with another of those heart-melting smiles and met her eyes without a hint of triumph. If she'd been played, at least it was by an expert in the game.

Sutton pushed open the door to the CID room and entered, Mia on his heels. Everyone turned to stare at them: Bycroft, the two male detective constables and DS Liz Murphy, who was reputedly tougher than any of the guys.

"Thought you must have quit for the night, sir," said Bycroft.

"I had something to sort out." Sutton moved to the front of the room and perched on a desk. "The DCI's asked us to run with this one, and he's had Mia seconded to us. This case is heavily dependent on forensic evidence, so I think the DCI's right, she can contribute a lot. By the way, it was Mia that recaptured our absconding old lady and saved us a lot of grief."

The suspicion relaxed into smiles and muttered greetings. As Mia sidled into a vacant seat she realised Sutton had sheltered her from being tarred by his own unpopularity.

"We need to do some rescheduling," said Sutton. "Who's got stuff that can't be shelved or passed to uniformed?"

Mia's attention drifted as they discussed reallocation until Sutton said, "Is that it?"

"I've got something I've been working on long-term," said Liz Murphy and the rest of the team groaned.

Sutton glared them into silence. "Tell me, Liz."

"There's this group of travellers that tour the area, violent bastards up to all the scams. I reckon they're into child prostitution. I've been working with Vice and the Child Protection people."

"Okay, keep tabs on it but don't spend too long unless something breaks. And tread carefully. We don't need racial harassment charges hurled our way."

"I'll watch it, but these aren't Romanies."

"Since when have the Media been interested in accuracy when they're throwing muck at us? Remind me when things are less frantic and I'll see if I can get you more manpower."

She looked surprised then flashed him a smile, "Thanks Guv. By the way, they were camped on the waste ground near Bridge Road not long ago."

"Do you think that's got any relevance to our case?"

"No, that's why I didn't mention it before." The unspoken message was clear, 'I'm a good, conscientious cop and I'm not pulling any stunts.' Mia thought Liz was probably as clever a manipulator as Sutton himself.

They reached the Bridge Road case. Sutton outlined what they knew, which was very little; what they'd deduced, which was rather more; and what they needed to find out, a depressingly long list. At last he asked, "Does anyone know if Lucy Logan is fit for questioning?"

"I got the police doctor to take a look at her and he's worried about her mental problems," said Bycroft. "We're still waiting for Social Services to show up."

"Why doesn't that surprise me? Have you tried to talk to her?"

"I tried, Liz tried, the doctor tried. All we could get was some garbage about her wanting the priestess."

"What?"

"The priestess of the sacred ritual who'll bring her babies to her in a carved sarcophagus," said Liz. "That make any sense to you, sir?"

Mia cringed as she waited for Sutton's reply. Cops were merciless piss-takers and she knew she was destined to spend the rest of her professional life labelled 'The Priestess.'

He glanced towards her, his blue eyes alight with mischief, then he turned back to the team. "No. What about you, Mia? Ring any bells with you?"

"No, but I think she knows the identity of the dead man, don't you?"

She saw his bewilderment and realised that unwittingly she'd got her revenge for that teasing look. He must have been feeling too out of it in the alley to process what was said. "You must have been out of earshot, sir. She said something about the dead man being the oppressor who'd been sacrificed."

"What the hell did she mean by that?"

35

"I don't know, but I think we should find out when and how those cats died."

Sutton nodded. "I'm afraid you're right. Tomorrow we'll try to interview her. Anyone got any other suggestions about how to discover the identity of our dead man?"

"I've made a list of the people who used to live there, sir," offered Dave Bycroft. "We've got addresses for most of them."

"Any old men amongst them?"

"Three at least. It ended up as an old people's street. The young ones took the money and moved on. We'll start visiting them tomorrow, if that suits you, sir? I mean we could do it tonight, but it's late for banging on pensioners' doors." The insolence was back in Bycroft's voice, overlaid by excessive deference.

"Tomorrow's fine."

"No problem, sir. That's an advantage of being an old hand who knows the area, you don't need to get your information second-hand."

Mia saw Sutton's lips tighten. "That's true, Sergeant. That's why an efficient team needs the old hands to support those who aren't content to stagnate within their comfort zone."

There was a nasty, slow-burning silence. Sutton stood up. "Briefing eight a.m. tomorrow. Goodnight everyone." He left.

Mia decided discretion was the better part of valour and scuttled after him.

He glanced over his shoulder. "You decided to stick with me? I thought you might hang around to join in the slagging off."

"Why should I? You covered my back in there. But is it a good idea to goad Bycroft like that?"

"What should I do? Lie down while he walks all over me?"

He strode along the corridor and Mia had to trot to keep up. "If you're not careful he'll take a swing at you."

36

"It'd be worth it to get rid of the bastard. And I didn't mean that, so you needn't note it down for any future disciplinary hearings."

"I don't snitch."

He halted so abruptly that she carried on for several paces, then swung round to stare at him. "Sorry. You've got a total right to be pissed off. First I hijack you into working with the detective team from hell, then I take my bad-temper out on you."

That was exactly what Mia had been thinking, and again he'd disarmed her by saying it first. "Do you want a lift home?"

"I'm in the Lodging House. I haven't had time to flat-hunt." The Lodging House was the block of en-suite rooms that housed young single cops. "Thanks, I'd appreciate a lift."

Mia pulled up outside the Lodging House. Sutton thanked her and hauled himself out of her car, then he lurched, leaning on the bonnet to stay on his feet.

Mia jumped out. "I'll come in with you."

She held his good arm and walked with him along the corridors to an impersonal bedsit. There were four large boxes stacked in a corner. On top of them stood a battered violin case.

"Sorry about the mess," he said. "It's not worth unpacking. I plan to move out soon."

"Do you play?" she asked, nodding to the violin.

"A bit."

Mia wondered what sort of music he played but she didn't ask. If he described some high-flown classical stuff she'd have to admit her ignorance.

Have you got your own place?" he asked.

"Yes, I've got a semi on the edge of town." Wanting a house was the reason she'd entered the police force. As an archaeologist she'd never been unemployed but three-month contracts don't get you a mortgage.

She watched him fumbling with his shirt buttons.

"Do you need some help?"

"Please. My fingers aren't working properly."

She undid the buttons and helped him to ease off his shirt. His left elbow was swollen and discoloured but, apart from that, he had lean, well-muscled arms and torso, and smooth, unblemished skin, not deeply tanned but not milk white. Unlike his face.

"Steady!" She guided him to the bed and helped him to sit down.

He ran his good hand over his face and let out his breath in a long-drawn, "Phew!" After a moment he looked up and smiled. "Sorry. I went pretty woozy."

"That's what comes of pretending you're Superman."

"Wrong comic book series. I'm the Boy Wonder according to the rest of CID."

Despite the flippancy, he sounded miserable.

"Is there anything else you need?"

"The painkillers they gave me are in my jacket pocket."

She found them, opened the container and gave him one. "Is there anything else I can do?"

"No thanks. I'm good. Mia, you're a star."

"I'll pick you up in the morning."

"No, that's okay, I'll walk."

"Give me a ring if you change your mind."

"Thanks. Could you put your number in my phone?"

As she keyed in her fingers were stiff and nervous. It was years since she'd taken a guy's phone and put her numbers in; she usually gave out a business card.

She went back to her car, blanking the stares of off-duty constables.

She drove on auto-pilot, her mind picking over what she'd taken on. She must have been crazy. This was way out of her comfort zone. When she turned into her drive, she shelved all other concerns for the more immediate one of getting safely into her house. The security lights came on and she parked as near as possible to her front door. But somehow, tonight, it didn't seem close enough.

As she sat there she was sure she saw a movement in the bushes on the side of her garden where it ran parallel with the road. She stared harder, straining to pierce the darkness. Surely there was a deeper blackness there? She traced the shape of a person. Or was it her imagination? Trees took on a different life at night, especially when the viewer was afraid.

She cradled her mobile. There were no lights showing in the next-door house, so it seemed likely they were in bed. Anyway, they were in their seventies and frail. She could phone Adam or Trevor, but they'd take at least twenty minutes to arrive and the chances were they'd over-rule her and phone for uniformed to check it out. Better to dial triple nine herself. Hundreds of women were doing that every night. But if there was someone watching her, they'd disappear at the first sound of a siren and, by tomorrow morning, it would be all round the Station that Mia was losing it. Driving round to her mother's house would keep her safe but it would worry Mum and she'd want Mia to move back with her. She wouldn't be frightened out of living in her own home.

The security lights were on a timer, they could go off at any time and she'd be left sitting in the dark, staring at the shadows, waiting for them to shift. Now or never. Heart pounding, jaw clenched, Mia held her house keys ready and flung open her car door.

Chapter 4

Safely inside her house. Door slammed shut and bolted, Mia leaned back against it, panting and shaking and despising herself for being such a wimp. Pulling herself on line, she reset the alarm system, angry that her hands were trembling.

Her mother had begged her to install the state of the art security and had insisted on paying for it. Now more than ever, Mia was grateful for its reassurance but resentful of the fear that made her rely on it.

She went round the house, closing curtains and checking window locks. Entering her living room, the first thing she saw was Robinson, the teddy bear she'd bought the weekend she worked in the trenches on a Time Team dig. He smirked at her, infuriatingly smug. She picked him up and kicked him across the room.

The next morning she felt better. She'd had a good night's sleep, thanks to an indulgent supper and a long, hot, scented bath. She dressed in trousers and a soft grey jumper, the same shade as her eyes. As she brushed her shoulder-length, brown hair she felt pleased she didn't have to tie it back to avoid contaminating evidence or trailing in something vile.

Robinson was still lying, upside down, on the floor. She told herself the long-suffering expression on his face was a product of her guilty imagination, but she picked him up, retied his knitted scarf, and sat him on the kitchen table while she ate breakfast.

Mindful of her calorie-loaded supper she selected the dismal cereal that, so far, had failed in its promises to give her either a supermodel figure or an athlete's stamina.

Her phone rang. She snatched it up certain it would be a summons back to SOCO. It had been early morning when the murdered women had been found.

"Mia?"

"Mum! Is everything okay?"

"Fine, I just thought I'd say hello before you went to work and see if you wanted to come round for dinner tonight."

Which meant she'd wanted to check Mia was okay. Since Mum's arthritis had got bad she didn't sleep well and Mia knew she often lay awake worrying at night.

"I'm fine, Mum, and I'd love to come for dinner if I can get off duty in time. I've got a new job, although it's only temporary. I've been seconded to CID." Swiftly she outlined the story behind her move. Inevitably, Oliver Sutton's name cropped up more than once.

"So what's he like?" asked Mum.

"Clever, tough, ambitious, manipulative." Mia ran out of adjectives and stopped.

"Good-looking?"

"That's not the point. He's my senior officer." Mia realised her protestations had a resoundingly hollow sound. "Yeah, he's quite good-looking. Tall and fair." She remembered his long, slender, sensitive hands, but that was too much information, even for her mum. "I'd better go. I don't want to be late."

When she reached the Station, her first stop was the Scene of Crimes Office to make sure her previous work was covered. Adam greeted her with a grin. "Moving into the Big League?"

She stuck her tongue out at him. "You know how it is, class will tell."

Trevor was less amused. "I hope you're pleased with yourself. Wangling a transfer is going to leave us even more short-staffed."

She met his glare full on. "Trevor, I didn't arrange it. It was the DCI. If you didn't want me to be seconded, you should have told him it wasn't possible."

The inspector's beefy face darkened. "It's not that simple."

41

"I can do more overtime if you want, Trev," offered Adam.

"How come? Last week you turned me down three times."

"Jan and I decided she and Toby should go back to her parents' house until things quieten down. She's getting jumpy every time I'm late and I can't concentrate for fear something's happening to her. I drove her there last night."

"Oh Adam!" Mia knew how much he and Jan adored each other and their infant son.

He shrugged. "It's only an hour's drive."

Mia didn't offer any more sympathy. Adam was making the best of things and she wouldn't undermine him. At least his diversion had softened their manager. She capitalised on this and said, "I'm sorry, Trev. I promise I didn't ask to be seconded to CID."

"That's okay, Mia. I didn't mean to yell at you. I guess the stress is getting to us all."

"I know." As well as the Serious Crimes Team, they'd brought in a few extra forensic specialists to augment the overburdened local teams but, all the same, the whole force was stretched to breaking point.

"I'll stay as CSM for Bridge Road if that'll help," she offered.

"Thanks. I can't spare Adam to go out there today. It'll have to be Geoff and Chantelle, if and when she turns up."

"Fine." In the circumstances Mia couldn't argue.

Trevor picked up on her tone. "Okay, I know Geoff tends to pace himself."

"I don't mind him pacing himself but does he have to use a sloth to set the rate?"

Trevor suffered more than anyone from Geoff's stolid refusal to get his arse in gear. He laughed at Mia's remark, then winced and rubbed his chest.

"You ought to cut out the beer and pies," said Adam. He picked up the giant pack of Rennies they'd purchased specifically for Trevor and lobbed them across to him.

"It ain't what I eat, it's stress," growled Trevor.

Mia thought that was at least partially true. Many cops suffered from stress-related conditions, especially the ones like Trev who had no domestic life. It wasn't surprising health suffered after years of hard boozing, quick food and irregular hours.

"I've got me routine medical coming up soon. I don't fancy being pushed into early retirement."

Adam said with forced cheerfulness, "We'll have to get you out jogging."

"Ha bloody ha."

"Seriously Trev, some exercise might help," persisted Mia. "Did you ever play any sports?"

"I used to enjoy a round of golf."

"Can't you take it up again?"

"I haven't got a partner. It's no pleasure going on the off-chance someone'll give you a game." Trevor glared as Chantelle slipped into the room. "You're late."

"I'm sorry. I overslept." Chantelle slid her cat basket discreetly under her desk. "I've been sleeping badly. I keep jumping awake, thinking someone's breaking in."

Mia had known a few jumping awake moments herself, so she didn't point out there were no signs of forced entry at the three victims' homes.

"Mia's been seconded for a while and I need everyone to put in more overtime," said Trevor.

"I can't!"

"What do you mean you…?" Trevor clipped off the words and Mia knew he was remembering the number of times Chantelle had reported him to HR.

Chantelle's eyes swam with tears. "I hate going home after dark. It's isolated in the car park and I hate walking into the building alone. What if I go up in the lift and the psychopath gets in? And often the lift isn't working and going up the stairs is even worse."

43

This Mia could empathise with, especially after her own fear last night. "Trevor, couldn't you arrange for someone to escort Chantelle to her door if she works late?"

"I'll do it if I'm around," offered Adam.

Trevor nodded grudgingly. "I'll get something sorted. I could do it myself sometimes."

"Fine," approved Mia, ignoring his grumpy tone. Trevor's bulk should deter any predator. Although it was to be hoped the lift was working, walking up six floors might easily kill him.

Chantelle gave a watery smile. "Thank you. I'm sorry to be a nuisance, Trevor."

"That's all right. I didn't say you're a nuisance."

Mia watched him hover between bad-temper and wariness and decided to build a few bridges. "Trevor didn't mean to be sharp with you, Chantelle. He's not well. He's stressed and his stomach's bad. I'd appreciate it if you kept an eye on him for me."

"I'm not sure..." Chantelle looked doubtful, but apparently her hesitation was merely in the selection of healing teas. "I'll make you some peppermint tea, Trevor, that should help your digestion, although camomile's excellent for stress."

Mia saw Trevor's expression and decided this was a good time to leave.

Oliver Sutton looked up from his desk and grinned at Mia. "Hi. You ready for another day full of aggro, cats and bones?"

"Wouldn't miss it. How's the arm?"

"Much better. Team briefing in five minutes. Then we'll interview the old girl."

"That's something to look forward to." She left him and headed along to the Ladies.

There were three cops in the area outside the cubicles, Liz Murphy and two uniformed officers. Their chatter ended abruptly as Mia entered but she caught the words, "Only

44

met him yesterday…" Perhaps she was paranoid but she was certain they'd been talking about her. The uniformed women left but Liz stood her ground.

"You got something you want to say to me?" Mia realised she'd spoken too aggressively. The detective sergeant made her nervous, which caused her to over-compensate.

"Should I have?"

"You seem to have plenty to say about me. How about you try some of it to my face?"

Clearly that took Liz by surprise. "You need to remember the fastest way up isn't necessarily the most permanent, or the one that makes you friends." She shouldered her way past Mia and left.

As Mia approached the CID room, she could hear Dave Bycroft holding forth. "You can tell what a sleazy bastard he is. He's not content with screwing the silly bitch, he has to wangle her onto our team. Well he's not getting away with it. I've reported him and all hell's going to break loose. With any luck he'll get suspended."

Poised outside the door, Mia knew two conflicting impulses. One was to run away, send in her notice and never see any of these bastard cops again. The second was stronger; it was to march into the office and throw the furniture at Bycroft.

She compromised. She stormed into the office and hurled words. "If you want to see a sleazy bastard try looking in the mirror. I'm not screwing DI Sutton and when it comes to inappropriate behaviour how about that Massage Parlour in Bruton Street? You're a corrupt, hypocritical loser! And what's more you're bloody stupid!"

"And you're insubordinate." The voice from the doorway made Mia jump. DCI Craig stalked into the room. He wasn't a tall man and he was quiet in dress and manner, and yet he dominated the assembled cops.

His fierce, hazel eyes rested on Mia. "Constables do not

45

tell sergeants that they're stupid losers. That's the job of their superior officers." The gaze moved on to Bycroft, "Thank you for your report, Sergeant. I appreciate the spirit it was offered in. Perhaps you'd care to hear the explanation DI Sutton gave me for Constable Trent's presence in his room?"

In the silence that followed, Mia became aware of Sutton lurking in the doorway, he looked angry and miserable.

"Sir," said Bycroft.

"In the course of his duties yesterday, DI Sutton injured his arm sufficiently badly to require hospital treatment. He was unable to drive and in severe pain. DC Trent drove him home and assisted him to his room." Again the cold look turned on Mia. "DI Sutton has assured me nothing of an intimate nature occurred?"

"No sir. I made sure the DI was okay and left."

"In that case you all owe Constable Trent and DI Sutton apologies."

The muttered medley of 'sorry' swept over Mia but she didn't raise her eyes.

"And now for the thing that concerns me most." The DCI swept on. "If you can't support your senior officer you're not a team I want working under me. Especially when we've got the Media watching us. Any more trouble and I'll make whatever changes I feel necessary."

He turned on his heel and strode towards the door. As he passed Sutton he said something in a sharp undertone. The DCI left and Sutton removed a sling from his pocket and draped it around his neck. Teeth gritted, he used his good hand to manoeuvre his injured arm into it. So much for his elbow being fine, thought Mia. She kept turned towards him, putting off the moment when she had to face the rest of CID.

He looked up and met her eyes. "Okay, I lied. It hurts like hell. And I couldn't open those childproof painkillers one-handed."

Mia cursed her own thoughtlessness, she should have left the container open for him.

"I apologise." Liz Murphy's voice forced Mia to turn round. "I was out of order."

"It's a mistake to judge everyone by yourself." Mia was still sore and ready to lash out. "I don't need to screw my way to promotion."

Liz stiffened, then she said, "Fair comment. You want to come out with us one evening? A group of us girls go clubbing most weekends."

"Yeah, that would be good." Clubbing wasn't Mia's idea of fun but she didn't want to be labelled as standoffish. If the invitation was followed through she'd claim a prior date or say she had to baby-sit her niece.

"Let's get this show on the road." Sutton walked into the body of the room and surveyed his sullen team. "I wish we could get this bad feeling sorted. We're not being a good team and, if the DCI sees us mucking up, we won't be a team at all."

"Much you care," muttered Bycroft.

"Of course I care! I don't go into anything to fail. Think of it logically, sergeant. You won't find it easy to take me down but if you work with me we'll turn this into the best CID team in Southern England. Then I'll get promotion and you'll get another crack at my job."

Mia watched as Dave Bycroft examined this proposition, obviously feeling it was flawed but unable to find the catch.

Sutton spoke quietly to the assembled team, "I may owe you lot an apology. I've been a bit tense since I got here. It's not been easy finding my feet with a major crime going on."

"Beautiful," muttered Liz in Mia's ear. "You've got to give it to him, he's bloody good."

Indeed, throughout the office, injured pride was softening into gracious forgiveness.

"I guess we've been a bit tough on you too, Guv." The change from 'sir' revealed Dave Bycroft's altered stance.

"Let's get back to work," said Sutton. "Have we tracked down any of those old men?"

Bycroft launched into details about the measures they were taking to find and interview the elderly residents who'd lived in Bridge Road. Of those surviving, most had stayed in town, but one enterprising quartet of friends had bought a villa in Spain.

"Any chance of a trip to the Costa del Sol to check them out?" asked Bycroft, who was growing matier by the minute.

"Sure, if you can swing it past the guys who hold the purse strings. I need an inventory of Missing Persons. I should have ordered that straight off."

"You did," said Bycroft. "I checked it last night. No-one suitable reported missing in the town."

"I ordered that? I must have been more out of it than I realised."

"How bad is your arm?"

"A bit sore. Could you open these for me, please, Dave?" He passed over the pillbox and Bycroft opened it. "If they knock me out you'll have to take over."

"No problem. Just say if you feel rough. One of you lot get a glass of water for the boss."

"With all the doves of peace flying round this office we'll be knee deep in bird shit," commented Liz, mirroring Mia's thoughts.

Lucy Logan didn't look or smell any better for her night in custody, nor was she being more co-operative. Sutton and Mia sat on one side of the interview table, Lucy and a reluctant Social Worker opposite them.

"Lucy, do you know the identity of the man buried in your back garden?" asked Sutton.

The mad eyes looked through him, swivelled slightly and focused on Mia. "Has the Priestess of the Bones brought the casket?"

"Not yet," said Mia, mentally measuring the distance across the table. "Not until you've answered our questions."

"Ask."

"Do you know who's buried in your back garden?"

"The Evil One. The slaughterer of my babies."

"Did you kill him?" The question slipped out.

"He was struck down. Vengeance is divine. I want the casket to be carved in symbolic patterns and inlaid with gold."

"It's too soon to be describing caskets, we need to know who he was and how he died," snapped Sutton.

Lucy ignored him but, when Mia asked the question, she repeated, "He was struck down."

"We need a name," prompted Sutton.

Obediently Mia said, "You heard that, Lucy. Tell us the name of the man who was buried in your garden."

"The Evil Ones have no names." She began to describe the exact carvings she required on the casket.

Chapter 5

"That was fun," said Sutton, as they returned to the CID office.

"I'm sorry. I guess my questioning technique's not up to much." Mia thought how much easier it was to examine the physical evidence and let it reveal the truth.

"It was more effective than mine," said Sutton. "At least she answered you."

"In her own weird way. What happens to her now?"

"We charge her with assaulting a police officer and get her stowed somewhere for assessment."

"I suppose someone else has to interview her about the assault on you?"

"Of course they do. We were pushing it to talk to her about the buried body. Why? Did you enjoy your time with her so much that you want another go?"

"No way. It's just that Priestess business. I don't want the rest to hear about that."

"It's okay, it's too weird for anyone to suss out." He smiled as Bycroft approached, "You got any information for me, Dave?"

"Just the details of complaints made to the Council by her next-door neighbours. It must have been hell living next to all them cats."

"Did the Council follow through on the complaints?"

"They sent a mediator round. Our chaps were called a couple of times as well but there wasn't much they could do. By then the neighbours were being as threatening as the old girl."

"What happened to the neighbours? Are they still living round here?"

"No. The wife died of cancer eight years ago and the old boy, William Davies, sold up and moved in with his daughter.

He lived with her a few months then went back to Wales. I've tracked down two old dears who lived at 7 Bridge Road. They might fill in some background details. I've phoned and they've agreed to see me."

"I'll take that interview and Mia can drive me. I want to familiarise myself with the town and you're needed here. With me crocked up your time's valuable."

"Right you are, Guv. The name's Whittaker, Alice and Emily. Here's the address. It's one of those sheltered flats."

"Cheers. Anything else?"

"You asked me to check out if any of the contractors has a record."

"You've had time to do that too? Well done."

Mia thought the praise unwarranted. This burst of efficiency showed what Bycroft could do when he wasn't being a pain.

"There's nothing on the archaeologist kid."

Sutton nodded. "He seemed harmless enough. What about the contractors?"

"The usual. Drunk and disorderlies and driving without tax, insurance and under the influence. That cocky bastard you talked to is the only one who's actually been inside."

"Dennis Plummer?"

"That's right. Him and his cousin, Mike Plummer, own the firm. They could lose a fortune in penalties if those houses don't come down in time."

"What's Plummer been inside for?"

"GBH. He got off light, only did three months. He's a vicious bastard when he's drunk. His ex-wife's just taken him to court to change the access to his kids."

"Why's that?"

"Apparently he turned up drunk at Brownies to collect his daughter and got abusive when the woman in charge refused to let her go with him." Bycroft's voice was heavy with loathing, whatever his faults Mia knew he was a devoted dad.

"What about the cousin?"

"No, he's clean."

"Right. Thanks Dave."

Bycroft said, "Mia, could I have a word?" He waited until Sutton was safely in his office. "About what you said before… about Bruton Street… how did you know?"

Mia thought back. In her rage the words had appeared without provenance from some corner of her brain. "It was about a year ago. I was working on car crime. The woman whose car had been vandalised was the stroppy sort. She worked in the Massage Parlour and she told me how I'd better watch my step because a Detective Sergeant in my station was a very close friend of hers. I said I didn't care whether she was a pal of the Chief Constable, and she got mad and mentioned your name."

Bycroft was red and sweating. "What happened then?"

"I warned her if she carried on like that I'd have to declare her workplace a Crime Scene as well as the car, so she shut up."

"Did you tell anyone about it?"

"Of course not. I'd never have mentioned it if you hadn't bad mouthed me."

"I'm sorry." This time the apology sounded genuine. "Mia, it wasn't something I'd done before. My wife and I were going through a bad patch but we're doing better now."

Mia shrugged. "I'll keep quiet."

"The only one who's likely to push it is Liz. She's got a wicked tongue on her."

"I'd noticed." Mia grinned at him and he smiled sheepishly. She'd rather have Dave Bycroft on her side, but that didn't mean she'd forgiven Oliver Sutton for being so double-faced. One minute Bycroft was the enemy, the next he was acting like they were best mates.

When she entered Sutton's office he was struggling to put on his coat and she stood in the doorway to watch the show. He'd got his good arm into the sleeve but was less successful when it came to looping the other side over his shoulder.

"Could you give me a hand?" he asked.

"Why don't you ask Dave Bycroft to help or is his time too valuable?" If Sutton didn't like her attitude he could send her back to SOCO.

He stared at her, then abandoned his struggles. "I thought I could keep a lid on things in CID by being tough but, since the DCI's weighed in, the only way to make this investigation work is to get Bycroft on my side."

Mia felt stupid. It was as though the aggro and weirdness of the morning had clogged her mind. She crossed the room, arranged his coat over his shoulder and buttoned it for him. "Sorry. I hate office politics."

"Me too." He sounded sincere but Mia wasn't convinced. Could anyone hate something they were so good at?

The bright, modern flat was warm and comfortable and Alice and Emily Whittaker seemed delighted to see them. "Of course we'll tell you anything we can but you must eat a little lunch first. Would sandwiches and cake be sufficient for you?"

"Thank you," said Sutton, "But please don't bother."

"It's no trouble at all. Come and sit down. You look so tired. Emily, find a cushion to support the poor boy's arm."

Mia noted without surprise that Sutton received more of the grandmotherly fussing than she did. As he was ushered to an armchair, the smile he gave Mia was mischievous and intimate, inviting her to share the joke. She grinned back at him, then wondered if he'd put her in the same category as Dave Bycroft, someone he needed to keep sweet.

When, at last, they got onto questioning, Sutton let the chatter flow, gently redirecting it if it veered too far off route. The two old ladies were so discursive that Mia was grateful she wasn't required to take notes. They'd been happy to let Sutton record them.

"It's like when the nice lady from the Local History Society comes round."

Perhaps it was the memory of Local History that caused them to dwell on their youth and how different things were then. "Oh yes, we lived in Bridge Road all our lives. All through the War and the bombing," explained Emily. "I always thought how strange it was that Hitler couldn't destroy our houses but the Plummer boys can. Tell me, who was the unfortunate man Lucy killed and buried in her back garden?"

"How did you…?" asked Sutton.

Mia realised that from where he was sitting he couldn't see the local paper on a side table. It was folded back to reveal the headline: Man's Body Found In Cat Woman's Garden. "It's in the local paper." She held it up for him.

"Oh I see. We have no evidence Miss Logan killed the man found in Bridge Road."

"I'm sure you will have soon," said Alice encouragingly.

"Tell me about Lucy," said Sutton. "Was she crazy about animals back then?"

"No that was later, after her parents died. They'd never allow Lucy to keep pets, so of course, as soon as possible, she went to the other extreme. So regrettable," said Emily.

"I hear her cats caused a lot of unpleasantness?" said Sutton.

"Disgusting, dirty creatures." That was Alice.

"Did you have problems with her?"

"We all did, everybody in the street. I've often thought it was a pity we had scrubland behind our gardens. A really fast road would have got rid of even more of them."

"Were many cats killed on the road in front of the house?" Sutton sounded surprised. Bridge Road had a speed limit of thirty miles per hour.

"There's a slight hill before you get there," explained Emily. "A lot of people used to freewheel down it and then accelerate and try to kill a cat."

"Good hunting to them," said Alice viciously.

Appalled, Mia tried to imagine what Lucy had felt like, besieged from every side.

"You're not pet lovers then?" she said, allowing a sarcastic edge to her voice.

"We had a tortoise for many years," said Alice. "We were very fond of that." Her lips quivered. "It was attacked by one of Lucy's wicked cats and died. One of the local children told us what had happened."

"I'm sorry." Mia felt her sarcasm rebound straight back on her.

"You don't understand what it was like to live near Lucy," said Emily. "Those cats got everywhere, even into the house if we didn't keep all the doors and windows closed."

"And it effected house prices," said Alice. "It made it appallingly difficult to sell. We were so glad when the construction company offered to buy us out."

"You didn't mind leaving your childhood home?"

"Not at all. This is so comfortable and easy to keep clean. We made certain beforehand that no pets are allowed." Both old ladies looked proudly around their living room.

"But Lucy wasn't so reasonable?"

"Lucy has never been reasonable in her life. Of course she took the opportunity to make a fuss. So hysterical. She only does it to show off. She even had her picture in the local newspaper. We were terrified the developers would withdraw their offers."

"Yes indeed, we snatched it up as soon as possible."

"And then, in the end, she got more than us for her property, dirt, cat fleas and all." Alice's voice rose in indignation. "She probably planned that all along."

They branched off into details about Lucy's unforgivable behaviour and deviousness, with examples to illustrate their case. The diversion spanned several decades. Mia thought if Lucy Logan had been found dead they'd have no shortage of suspects, in fact she'd have gone for a collaborative effort by the entire neighbourhood.

She shifted slightly to try and see if Sutton's eyes were shut. She was afraid he'd dozed off, overcome by the heat of the room, the rambling conversation and his painkiller.

"… And of course, poor Mr Davies was so proud of his garden…"

"Is that William Davies, the man who lived next door to Lucy?" Sutton's quiet voice cut in.

"That's right. He and his wife moved in soon after the War. He came from Wales but he said there were no jobs there."

"But he went back there in the end, didn't he?" persisted Sutton.

"Yes. So nice for him but it must have upset poor Joy," said Emily.

"Joy?"

"His daughter. His only child. He moved in with her when he left Bridge Road. We happened to meet her not long ago and she told us he'd gone back to Wales."

"Such a pity," said Alice. "He could have applied for one of the flats in this building, then we could have made sure he wasn't lonely."

"Yes dear." Mia thought there was a certain dryness in Emily's tone.

"Does Joy live alone now?" asked Sutton.

Emily smiled at him. "Oh no. She's a widow, bless her, but her two younger children are still at home. She's a nice woman. Mind you she's put on a terrible lot of weight. I was sorry to see she'd let herself go like that."

"Seems odd to move so far away when you've got a home with your only child."

"Maybe. But Mr Davies was a man who liked things done the way he wanted. He gave his orders and expected everyone to stand to attention."

"Emily, you don't know that!" protested her sister.

"Of course I do." She turned back to Sutton, "His wife, Connie, used to come round for a chat, but she'd always make sure she was back in good time to get his tea."

"Emily, they were devoted to each other. Think of the way he nursed her through her last illness, with just the bit of help Joy could give him."

"Alice has always had a rose-tinted view of marriage," explained Emily. "Personally, I think a good book and a bar of fruit and nut chocolate have a lot to recommend them." She twinkled at Mia, who grinned back at her.

"And Mr Davies didn't get on with Lucy Logan?" Sutton kicked the ball back into play.

"Of course he didn't. And who can blame him?" said Emily. "He complained to the Council and the Police and the Social Services, but they were so wishy-washy nothing was ever done."

"He must have been angry," said Sutton.

"Furious. Especially when he discovered Joy had been sneaking over to Lucy's house to play with the kittens. Connie was so upset. We tried to tell her it was one of those silly rebellious phases girls go through but I don't think William Davies ever forgave Lucy for it, along with everything else."

Mia was appalled by the hatred that had festered in the neighbourhood for years.

"So this enmity continued?" asked Sutton.

"It got worse," said Emily. "Especially when Connie got cancer. Mr Davies blamed Lucy. He said it was because of the stress and the infections people caught from dirty cats. I suppose he had to blame someone. It was then he threatened…"

Sutton sat forward, suddenly intent. "Threatened what?"

Emily hesitated, biting her lower lip. "He threatened to poison her cats."

"The timeline's wrong," said Mia as they got back to her car. "The old ladies said Lucy still had her cats when they left, and William Davies had moved out by then."

"I know," snapped Sutton.

"So he can't have killed those cats. Unless you think he came back to do it."

She meant it as sarcasm but Sutton said, "Maybe he did. I wouldn't put anything past any of them when it comes to nastiness."

"I thought we'd never get away from those old girls."

"It's no good hurrying witnesses like them and I wanted to get the feeling of the Bridge Road community. What did you make of the set-up down there?"

Mia hated it when people threw questions like that at her. "Stagnation. The people who wanted to stay there resented the cesspit at the end. Others must have been even angrier when they couldn't sell because of Lucy's cat sanctuary."

"When people feel trapped it builds up a lot of hatred," agreed Sutton.

"But it wasn't Lucy's body in that hole."

"Which brings us back to the man who threatened to kill her cats." He got out his mobile. "Dave? It's Sutton. You spoke to William Davies' daughter. What's the address of that nursing home he moved to?... Phone number then?... I see. No, that's okay. Give me the daughter's address. I'll call in and ask her."

He scribbled down the address, keyed off and said, "Would you believe Bycroft hadn't got the name, address or phone number of the nursing home, much less made sure the old boy was really there?"

"Yes." To Mia it seemed inevitable.

Sutton sighed. "Davies' daughter lives in a place called Foxcote. Is that one of the villages north of town?"

"It used to be. Now it's one of the suburbs. I live out that way myself." They were within half a mile of Bridge Road. "Could we drop in on the crime scene? I'm still CSM."

"Sure."

They parked in the same place as yesterday behind a patrol car and SOCO van but no officers were visible on the scene. "Where is everyone?" said Mia.

"God knows. This force makes the Keystone Cops look good."

"Don't touch me!" Chantelle's voice, shrill with terror, echoed from the tent.

Chapter 6

"That's not friendly, darlin'." Mia recognised the voice. It was the lairy builder they'd talked to yesterday. She laboured after Sutton as he ran, slithering and squelching on the rain-slicked mud and thought that this case was falling into a pattern she could do without.

Sutton wrenched open the flap of the tent to reveal Chantelle cowering on the ground with Dennis Plummer standing over her. "What the hell do you think you're doing?"

"Just asking the pretty lady for a date. No harm in that." Plummer turned to face him.

"Get out of the crime tent," snapped Sutton.

"You gonna make me? You bloody one-armed bandit." Plummer looked meaningfully at Sutton's sling. He was holding a beer bottle and his slurred voice and insolent smirk showed all the bravado of the lairy drunk.

"I'll do it if I have to." Sutton sounded remarkably calm.

"What, you and Miss Smart-mouth Criminalist there?" He scowled at Mia. "You're no way as sexy as your mate." He glanced down at Chantelle. "I got a real hard on for you, darlin'. Wanna feel?"

Chantelle whimpered. Mia saw Sutton's fist clench and willed him not to throw that punch. With his injured arm he wouldn't stand a chance. Plummer must have picked up on the threat. He smashed the beer bottle and thrust the jagged glass inches from Sutton's face.

"That's a bad idea, Dennis. Put the bottle down or you're looking at serious prison time."

Sutton's quiet words seemed to wind Plummer deeper into alcoholic rage. "You bloody bastard with your superior smirk. Lookin' down on an ordinary working bloke. You won't look so smug when I've finished with you."

"Drop that!" The crisp voice made everybody jump.

For a moment Mia thought Plummer would lunge forward. She saw Sutton brace himself to fend off the blow. It never came. A burly figure shoved his way into the tent and Dennis dropped the bottle and staggered back.

Mia had never been so glad to see Trevor. A glance confirmed what she'd heard in his tone, the flabby desk jockey had disappeared and an uniformed, tough, if ponderous, cop stood in his place. Best of all he was holding a riot stick, like a man who'd be delighted to show his skill.

"What's going on?"

"He's drunk," said Sutton. "He frightened Chantelle." He glanced down at her, "Are you okay? Did he touch you?"

She shook her head. "Not really. He tried to kiss me. That's when I tripped over. I'm not hurt." Mia helped her to her feet and Chantelle clung to her.

"Turn round." Trevor handcuffed Dennis Plummer, speaking the words of the caution as he did so.

"Chantelle, where did the cops go?" said Sutton.

"There was an emergency call so they went off to answer it. Geoff had already packed up and gone and I was scared. That's why I phoned you, Trevor. Then he turned up." She glanced at Plummer and shuddered.

"I won't have my officers put at risk like this." Trevor's tone was grim.

"I agree." Sutton looked over his shoulder. "The pride of the uniformed division are coming now. Do you want to deal with them, Inspector, or shall I?"

"I'll talk to them later, when we've got this prize specimen booked in. What I've got to say is going to take some time." Trevor shoved Dennis towards the officers. "Take him and book him. Assault will do for starters."

"Hang on a second," said Sutton. "What was the call that took you away from here?"

The younger policeman turned back to explain, "Assault on a woman, in that tower block over there. Only, it seems like a false alarm. The rest of the guys are still searching."

"You shouldn't have left your post."

The constable looked mutinous. "Control heard the woman screaming down the phone. We were nearest and thought we could catch the bastard."

"And instead you nearly allowed a colleague to be raped," said Sutton icily.

"Who said anything about rape?" Plummer wrenched free to make the protest. "I don't do stuff like that."

Sutton's gaze was as hard as sapphires. "If I find you made a hoax call, I'll crucify you." Then to the uniformed cops, "Take him away." Sutton turned to Trevor, "Thanks Inspector."

"No problem. Does me good to get out of the office. Chantelle, how much more you got to do here?"

"I'd just finished."

"That's it," said Mia, who'd been photographing Dennis Plummer's bottle and gathering it and the broken fragments into evidence bags. "We can get uniformed to deal with the tent and markers. The rest of the evidence is ready to transport."

"Let's go," said Trevor. "Chantelle, I'll drive the van back with you and send someone to collect my car."

As they trudged across the mud, Mia said, "Thanks Trev."

He grinned at her, pleased to be the hero of the hour. "No problem."

Chantelle was still shaking. "Thank you Trevor. I'm so grateful you came."

"Of course I came as soon as you phoned me. I won't have any of my officers put at risk. Not that I knew you were going to be at risk when I sent you here." The final disclaimer was obviously prompted by fear that Chantelle would still slap in a complaint.

Mia saw Sutton was frowning. "What's wrong?"

"Nothing. I caught a glimpse of someone lurking. He's gone between the next row of houses. I think it was Dennis

61

Plummer's cousin. I wonder what he's doing here?"

"You want us to catch him and ask?" She made the offer with more bravado than she felt.

"No. We've got no grounds for that."

"You're the boss." Mia knew she'd spoken too willingly and, from his grin, Sutton had noticed it.

"Only when it suits you," he replied.

In the car, Mia waited to reverse until Trevor and Chantelle had driven away. Reaction had set in and she was shaking so badly she fumbled the gears.

"Steady." Sutton's fingers closed reassuringly over her hand.

"I'm sorry."

"Don't be. You did great."

"I didn't do anything."

"You stood your ground. You didn't let the bastard panic you."

"I was scared."

"So was I."

"You were?"

He removed his hand from hers and held it out flat in front of her. It was trembling. "I've always hated violent drunks. They're unpredictable. And broken bottles scare me even more than knives. I've got a scar from an encounter with a bottle-wielding drunk when I was first on the beat."

"You have?" Mia wondered where it was. She'd seen his upper torso when she'd helped him undress last night.

He must have read her thoughts. A grin relaxed his tense features and he indicated the area just above his right knee.

"They offered you work-experience arresting drunk pygmies?" she enquired.

"No, you lairy woman. It was a falling-down-and-playing-possum drunk, who caught me unawares and lunged upwards."

"If he was lunging upwards, it could have been a lot worse than a scarred knee."

62

He stared at her and began to laugh. "Thank you, Mia. In my darkest hours I'll hang onto that thought."

This time, as she drove away, Mia put the car in gear with her usual efficiency. "Why do you want to see William Davies' daughter yourself?" she asked. Although it was obvious Sutton spent less time in the office than most DIs.

"I don't want to go back to the Station. The atmosphere's getting to me."

Tough, ambitious, ruthless, and clever; but perhaps he was lonely and miserable as well. It couldn't be easy to continually force yourself upwards out of your comfort zone.

"This is it." She pulled up outside a suburban semi, not unlike her own.

The woman who opened the door was fat and grey-haired. She looked old to be the mother of the teenage girl who came downstairs, surveying them suspiciously.

"Mrs Marshall? I'm Detective Inspector Sutton and this is Detective Constable Trent. I'm sorry to bother you. My sergeant phoned you earlier, but I've got a few more questions."

"Of course. Please come in." Despite the welcoming words she seemed nervous.

"Are you all right, Mum?" The girl glared at them.

"I'm fine. Go on upstairs. You've got homework to do." She led Sutton and Mia into a cluttered sitting room. "I'm sorry about the mess. Please sit down."

The obvious query was, 'Where do you suggest?' Sutton tried to manipulate a pile of gardening magazines from the sofa one-handed, but they slipped from his grasp. Mia picked them up and piled them on the floor and they both sat down.

"I don't know what I can tell you." Joy perched on the edge of the other sofa, next to a large, handsome black cat.

"I'd like some background on Lucy Logan. I understand you lived next door to her for years," said Sutton.

Joy smiled. "Lucy wasn't as bad as people made out."

"Really?"

"She was a kind old lady, always nice to me."

"But then you're a cat lover."

"Yes, I always have been." She shifted round to tickle the cat's neck. It opened its eyes and purred, then patted her hand with one large velvet paw, playing with her ring.

"No, that's naughty, darling."

"That's a pretty ring. The stones spell out a word, don't they?" asked Mia.

"That's right: ruby, emerald, garnet, amethyst, ruby and diamond… regard. My husband's mother gave it to me when our first daughter was born. She was a lovely lady, my mother-in-law." She held out her hand for Mia to see the ring.

"It's beautiful." Although not perfect, the ruby that started the word was smaller and paler than the one towards the end.

Joy smiled and returned to caressing her cat.

"He's a handsome fellow," said Sutton. "Have you had him long?"

"Around five years."

"Your parents didn't like cats?"

"They didn't care for any animals."

"Your father quarrelled with Lucy Logan about her cats?"

"Everybody did."

"Apart from you?"

"I don't quarrel with people."

Mia saw Sutton struggling to keep a dialogue going that involved him asking questions and Joy Marshall absorbing them and giving the minimum of information back. Mia would have helped him if she could but she didn't know where his questioning was heading.

"Your father had a fish pond in his garden?" continued Sutton.

"Yes."

"So he liked fish?"

"He liked his garden."

"Yes?" Sutton looked puzzled.

"The fish were ornaments."

"It's lucky Lucy's cats didn't get them," said Sutton. Joy shuddered and his voice sharpened, "Or did they? Was that another point of contention between your father and Lucy?"

"No." Her voice was still a monotone but her expression was that of a woman looking back at a nightmare. "It was the fish that were vicious. Once a kitten... fell... in the pond. It was horrible!"

"I didn't mean to upset you."

The barriers were back in place. "That's all right. It was a long time ago."

"Your father lived with you when he left Bridge Road?"

"Yes."

"When was that? And how long was it for?"

"Six years ago. He lived here for almost eight months... seven months and three weeks."

"And why did he leave?"

"He wasn't happy here."

"Why wasn't he happy, Joy?"

"He didn't like the girls having friends round, or the untidiness, or me going out, or the way I cooked, or the things I liked watching on television, or the girls playing their music in their rooms, or my garden, or my cats." The list, which had seemed set to go on forever, came to a halt as abruptly as it began.

"How many cats did you have?" asked Sutton, clearly suspecting a similarity to Lucy.

"Two... pedigree Siamese. My father said they looked like giant rats but I loved them."

"You and your father both liked gardening?" He gestured to the pile of magazines. "Wasn't that a bond?"

"No."

"Why not?" There was an exasperated note in Sutton's voice.

"I didn't do things the way he wanted me to."

"In what way?"

"He didn't like my wild garden or lots of colours. He liked order and control."

"So he went to live in a nursing home?"

"That's right."

"Did you go to Wales with him when he went to the nursing home?"

"Yes, my eldest daughter and I drove him down with his things. It was a relief to have him settled. My daughters and I were going off on holiday, the first time we'd got away since my husband died, and I don't know who I'd have got to look after Dad."

"Couldn't he have looked after himself for a short while?"

"He didn't want to. 'Why keep a dog and bark yourself,' that's what he used to say."

"Did he take much with him?" continued Sutton. Mia thought his questions were getting wilder, not aiming for any mark but praying he'd hit one by sheer luck.

"He took two suitcases, an umbrella and a shopping bag that had belonged to my mother."

"When did you last see your father?"

Caught unawares, Mia choked back a giggle. Joy smiled, but Sutton glared.

"When did you last see your father?" he repeated.

Joy's amusement vanished at the sharpness in his tone. "Why then, of course."

"You mean, you haven't seen him in the past five years?"

"No. I didn't expect to."

"You've had letters? Spoken to him on the phone?"

"Oh no. My father said he was cutting me off. He wasn't a man who ever forgave."

"But what was there to forgive?"

For the first time in the interview Joy's voice had an edge to it, "For not being my mother."

66

Sutton looked totally out of his depth. Mia weighed in with a practical question, "Have you got the address of the nursing home?"

"Of course. I send him cards on Christmas and his birthday, and when my oldest daughter had her baby, but he never replies." She got up and crossed to a writing desk, took out an address book, opened it and removed a small brochure.

"Thank you." Mia was surprised by this burst of efficiency. She glanced at the brochure. "The Mountain Ash Residential Home. That's an attractive name."

Again Joy surprised her, this time by the mischief in her smile. "That's what my father thought. He had visions of a beautiful mountain covered in silver-leafed trees."

"And?"

"In South Wales it meant a mountain of ash; a slag heap created by the mining. I could see how angry Dad was when he got there but he couldn't say anything. It was his mistake and he'd never admit to being wrong."

Mia took out her notebook to write the address but Joy said, "You can take it. There's no sense in me writing any more."

"One last question," said Mia, "When your father lived in this town, which doctor and dentist did he attend?"

"The surgery at West Shore Road. I'm sorry, I can't remember either of their names."

They got up to leave. Joy said, "I should have offered you a drink. Would you like something now?"

"No, thank you. And thank you for your help." Sutton waited until the front door was closed before he said, "I'd like it placed on record I'm not enjoying this case."

"Hang on a minute." Mia stepped off the path and headed towards the side garden.

"What are you doing?" Sutton followed her.

"I spotted this on the way in." Mia squatted down and brushed aside wet leaves to reveal a stone slab, carved with the names Yen and Chang.

"Sounds Chinese," said Sutton. "Or Siamese. I guess they were her cats. And no, you can't dig them up, you've got enough cat bones already."

Mia peered at the date carved under the two names. "According to this stone, they died nearly six years ago. That puts their deaths right in the timescale we're looking at. I don't want any more cat bones but I'd like to know how they died."

Chapter 7

"Where now?" asked Mia as she started up the car.

"I don't want to be a quitter but you'd better drop me off at the Lodging House."

"Are you okay?"

"Not really. It's this arm. If I don't straighten it soon I don't think I ever will."

Mia didn't suggest he took the sling off and straightened it there and then. The last thing she needed was a senior cop fainting in her car outside a witness' house. But it was rush hour, and the drive back would take ages.

"My place is a couple of minutes away. We could go there and have a break." It was an offer she'd never made lightly to anyone, especially her police colleagues. Adam and his wife had been round several times but none of the others had set foot in her home.

Inside the house, she helped Sutton take off his coat and showed him to a chair in front of the gas fire.

He took his painkillers out of his jacket pocket. "Could you open these?"

She got one out, gave it to him and fetched him a drink of water. Then she found a small, empty herb container with an easy-to-open lid and transferred the rest of his pills. As she put the kettle on to make a drink, she thought this was so not her; she didn't do nurturing, at least not for the guys who'd passed through her life. That brought her up short. Sutton wasn't a man in her life, not in that sort of way. Looking out for him was the same as her asking her mum's advice about medicine for Trevor. They were both colleagues and there was no difference, give or take eighteen years and six stone in weight.

As she returned to the living room Sutton looked up at her and smiled. It was a nice smile but she read smugness in it. "You're good at getting women to fuss over you."

He looked startled. "I guess I'm used to it. I've got four sisters."

"Four!"

"Three older stepsisters and one younger half-sister," he elaborated. "My mum married a widower when I was five, so I had three, ready-made, bossy women inserted into my life, as well as my mum. Dad and I just do what we're told." Despite the complaint, Mia could hear the affection in his tone.

"I've only got Mum and my sister and niece. Dad died ten years ago. My sister's twelve years younger than me, so I suppose I'm the bossy big sister in my family."

"I'd never have guessed." He leaned back in his chair and sighed. "I wonder if all the people who lived in Bridge Road were as weird as Joy and old Lucy."

Mia remembered the research she'd done into the area when she was working on the plague pit. She knew it was fanciful but she said what she was thinking anyway, "In medieval times it was actually a hamlet, the only piece of land between two inlets. It was called Brycg. That's Old English for Bridge. When the Black Death struck, Brycg was contaminated first." She broke off, embarrassed that she was lecturing a senior cop about medieval history.

"Go on." Sutton sounded interested.

"The inhabitants of the neighbouring hamlets destroyed the bridges and cut off Brycg. Records say everyone in the hamlet died."

"And you're wondering if there's some sort of residual communal memory still at work in Bridge Road?"

Mia felt stupid. "It's idiotic. It's just that the place feels so… blighted."

"It's not idiotic. It would make a fascinating social psychology study. There are places like that, where the past seems close to the surface, but most of them are rural and isolated." He grinned at her. "Now you've got me jumping

70

on my hobby-horse and galloping away."

"Did you study psychology at uni?"

"Yeah."

Mia thought that made total sense.

"That weird interview with Joy Marshall makes your case as far as I'm concerned," continued Sutton. "I hated the way she answered everything without telling me anything. And she didn't ask what it was about."

"I know, but I don't think she's a stupid woman."

"It was driving me crazy. She was answering but I didn't feel I was getting any response."

"I felt that too."

"You were getting on well with her. In fact you were giggling away together towards the end. What was so funny?"

"It was what you said."

"What I said?"

"'When did you last see your father?'" She had a bad feeling she'd have to explain this was the title of a painting about the interrogation of Charles I's children.

To her relief, he grinned. "Did I really say that?"

"Twice. Where were you going with all those questions about the fishpond?"

"I keep thinking the pond's significant."

"You think he died there?"

He started to shrug, then winced and abandoned the move. "I don't know."

"He had no clothes on. Unless he was suffering from dementia, no old man would go nude bathing in a garden pond full of Koi carp."

He glared at her. "Thanks for that. Why don't you just say, in your opinion, I can't detect my way out of a paper bag?"

Mia awarded herself full marks for logic and minus points for tact. "I didn't mean that. It's hard to think things through when you're in pain."

"I guess so. I'm not usually over-sensitive." He forced

71

a smile. "I feel like that picture you painted of the old guy."

"What?"

"Naked, exposed and swimming with carnivorous fish. It's no good putting it off any longer, I'd better straighten this arm." Gingerly he removed the sling and tried. He got it about three-quarters straight then stopped.

"It'll be better when the painkiller kicks in. Do you want tea or coffee?"

"Coffee please, and have you got anything sweet to eat? I need a sugar fix."

"Me too." She made a cafetiere of Fairtrade coffee and opened the box of Belgian chocolates she'd been saving for a special indulgence day.

"Very nice," commented Sutton.

"They're from a colleague I did some bone analysis for... archaeology, not crime."

"You keep up your archaeology?"

"Yeah. I don't do badly out of my private work, but I never seem to have enough time."

"Tell me about it. Hobbies have to take second place. Not that I'll be playing the fiddle for a while."

"Do you play in an orchestra?"

"In a folk-rock band. There are three of us. We perform at folk clubs and ceildhs."

"Cool." That was more interesting than most cops' hobbies. Not that she was in a position to criticise, most people thought a fascination with medieval middens was weird.

Eventually, teeth gritted, Sutton managed to straighten his arm. "Now that's sorted, we ought to get back to work."

"We don't have to go to the office. You can phone to check on William Davies from here."

"Thanks."

He rang through to the nursing home, gave his name and rank and asked to speak to Mr William Davies. This caused some confusion, Davies being a common name in Wales. After long explanations Sutton covered the receiver and said, "He's not there any more but they're fetching a care assistant who knew him."

"Would it help if we put it on speaker phone? Then I can take notes."

"Good idea."

They waited until a brisk voice said, "Hello?"

Wearily Sutton again explained what they wished to know.

"William Davies from England? I remember him, poor man."

"Why poor?" asked Sutton.

"He's the sort who must have his own way and doesn't know what to do with it when he gets it. Only here two weeks and a lot of trouble he made. Nothing was right for him, the food, the television, the entertainment the local schools put on. And a few of our residents aren't as with it as they used to be, and he was unkind to them."

"You didn't like him, did you?"

"I don't see how anybody could."

"Do you remember him leaving?"

"Oh yes. He packed his bags and called a taxi to take him to the station. There was quite a to-do with our Care Manager, the one before this one, because he wanted a refund on the two months he'd paid in advance and she said he wasn't entitled. He was real angry but she had the cash already and she won. She told me he had plenty put away and, from what she'd heard, he hadn't paid his poor daughter in all the months he'd been there. Real skinflint he could be. But it wasn't about money, it was about power."

"You seem to have got him sussed very quickly."

"In this job you see it all the time, old people trying to keep control over their families. Silly really. It never works, making people resentful. But that William Davies, he was the worst I've seen in twenty years of working here. He wouldn't let anyone call him by his first name. Mr Davies he was, to staff and residents."

"And did he call you by your first names?"

She snorted indignantly. "Not so polite as that. 'My good woman' to people of my age or 'girl' to the younger care assistants."

"Did he say where he was going when he left?"

"He said he was going home, where he'd be looked after proper."

"Home to his daughter?"

"That's what we assumed. Real browbeaten she was, poor soul. I said to the Care Manager she ought to phone and warn her he was on his way."

"And did she?"

"I don't know."

"Where's that Care Manager now?"

"Passed on. A stroke it was. Two years ago."

"I see. Thanks for being so helpful."

"You're welcome. But what's it all about? Did the old devil end up in trouble?"

"Possibly."

"Ah well, I always said he would."

Sutton rang off and stared bleakly at Mia. "I'll get onto the dental surgery and ask for a copy of William Davies' records."

Ten minutes later he came off the phone. "That's sorted, subject to the usual paperwork. Hopefully we'll be able to link his records to the skull."

"Unless it's not him," suggested Mia.

"If it's not then where the hell is he?"

"Maybe he's gone off with a voluptuous widow to live in a cat-free Paradise."

"Don't even joke about it. I don't want to start again from square one. Assuming it's William Davies, I wonder whether he did turn up at his daughter's house."

"She said they went away on holiday. I bet she didn't tell her father in case he tried to ruin it. Hang on. I've got an idea."

She phoned through to the only travel agent in Foxcote High Street and asked to speak to the manageress. After a few minutes conversation she rung off and said, "That's confirmed. She looked up her records. Joy and her daughters went to Spain the day before William left the nursing home and they came home two weeks later."

"How the hell did you do that?"

"I thought Joy was the sort of person to book at a local travel agent and I went to school with the manageress. Dave Bycroft's not the only one with local contacts."

"It feels like I'm the only person without any." Sutton sounded sour. "How about using another of your contacts and asking that archaeologist kid to meet us for a drink?"

"Why?"

"Those builders used to live in Bridge Road and I want to know more about them. The kid will be more use if he isn't uptight."

"He'd have been okay yesterday if you hadn't glowered and growled at him." She leapt into insubordination again.

He took her comment well. "I know. My arm hurt. Thanks for helping out."

"No problem." She found Tim Lewis' business card and arranged to meet him, in half an hour, at a pub that was frequented by SOCO and uniformed cops.

As they went out to the car she saw the bushes moving and stiffened instinctively.

"Yeah, they're getting to me that way too," said Sutton.

"What?"

"Cats." He nodded towards a scraggy old tortoiseshell lurking in the undergrowth.

Mia laughed, relieved and a bit embarrassed. Perhaps last night's panic had been caused by a harmless animal. She imagined the piss-taking if she'd dialled triple nine.

"That's Moggy from next door," she said. "She's incredibly ancient and almost blind. She's not allowed out.

I'd better take her back." She scooted across the garden and swooped before Sutton could object. She knew what happened when Moggy went walkabout and had no wish to be greeted by her elderly next door neighbours when she got home with the plea to help them hunt for their runaway.

As she straightened, the cat in her arms, she noticed the ground three feet from where she stood. The soft mud bore the scuffled marks of shoeprints, a man's size, large and broad.

Chapter 8

An hour later, sitting in the pub, Mia still wondered if she should have told Sutton about the footprints. Her instinct to keep quiet had been based on a wish not to seem neurotic. As the fear in the town deepened, many women were dialling 999, some of them phoning every night, because they imagined a killer was stalking them. It would be a dark day when police officers joined their fearful ranks. There could be hundreds of innocent reasons why a man had stepped into her garden, although she couldn't think of any of them off hand. At least she didn't have to worry about going home alone tonight. Mum always expected her to stay over after dinner... that way she could drink.

She forced herself to concentrate on Sutton's interview with Tim Lewis and watched with a mixture of amusement and irritation as Sutton turned his considerable charm onto the younger man. With his arm back in its sling he was the hero cop. Even drinking orange juice he was the coolest guy in the place. Within two minutes the young archaeologist was chatting away, eager to tell Sutton anything he wanted to know.

"It took guts to stand up to those builders, Tim. Did they give you a hard time?"

"Mike was okay but Dennis got nasty. He wanted me to ignore it. If they don't make their deadline they'll be in bad financial trouble. But I couldn't ignore a dead body, could I?"

"Of course not. Why did the builders start at that end of the road? Was there some technical reason or was it chance?"

"Mike said it was probably better to start there because they'd get rid of the loony old girl that kept coming round."

Fleetingly Mia met Sutton's eyes and knew they were thinking the same thing: Dennis and Mike had known more about Lucy than they'd let on.

"Thanks for your help, Tim," said Sutton.

"You're welcome." Nevertheless the boy looked miserable.

"Was this your first body, other than ancient burials?" asked Mia.

"Yes. I don't want to work on watching briefs anymore. I wondered… you must have lots of contacts. You wouldn't put a word in for me, would you?"

"Possibly, but it would be better to get over any squeamishness. What's your specialist area?" As they talked archaeology she kept a wary eye on Sutton but he seemed content to wait.

At last she said, "We must be going. The DI needs to brief his team."

As they left the pub, she said, "Thanks for giving me time with the kid. I wanted to check he was academically sound before I mentioned him to any of my mates."

"It was interesting. I learned quite a bit."

"You were interested in Roman pottery?"

"That too."

Mia wondered if he'd been sussing out Tim or her.

"Do you wish you'd stayed in archaeology, Mia?"

"Sometimes. But I couldn't get a decent permanent job round here and I want to stay in the area, my mum's crippled with arthritis and my sister's a single-parent." In Sutton's eyes that must make her a loser like Dave Bycroft.

"I guess I'm lucky, not having any ties."

Mia shrugged. "That depends on how you define lucky."

In the CID office Dave Bycroft came hurrying over. "The DCI wanted you to report to him as soon as you got in, Guv."

"Right. Call a team meeting for an hour's time. There's been a development. If you walk along with me, Dave, I'll tell you what we've got."

The delay suited Mia. She wanted to check that Trevor and Chantelle were okay. She headed for SOCO.

"I'm glad you're here!" exclaimed Adam as she walked in the door. "This place has become seriously weird."

"In what way?" In fact, as she entered the room, Mia had smelled one strange thing and spotted another. The office was heavily scented with lavender and Chantelle was sitting next to Trevor, holding his hand.

"A strange alternative medicine sort of weird," elaborated Adam.

"It's not weird," protested Chantelle. She glared at Mia. "Surely you've heard of reflexology?"

"I've heard of it," admitted Mia, perching on a corner of Trevor's desk. "But that doesn't mean I know much about it." Now she could see Chantelle was rubbing Trevor's left hand between the forefinger and thumb.

"There are reflex points all over the body and massaging them can ease pain in other places," explained Chantelle.

"I saw a programme about it on TV, but I thought it was feet you had to rub."

"Trevor wasn't comfortable with that."

"If Trev removes his shoes, they'll declare the office a Biological Hazard Area," said Adam.

"She says she can cure my indigestion by rubbing my hands," said Trevor.

"Not cure, alleviate it."

"You seem to know a lot about reflexology?" said Mia.

"It was what I used to do, reflexology, aromatherapy and therapeutic massage."

"Why did you give it up?"

Chantelle shrugged. "It was time to try something new."

"But do things like reflexology work? I'm not being funny, Chantelle, I want to know."

"Of course it does."

"Has it helped you, Trev?"

He cast an apologetic glance at Chantelle. "Not really."

"That reminds me." Mia delved in her bag and produced a medicine bottle. "I asked my mum and she recommended

79

this. She used to be a pharmacist you know."

Trevor looked surprised. "You told your mum about me?"

"I was worried about you."

"Ta luv. Nice of you to care."

"Mum said you ought to see a doctor." Mia knew he wouldn't but she'd done her duty and, more important, done what she was told.

She pinched the teaspoon from Trevor's saucer and poured him a dose of thick, off-white liquid. Obediently he opened his mouth and swallowed.

What's it taste like, Trev?" enquired Adam.

"Horrible. Just like real medicine."

Chantelle's mouth closed to a hard, thin line. She stood up and stalked out of the room.

"The tragedy queen strikes again," said Adam.

"That's not fair," said Trevor. "She's bound to be feeling fragile and I guess I hurt her feelings. You'd best go and check she's alright, Mia."

Mia didn't ask why she'd drawn the short straw; the chances were Chantelle had taken refuge in the loo. Reluctantly she went along the corridor and into the Ladies. Chantelle was standing in the communal area. She kept her back turned.

"Are you okay, Chantelle?"

"Yes!" The hostility in the word made Mia blink.

"Are you sure? I may be over-sensitive but I get the impression something's wrong."

"I'm sick of your clique."

"Our what?"

"You all laugh at me and talk behind my back and Trevor's always picking on me because I'm a woman. The only reason he's nice to you is because you suck up to him."

"That's garbage! We don't like you because you're a troublemaker and Trevor only picks on you when you don't do your job."

"Oh!" Chantelle stared at her open-mouthed.

"He gives you every chance he possibly can. Don't you realise how brave it was of him to let you try out reflexology on him when he was terrified you'd throw another tantrum and put in a complaint?"

"That's why the healing wouldn't work, because he was so tense." Chantelle seemed genuinely horrified.

"Of course he was tense! The stress you're causing him is making him ill." Mia reigned back on her temper. "As a team we don't like people who keep running to HR with a load of lies. We're sick of you. And don't start crying again!" To her surprise, Chantelle bit her lip and blinked back her tears. "Why don't you get on with the job? The first few weeks you were here we thought you were pretty good."

"And then Trevor reprimanded me for something I didn't do." Chantelle sounded bitter.

Mia felt puzzled, then she thought back. "You mean those files that got misplaced? So the CPS had to drop the case?"

"I didn't misplace them. I left them on Steve's desk. He must have got it wrong, but Trevor blamed me."

Mia thought that could very well be true. Steve was a supervisor because of length of service rather than talent and he was notoriously slapdash. But even the best of cops tended to hang together.

"It may not have been fair but is it worth making enemies of everyone? It can't be much fun for you?"

Chantelle hesitated. "My father said I'd never get respect from men in a proper job because I was a girl. He said people would always put me down unless I stood up for my rights."

Mia thought that made no sense at all. "What did your mum think?"

"She died when I was fifteen, but she always used to tell me Dad knew best."

"I see." In fact she saw a lot more than Chantelle realised.

"Then Dad got cancer and I knew he hadn't got long,"

continued Chantelle. "I wanted to be a scientist and make him proud of me but all the time he'd tell me to stand up for myself because cops were sexist."

Mia noted the past tense. "Is he still alive?"

"No. He died six months ago."

And Chantelle hadn't told anyone at work about her loss. Mia felt sorry for her.

"I've made such a mess of everything," sobbed Chantelle. "I'll have to leave. I can't be angry with Trevor anymore. He was so brave today and so kind."

Mia knew a moment's temptation. The office without Chantelle would be bliss, but telling her to go would be a lousy thing to do and HR were bound to blame Trevor and his team. "There's no need to leave. How about we all make a fresh start?"

"I'd like that." Chantelle kept on crying.

Mia watched her helplessly, then thought, 'What would I do if this wasn't Chantelle?' Stiffly she put her arms round her and muttered soothing words.

At last Chantelle wiped her eyes and straightened up. "I'm sorry."

"That's okay. You'd better wash your face."

Chantelle obeyed but didn't renew her make-up. Without it she looked older but much pleasanter. "Ready," she said.

Chantelle went through with the reconciliation better than Mia had expected. Standing in a little girl pose, hands twisting together in front of her, she said how sorry she was she'd caused so much trouble. She explained about the death of her father and how isolated she'd become.

Mia noted that Trevor seemed more sympathetic than she'd been. She caught Adam's gaze and he winked. If she was a cynic it was nice to know she was in good company.

"Mia said your colic was due to stress and I'd caused it," said Chantelle.

"I wouldn't put it like that," said Trevor warily.

"You mean you wouldn't say it because you're scared I'll

make more trouble? I'm sorry. I didn't mean to make you ill, Trevor."

Mia dredged up a memory of something Chantelle had mentioned in the early days of their acquaintanceship, when they'd still tried to chat. "Trev needs a golf partner. You play don't you, Chantelle?"

"I used to. My father taught me, but I haven't played for years." Chantelle smiled shyly at Trevor. "I'd love to take it up again, but I'm sure you're too good to partner me."

"No, not at all. I mean I'm not that good but I'd enjoy a game sometime."

"Who wants coffee?" asked Mia, desperately trying to keep her voice steady.

"Chamomile tea for Trevor and me, please," said Chantelle.

Adam joined her beside the kettle as Trevor and Chantelle plunged into a discussion of irons and greens. "What have you done?" he enquired softly, his voice shaking with laughter.

Mia refused to meet his eyes. One lapse and they'd both be rolling on the floor. "I don't know, but I think I may have created a monster."

Chapter 9

Mia got in early on Thursday morning, determined to persuade Sutton to allow her enough free time to work the crime scene. She breezed into his office and walked into an intimate moment.

Sutton was sitting at his desk, behind him stood a young woman, leaning over to arrange his tie. She was so close her hair brushed against his cheek. As Mia stopped in the doorway, she looked up and smiled, then darted round to survey Sutton. "That's okay."

"Cheers Tash." He grinned at Mia. "'Morning Mia. Meet Natasha Wendover. She's come down from the seriously scary North to check up on me. Tash, this is Mia Trent, the unfortunate woman who's taken over your role as my minder." Despite his breezy manner Mia thought he seemed ill at ease.

"Cheshire is so not scary," retorted Tash. "At least only to a city boy like you. You're the only cop I know who wears riot gear to round up a herd of cows."

If Sutton was uncomfortable, Tash seemed supremely confident.

"Have you known DI Sutton long?" Mia knew her question sounded stilted.

"For years. Ever since we were both hopeful young DCs."

Mia thought that uniform for CID officers would be a distinct advantage. Tash was dressed in a smoke grey suit that emphasised her lovely figure and her long fair hair was fluffed out around her heart-shaped face. Police uniform and a severe hairstyle would cut down on her charms, and it would tell Mia whether she should call her 'ma'am.'

Sutton came to her rescue. "Tash has just made detective sergeant."

"Congratulations." Mia hoped she didn't sound as

grudging as she felt.

"More luck than judgement." Tash nodded towards Sutton, "This is the guy who showed me how to keep my eye on the ball. Stick with him and you'll get promotion in record time."

"Mia doesn't want promotion as a detective," said Sutton. "She's a Forensics expert."

"Cool. That must be so useful."

Condescending cow! "Are you staying down here long?"

"Just as long as it takes Ollie to get his act together. You ready yet?"

"As I'll ever be." Sutton stood up.

"But?… What?..." Mia hated being reduced to blithering.

"I'm sorry, Mia. There's something important I've got to do today. I'll try to get back this evening or first thing tomorrow."

She couldn't believe he'd skive off in the middle of a case. "Any instructions for me, sir?"

"No. I'm sure you've got plenty to do."

"Right." She turned on her heel and left.

Instinct took her down to SOCO. The last place she wanted to be was the CID office with everyone smirking and asking where the Boy Wonder had flown off to and if that was Superwoman who'd dropped by to pick him up.

It didn't improve her temper to be greeted by the sight of Pixie, Chantelle's cat, curled up on Trevor's desk. Apart from Pixie and Trevor the office was deserted.

"Don't look like that," he said defensively. "It's cruel keeping him trapped in his basket all day." He tickled Pixie with his pen and the cat rolled over and pounced on it with velvet paws.

Mia reached over and stroked the cat. Despite her bad mood she smiled as he purred contentedly. He was a handsome creature, with glowing ginger fur and a placid temperament that was amazing in anyone living twenty-four seven with Chantelle. Mia liked everything about him apart from his ridiculous name but there was a time and place for everything. "I agree but I was thinking of not bringing him into work rather than giving him free-run of the office."

"I talked to Chantelle about that. I've given her a week to make other arrangements for him, then he's got to be out of here."

"And she agreed?"

"Yeah. I don't know what you said to her yesterday but I appreciate it. I know it's not your job to sort out the other staff." He looked at her thoughtfully. "Though it could be, if you went for your sergeant's exam. If they retire me, I'd go a lot happier knowing you were keeping the place up to scratch. The exams shouldn't be a problem for a smart girl like you. You'd make inspector in no time."

Mia had to admit it would be good to equal Sutton and outrank his pal, Tash. "But you don't want to retire."

"I don't reckon I'm going to get much choice."

Mia surveyed the pork pie, Scotch egg and iced doughnut that lay on a side-table, out of reach of the cat. "I'll make a bargain. You get some exercise and cut out the pies and cakes and I'll go for my sergeant's exams."

"I suppose I should." He cast a longing look at his junk food.

"Trev, you do know the additives in this stuff are addictive?"

"You're winding me up!"

"Really I'm not." She turned her head as Chantelle entered the room and made a conscious effort not to clam up. "We're talking about how bad the additives are in pre-packaged food."

Chantelle nodded vigorously. "They're terrible! They attack your immune system and make you prone to all sorts of diseases, and cause constipation and add to the risk of diabetes. And the amount of salt increases the likelihood of heart attacks and strokes."

"Ease off," begged Mia. "You're scaring Trev."

To her surprise Chantelle took this in good part. "I'm

sorry, Trevor, but I feel strongly about additives."

"I noticed," said Trevor. "But I guess you're right. I don't eat properly." He glared at Mia. "Did you drop in to stir things or are you planning to do some work?"

"I'm planning to do a lot of work. I want this case solved as soon as possible."

"Going all out to impress the new DI?"

"No, I'm going all out to get away from him."

Putting together cat bones was a tedious job, like doing several 3-D jigsaw puzzles at the same time, with an unknown quantity of bits broken or missing. After some hours Mia could be reasonably sure none of the cats had been killed by physical trauma. That left the cause of death as drowning or poison or possibly electrocution, which didn't help a lot.

Trevor put his head round the workroom door and said, "Dave Bycroft's here with dental records for the Bridge Road victim."

Reluctantly, Mia went to collect them. Bycroft looked infuriatingly smug. "Check these for me straightaway, Mia."

"For you?"

"Of course for me. I'm senior officer on the case while the DI's away."

"He'll be back by this evening." She wondered why she felt any loyalty to Sutton.

"Maybe I'll have the case wrapped up by then. That's why I don't want to waste time getting the pathologist to do a comparison with the skull. You can make the ID from your records and I'll go and talk to that crazy old girl and get a confession out of her."

"Be careful, she's very vulnerable."

"The loony game won't work with Liz and me. We had enough of her nonsense the other day. You planning to do that dental comparison any time this year?"

Seething, Mia followed Bycroft and Trevor back into the office to compare the charts.

She checked through carefully, then said, "The dentistry matches, although the jaw we found has lost two teeth on the top left front."

"Must be in that hole we found him in. You probably got them mixed up with the cat bones."

"No we didn't. We've documented everything in there."

"Must've missed them. You lot are always mucking up and blaming working cops."

"Who do you think you are, talking to my officer like that?" Trevor's interruption startled them both.

Bycroft scowled. "She's seconded to CID and I'll talk to her how I want."

Mia thought the sergeant must have short-term memory problems; the words 'Bruton Street' and 'massage parlour' hovered on her lips.

Trevor slammed to his feet. "You treat a senior officer with respect! I allowed Mia to work this case as assistant to DI Sutton and her secondment's directly to him. Anytime she's in SOCO she's my officer. That was what DCI Craig and I agreed. If you want to argue with him, we'll go straight along to his office." He moved towards the door.

"No need for that," said Bycroft hastily.

Trevor remained standing. "I've been thinking I ought to see him anyway. I'm not sure he knows about that fishpond business. My people are busy. I won't have their time wasted."

"I've warned the officers involved." Bycroft backed towards the door. "Mia, if you get any forensics information today, please pass it on."

"Anything I think will help you." Mia phrased the agreement cautiously. "What about William Davies' house?"

"You can start there if you want. We've got permission to go through it but I haven't got the time." The door closed behind him as he spoke.

Mia grinned at Trevor. "Would it be disrespectful to a senior officer if I kissed you?"

He chuckled, then cast a wary glance at Chantelle. She

looked embarrassed. "I don't mind if Mia kisses you. Please don't look like that, Trevor."

"Sorry, it's a habit."

"That doesn't make it better," said Mia.

"Doesn't it?… I'm sorry… I didn't mean…"

Mia cut across his confused apology, "Surely years in charge of Scene of Crimes has taught you, when you're in a hole, you stop digging. Tell me about you and DCI Craig agreeing the terms of my secondment. I seem to remember you were really cross about letting me go."

"Yeah, but Bycroft didn't know that. And he wouldn't risk me complaining to the DCI."

"I'm impressed. You're more devious than you appear to be."

"If that was a compliment, thanks. How are you getting on with this case? I want you back as soon as possible."

"I'm stuck regarding the forensics. There's nothing in the pit to tell us how he died. I don't think it's the primary scene and I'm not happy about how long ago he died."

"How do you mean?" Trevor was clearly struggling to keep up. Mia reminded herself that he wasn't forensics trained. The knowledge he'd picked up over the years was a bonus, not part of the job description.

"You mean the rate of decomposition is too far advanced? It doesn't tie in with when you know the victim was alive?" said Chantelle.

"That's right." Mia tried to conceal her surprise. She'd got into the habit of discounting Chantelle but of course she wouldn't have got the job without a relevant science degree. "The victim was known to be alive five years ago. Witnesses from the nursing home in Wales swear to that. But that degree of decomposition should take at least ten years, even allowing for the shallowness of the grave. The pathologist says some unknown conditions must have triggered the unnaturally fast rate of decomp. And she can't be certain whether the blow to the head killed him or not, although she thinks it's possible.

And the million dollar question is why was he naked?"

"For me the big question is why the Pensions people didn't pick up on him not drawing his money," said Trevor.

"DI Sutton got straight onto that. Apparently the money was automatically diverted into a savings account. That's all they'll tell us until we've got proof of death."

"That's banks for you. Cagey when the cops want their help, then leaving all their clients details on a laptop for any villain to pinch." Trevor rummaged through a pile of reports on his desk. "Geoff's given me his findings on the bit of the fish pond he processed. I wish we could have got the lot done, but we're snowed under. Do you need the rest of that scene processed? I had the tent left in place in case you did."

"I'll check what Geoff's listed and make a judgement call. I don't think it's important." Although she remembered Sutton had suggested the fishpond was somehow significant.

She sat at her desk, forking up pasta salad and reading through Geoff's report. Most of it was exactly what you'd expect to find in a disused fishpond: fish bones, snail shells, a residue of aquatic plants, rocks, the debris of the water pump and a fragment of splintered tooth.

"Tooth!" Trevor and Chantelle both turned to stare at her and she said, "I've just realised that I need to excavate the rest of that pond."

Chantelle hesitated then, to Mia's amazement, she said, "If Trevor can spare me, I'll help."

"I need the help but are you sure you're okay about going back?"

Chantelle nodded. "Yes, I've got to get over it."

As they pulled up in Bridge Road Mia felt relieved to see a patrol car with two uniformed officers waiting for them.

"We'd better start with the pond, while it's still light," she said. "Be careful you don't cut yourself on the broken pump."

They worked in silence, recording and processing

efficiently. Mia thought she could get to like this new, focused Chantelle.

"Mia, could I ask you a favour?"

Or maybe not. "What sort of favour?"

"I wondered if you and Trevor would come to dinner with me one evening? I don't want Trevor to think I'm laying some sort of trap for him."

So when did she turn into a chaperone? "Sure."

"I guess Adam will be going to see his wife but I could invite DI Sutton, if you like."

"No way! Why would I want to spend my off-duty time with him?"

Chantelle looked startled. "I thought he seemed lonely."

"He can stay lonely for all I care… Hold on." She held up a discoloured incisor. "I'm sure this is one of William Davies' missing teeth. If so, we've found our primary crimescene."

Encouraged, they worked for another hour and found splintered fragments of the other tooth.

"What's this?" Chantelle indicated a tiny red stone.

"Well spotted." Mia wondered why she noticed slivers of tooth and Chantelle homed in on a precious stone.

"I think it's a jewel but it might be glass."

Mia looked closer and felt her stomach tighten. "I'm sure it's a jewel. And I'm pretty sure I know where it came from."

Another half-hour's work yielded no results. Mia stood up and stepped outside the tent to stretch her cramped muscles. "That's it. We've finished the pond." She took a heavy iron key out of her pocket. "Now to check the house. I'm not happy about the batteries in this camera. I'll go and get new ones."

Her mind occupied with unravelling their discoveries, she hurried back to the van and got out new batteries. As she jumped out of the van she saw Dennis Plummer, standing across the road. A jolt of fear went through her.

"I wish you'd tell us if you're going off somewhere."

Mia whirled round. One of the uniformed cops stood there, looking aggrieved. "Inspector Mayfield warned us we've got to stay with you, but it works both ways, you know."

She turned again. The street opposite was empty. "Did you see him?"

"See who?"

"Dennis Plummer. He was standing over there."

"He must have made bail. That's why you're not supposed to go off on your own."

"Okay, you've made your point. Thanks for coming to look for me." She led the way back to 2 Bridge Road where Chantelle and the other cop were waiting.

She greeted Chantelle with a bright smile; no point in frightening her. "Let's look at the house."

"What are we looking for?"

"Any signs that the old boy came back here, and anything else that strikes you as odd."

In the wrought iron conservatory the shelving still held plant pots and seed trays full of dusty earth. Mia imagined William Davies walking out and leaving the plants to die.

"I can smell tobacco," said Chantelle.

Mia sniffed. "You're right."

"Didn't you notice it when you came in before?"

"I didn't come in here. DI Sutton told two of the DCs to check it out. If they smoke, they might not notice the smell, especially as the whole place stinks of mould."

"It's this." Chantelle had followed her nose and discovered an almost empty, glass milk bottle on a top shelf. Although plugged with a rag, it had fallen on its side and yellow-brown liquid had formed a puddle on the shelf.

Chantelle peered at it doubtfully. "There's a stick-on label on the bottle. It's discoloured but I think it says 'rose spray.'"

"Don't touch it! It's probably nicotine. That's what the old gardeners used to use. Double glove and put the bottle in a sealed safety-box. Nicotine is absorbed through the skin and it's lethal." Mia made sure Chantelle carried out her instructions and put up a hazardous substance warning. "We'll get someone in to clean up. Thank God no-one touched that stuff. "Let's see what other treats this house of horror has for us."

Chapter 10

There was a two-ringed camp cooker in the kitchen cupboard, along with a hurricane lamp and candles and a small selection of tinned food, brown speckled and pitted with rust. Apparently it was too grotty even for vandals and squatters to nick.

There was nothing else to be found downstairs, just dirt and decay, the trappings of abandonment. The smaller bedroom was empty but in the master bedroom there were more candles and men's clothes, neatly folded and put away. This meticulousness brought the old man to life in Mia's imagination. Poor, miserable, old sod.

As she moved back towards the door a board squeaked. She felt it shift under her foot. She rolled back the threadbare carpet to reveal a tiny trapdoor, which she swiftly levered up. "Eureka! Most of his personal papers must be here." She lifted out her find, taking photos before she bagged it up. She grinned at Chantelle and announced triumphantly, "There's two bankbooks, both for savings accounts. Now perhaps we'll discover where his money's gone."

Mia returned to the Station certain she'd discovered the primary crime scene and evidence to piece together a picture of the crime. Now it was down to interviewing suspects and getting confessions. She went to CID in the hope Sutton had returned but his room was dark and empty.

"You looking for me?" Dave Bycroft came out of the CID main office.

"I've left the preliminary report about today's findings on the DI's desk."

"Anything earth shattering?" He still sounded sulky after the run-in with Trev.

"We've found the victim's missing teeth in the fishpond,

so it seems likely that's our primary crime scene. Your constables hit it right by accident."

He scowled at her. "Don't get smart with me. You got anything useful to tell me?"

"It's all in there." She gestured towards the office.

"I'll look at it tomorrow." He glanced at his watch and strode away.

Mia strolled into the CID main office. "Bycroft's in a hurry," she remarked.

"Probably hoping to grab a shower before he goes to his kid's Parents' Evening." Liz looked up from her desk and grinned ruefully. "I stink!"

"The full Lucy Logan sensory experience?" Mia didn't try to hide her satisfaction.

"You're not kidding! I don't know why the mental health people haven't cleaned her up."

"Did you get the confession Bycroft wanted?"

"Oh yeah, she confessed to everything… the Hungerford massacre, the London tube bombings and shoplifting from Debenhams in 1973. The only thing she hasn't admitted to is being Jack the Ripper and killing that old guy you dug out of her garden. She drove Dave Bycroft crazy."

"Couldn't happen to a nicer guy. I saw Dennis Plummer hanging round Bridge Road today."

Liz scowled. "The bastard got police bail, but he shouldn't be near the crime scene, or approach you or Chantelle."

"He didn't actually approach me. Maybe he didn't know we were there. After all he has got a lot of money invested in Bridge Road." Mia tried for a casual tone, "Any idea when DI Sutton's due back?"

"No. We thought you'd be the one who could answer that."

"Afraid not. I think it's something to do with a former job up north."

"Yeah, I saw his former job when she picked him up. What I wouldn't give for legs and an arse like that. It's not surprising the Boy Wonder went off with her."

95

Mia made good her escape from the CID office. She felt uncertain what to do. She'd got some theories she wanted to share and it was only right that Sutton should hear them first. She got out her mobile and dialled Sutton's number.

He answered on the fifth ring. "Hello?"

"It's me, Mia."

"Mia? Is something wrong?"

"No. I wanted to talk to you about the case. I…"

"Could this wait? It's not a good time."

There was noise in the background, lots of voices talking and a woman screeching loudly; Mia guessed she was drunk. "No, that's fine. Sorry to bother you."

She keyed off. To hell with the rules, she'd follow this through by herself.

Rush hour traffic delayed her and it was already dark when she reached her destination. She hesitated before getting out of the car. Temper and pride were lousy reasons for breaking the rules. She imagined Sutton's reaction if she transgressed PACE and hindered prosecution. Not to mention placing herself at risk.

Her phone rang. The display read, 'Mum: Home.'

"Hi Mum. Everything okay?" The last time Mum had phoned her at work was three years ago when Dani was born.

"Fine love. Is this a bad time?"

"No, it's okay."

"I've been watching the news and I wanted to check whether DI Sutton was all right."

"Why shouldn't he be?" Had there been a motorway pile up or terrorist explosion since she'd spoken to him?

"The reporter said his name, and I thought there couldn't be two DIs called Oliver Sutton. He had his arm around that poor girl and he looked so upset."

So he and Tash had been in an accident. "Is he hurt? What happened?"

"Oh no, he wasn't hurt. I thought you'd know. It was

those twins who were kidnapped a few years ago, up near Manchester. One of them has died, at least they've turned off the Life Support machine."

"And Oliver was there?" Mia felt as if she'd stepped into quicksand.

"Yes. He had his arm around the twin that survived while the family spokesman was talking outside the hospital. I suppose he was involved in the original case."

"Yes, that makes sense." At least as much sense as anything did. "Thank you, Mum."

Thank you for stopping me from making the biggest mistake in my career. She keyed off and used her phone to log on to the news service. The death of the girl was still a major news item, although the crime had been committed over six years ago. Now she remembered. Gail and Katherine Briar had been twins, aged seventeen, and inseparable. They were together when they were abducted by the psychopath who'd been stalking them. He'd hardly touched them. Instead he'd buried them together in a wooden coffin, in wild woodland, in a shallow grave. They were in there for five days. There was a listening device in the coffin, so he could hear them sobbing and suffering and begging to be released. There were two hoses to the outside for them to breathe through. In theory that should have given them sufficient air, but Katherine's tube got clogged. Gail had tried to get her twin to share her tube but she'd become disorientated and Katherine had lapsed into a coma. When the police discovered them she was brain damaged. Now they'd given up hope and turned off Life Support. She saw a couple of shots of Sutton outside the hospital. His cold expression told her how distressed he was.

She entered the crowded pub, looking for her off-duty boozing mates. Her mobile rang. She debated whether to retreat outside to take the call, then compromised and sidled into a corner occupied only by a malignant looking, stuffed ferret in a glass case.

97

"Hello?"

"It's Oliver… Oliver Sutton. Sorry about not being able to talk before. Things were a bit… It wasn't a good time."

"No, I'm sorry. I shouldn't have phoned out of the blue like that. At that time I didn't know why you'd gone up North."

"And now you do?"

"I think so."

"When you rang I'd only just put my phone back on."

"After the hospital?"

"Yeah. They made us turn our phones off in case they mucked up the machines." He gave a shaky laugh. "Ironic, isn't it? When they were about to switch Katherine off."

"I'm so sorry, Oliver." Mia felt helpless.

"As soon as we got back to the house Gail fell apart… I'd expected that."

"Were you the Family Liaison Officer six years ago?"

"Sort of. What did you want to tell me about the Bridge Road case?"

"I've found the primary crimescene. Believe it or not, it was the fishpond." She smiled as he swore softly. "I've got a theory to run past you when you get back."

"What sort of theory? Have you told Bycroft?"

"I didn't think he'd listen to me. Don't worry, a day won't make any difference."

"For a second I was scared you'd tried to deal with it by yourself."

"Of course not. That would be stupid." How hypocritical was that?

"I assume you're not planning to tell me your theory over the phone?"

"I can't. I'm standing in the pub." The stuffed ferret had the feral look of a creature that would grass up anyone.

"Me too. Tash insisted on taking me for a stiffener before I start the journey back."

"Is she driving you?"

"She wants to but I'd rather take the train."

Mia imagined him going back to his police lodgings with the experiences of the day heavy upon him. "Oliver, if you want to come round to me when you get back, you're welcome… I thought you might want to talk… I'll be glad to listen…"

"I'm not the best of company."

"All the more reason you shouldn't be by yourself."

"I could be pretty late."

"It doesn't matter. I'll wait up until you arrive or until you phone to say you won't be coming."

"Thanks, Mia. I'd better go."

As she squeezed through the crowd someone pushed into her. "Sorry."

"No problem." Recognition hit, and with it wariness. This was her local and she'd never seen Mike Plummer here before.

He didn't move on. "Could I speak to you?"

"I guess." She was pretty sure he'd come here with that in mind.

"I wanted to say sorry, about Dennis and what he did the other day."

"It was my colleague who was traumatised. She's the one who deserves an apology"

"But she's with those other cops. I'm no good at talking to people in a crowd."

She shrugged and started to move away.

"Please wait. I need to explain about Dennis. Everything in his life's gone wrong in the last few years. He got in this pub fight and was banged up for assault. His wife threw him out and he isn't allowed to see his kids anymore, because some bitch of a Brownie worker phoned his wife to say he was drunk when he was picking up Zoe."

"You can't blame the woman for putting the kid's welfare first." Mia forced her protest into his monologue; after his slow start he was talking without pause. "Mr Plummer, why are you telling me this?"

99

He shrugged, his face sullen. "I thought you ought to know. When he gets like that he could do any crazy thing." He turned abruptly and shouldered his way through the crowd.

The table was full of off-duty SOCO officers and cops. They greeted Mia cheerfully but none of the guys offered her a seat, which was cool with her, equality should work both ways.

"You can share my chair if you like," said Chantelle. She looked blissfully happy, as if being asked to the pub with the team was the best thing that had happened to her for years.

"Or you can sit on my lap," suggested Trevor. "As long as you don't spill my beer."

"You reckon there's room on your lap for Mia and your gut?" said one of the uniformed sergeants, taking advantage of their off-duty status.

They all laughed. Trevor managed a grin, but the amusement didn't reach his eyes.

"You saying I've got a big arse, Frank?" Mia perched on the arm of Trevor's chair, retaining her balance by draping her arm over his shoulders.

"You're in there, Trev," said the self-appointed wit.

Mia's smile didn't slip. "Too right he is. I love cuddly guys."

"That new DI's going to have to put on a few stone then." Frank was pushing his luck.

"Mia, please take my chair."

The voice close to her ear startled her and she nearly fell off of the chair arm. She regained her balance and stood up. "Tim, hello. You made me jump."

"I brought this across for you. I couldn't see a lady standing when I'd got a chair."

And a lady certainly couldn't stand when he was ramming a chair behind her knees. He wedged her between Chantelle's and Trevor's chairs, an awkward position, half in the passageway. "Can I get you a drink, Mia?"

100

"Red wine please." Mia sighed as he hurried over to the bar. It was her own fault for having met Tim here with Sutton yesterday.

"You setting up a toy boy?" Trevor kept his voice low so that only Mia could hear.

"Do me a favour, I've got better taste than that." She saw the image of Oliver Sutton in his mind and warned, "Don't say it."

"I'm not saying nothing. I owe you for putting Frank Dawson in his place." He chuckled. "Cuddly men indeed."

Mia thought she'd rather have sex with Trev every day for a month than once with Tim the Geek. However, as the optimum was not screwing either of them, she didn't mention this.

Tim returned with her drink. As she'd feared, he stayed hovering behind her chair.

"Are you by yourself?" she asked, craning her neck to look up at him.

"Oh no, my mate's over there." He waved vaguely towards the scrum. "Is there any news about the body I found?"

"Not yet."

"When it's over, do you think you could tell me about it? It's kind of worrying me."

The words 'Get over it,' rang in Mia's mind. She changed the subject, "Did you tell Mike Plummer or his cousin that I use this pub?"

"I might have mentioned it. I'm sorry for Mike. It's hard for him, Dennis being so vile."

"There's no reason for him to keep clearing up Dennis' garbage."

"Mike told me Dennis' mum brought him up, so he feels as if he owes her."

Tim's breath was stale and she wished he'd stop breathing in her face. Trevor, who might have helped her, had been drawn into conversation with some of the other guys.

"Are you an archaeologist like Mia?" Chantelle smiled sweetly up at Tim.

"Yes that's right."

"How fascinating. Tell me about all the digs you've been on."

Eagerly he turned towards her and started to describe a Roman villa he'd helped excavate in Yorkshire. He made his part in the dig sound pivotal. Mia suspected, in his eagerness to impress Chantelle, he'd forgotten a fellow archaeologist was listening in.

"Lost your admirer then?" Trevor's breathy whisper tickled her ear.

She turned towards him and hissed, "Chantelle's doing me a favour."

"You get anything useful from digging out the rest of that pond?"

"I think I did. My report's on your desk. I'll know for certain how relevant it is after I've talked it through with DI Sutton."

"You know where he's been to today?"

"Yeah? Do you?"

"Saw it on the news, so I had a nosy through the reports on the case. It was him got them girls out of that coffin. That sort of thing stays with you." He stood up. "I'm off. Either of you girls want watching home I'll be glad to do it."

This time none of the other cops made lairy comments, the fear in the community was too cruel for anyone to mock.

"Please." Chantelle was already on her feet.

"What about you, Mia?"

"No need to go yet," said Frank. "We're going for pizza. We can see you home."

"No thanks. I'd love a pizza but I've got to go."

"Please stay, Mia. I'll look after you," pleaded Tim.

"I must get home."

"I'll go then. Goodbye Mia." Sulking, Tim walked away. As they crossed the car park, Mia saw a movement in the shadows and a glimpse of a white face and burly form. She looked again and the figure was gone.

They drove to her house in convoy, escorted her to her door and waited until she'd set her alarm. There was no message from Sutton on the answer-phone but, after a few seconds, her phone rang. She snatched it up. "Hello?" No-one spoke. "Hello? Oliver, is that you?" Still no speech, but she could hear the rustle of breathing. "Hello? Who's there? Oliver?"

The line went dead. She keyed in 1471 but the caller had withheld their number.

She felt rattled and hated herself for it. She rechecked her alarm system, then went upstairs to change. Remembering the gorgeous Tash, she put on a velvet caftan in shades of scarlet and gold and sprayed herself with perfume. A girl had to keep her confidence up somehow.

She curled up on the sofa with a glass of wine and watched The Lion In Winter, a historical classic that she still adored. Time plodded onwards and she wondered whether Sutton had gone straight back to his lodgings and had forgotten to phone.

The knock on her front door startled her. It came again. She got up and hurried into the hall. "Hello? Who's there? Oliver, is that you?"

She thought she heard a whispered, "Yes," but couldn't be sure.

She peered through the spy hole. There was no-one in sight. Could he have collapsed?

"Oliver, are you ill?" She thought she heard a muffled groan.

Her hand flew to the bolt but she controlled the impulse and stepped back. She picked up her mobile from the hall table and called Sutton's number. Suddenly she was afraid. She could hear Sutton's phone ringing in her ear but there was no sound of it outside.

Chapter 11

"Mia, hi. Sorry I didn't phone. I've slept most of the journey."

The voice was in her ear, and still there was no echo from the other side of the door.

"Where are you?"

"About twenty minutes away."

"Then you're not outside my door?"

"No." His voice sharpened, "But if someone is barricade yourself upstairs and call triple nine."

Mia fled upstairs to her bedroom and pushed a cupboard across to block the closed door.

She made her emergency call then stood beside the window, pressed against the wall. Five minutes later a squad car blue-lighted its way onto her drive. She recognised the two cops who got out and went downstairs to unbolt and open the front door.

"Pizza delivery, luv?" The patrol cop grinned as he handed her a flat box, labelled with the name of a popular take-away.

Automatically she accepted it. "But I didn't order pizza."

"Must be a mistake. Probably a credit card transaction, so the delivery boy didn't have to worry about getting paid. Someone's going to be mad when they don't get their food."

"Maybe." It occurred to her that Frank and the other guys might have sent her a pizza.

"We'll get on then, if everything's okay?"

"Yeah sure. Sorry you've been bothered."

"Better safe than sorry. I'll wait until I hear you bolt the door. If someone does come asking for their pizza, you chuck it out of an upper window, don't get lulled into opening the door."

"I won't. Thanks."

The patrol car had just gone when another car pulled up on the drive and Sutton and Tash got out.

"You okay?" he demanded as she opened the door.

"I'm fine. It was a false alarm. Someone left a pizza outside."

"Thank God for that!" Neither Sutton nor Tash raised even the glimmer of a smile.

Mia expected them to say goodnight and leave, but they didn't move. She stepped back from the doorway and they trooped inside.

In the living room, Sutton slumped onto the sofa. He'd lost his jacket and tie and his shirt was stained with sweat. He'd abandoned his sling but was moving his arm with care.

"Your stuff's still in my car," said Tash.

"Whatever." He looked shattered

"I thought you were coming by train," said Mia.

"That was before I realised how incapable he was," said Tash. "One drink and he was so pissed he'd lost all sense of direction. If I'd left him to it, he'd probably be in Scotland by now. I know it's cheeky, but could I beg a cup of coffee and a sandwich before I head back home?"

"You're going back tonight?"

"I'd better. The baby-sitter doesn't like me staying out all night. I have to do it too often for work."

"You know damn well Joe would rather you got home tomorrow than not at all," snapped Sutton. "I'll find you a hotel."

"You're welcome to stay here." Mia regretted the words as soon as they left her mouth.

"You sure?" Tash was clearly tempted.

"Think of me," said Sutton. "I'll feel hideously guilty if you go to sleep behind the wheel and get splattered all over the motorway?"

She blew him a kiss. "You really know how to sweet talk a girl. Thanks Mia. I'll give Joe a ring." She took her mobile out into the hall.

"Is Joe her partner?" asked Mia.

"Yeah, they're getting married at Christmas. They're taking Tiffany, that's their little girl, to Lapland with them on their honeymoon, to visit Father Christmas."

"What a lovely idea. Is Joe a cop as well?"

"No. He's a part-time music teacher and Tiffany's prime carer. Tash has always been more career minded than Joe."

"Will he really not mind Tash staying down here?"

"Of course not." He clicked onto the hidden part of Mia's question, "Joe and I have been mates since Uni. We formed a band and still play together when we can. It was me that introduced him and Tash. She sings with us."

Mia hated him knowing what she'd been thinking when her thoughts had been so cheap. "Sorry. I got things wrong. She's so gorgeous."

"Yeah, beautiful, sexy, smart and tough, and even bossier than you."

"I'll have to work on it then." She poured him a glass of wine. "You look wrecked."

"It's not been the best day I've ever known." He grinned at her. "I'm even glad to be back in Ledleigh."

"Want to talk about it?"

"I'm not sure."

"I didn't mean to be nosy."

"I know. I didn't mean to snub you, but it's hard to talk about something when you haven't got it straight yourself." He was silent for a minute then said quietly, "It was odd, going to the hospital. Katherine didn't look much different to when we got her out of that box. There was a greyish tinge to her skin and she looked so frail. The terrible part of today was she didn't seem like a person. It was as if she was just a thing." He downed his wine in one gulp.

"But it was the other one, Gail, that took me apart. One look and I was right back in the days when I kept wondering when I was going to get the call from her mum that this time she'd managed to do it… to top herself."

"Has she tried often?" Mia spoke softly.

"Yeah. Except I don't know if she's really trying or if it's some game of brinkmanship she's playing."

"Game?" queried Mia.

"Not like in having fun. More like offering herself to death time after time, waiting to be accepted."

"Is she playing this game with herself or with you and her family?"

He considered this. "I don't think it's anything to do with us."

"But surely she must relate to you? Otherwise why did she want you there today?"

He shrugged. "For a while it seemed like she was relating to me. I was the one who scooped her out of that hole and, for the first few weeks, I was the only one she'd communicate with. Not even her mum or dad, just me. That's why they wanted me there today. But, looking back, I don't think anyone has been real to her since it happened."

The empty glass cracked between his tense fingers and he swore.

"Have you cut yourself?"

"It's nothing, just a scratch." He sucked his finger. "Sorry about your glass."

"That doesn't matter." She passed him a tissue, then took the broken wineglass from him. "I'll get rid of this."

In the hall, Tash was talking on her phone but she said, "Yeah, love you too," and keyed off as Mia appeared. "How's he doing?" A nod of the head indicated Sutton.

"Fine, apart from crushing the odd glass."

"That good huh?" She followed Mia into the kitchen and watched as she dumped the broken glass and got out clean ones and a fresh bottle of wine. She smiled her gratitude as Mia passed her a drink. "Thanks for letting me stay tonight. And thanks for being here for Ollie. This business has really got to him."

"He's been pretty miserable anyway. His new team aren't

making it easy for him."

"Yeah, he said. I told him that's the trouble with going up like a rocket. It gets lonely in the stratosphere by yourself." She raised her glass in a mock toast. "And he told me he'd met one star since he'd been here."

Mia felt herself blush. Tash chuckled, "Sorry, I didn't mean to embarrass you. Every woman I know fancies Ollie. But it didn't take me long to realise I wouldn't have a hope."

Mia had just enough time to think, 'Oh Lord, he's gay!' before Tash continued, "Ollie will never mix business with pleasure. No way would he ever get involved with a colleague."

"Are you warning me off?"

"No, just warning you. Don't get me wrong, he's a diamond guy and I love him to bits, but he's nearly thirty and a hundred-per-cent committed to his job."

"And I'm thirty-two and a hundred-per-cent committed to my independence."

"That's okay then." Tash strolled towards the door. "Let's go and see how he's doing."

She wandered into the sitting room, put her glass down and leaned over the back of the sofa, massaging Sutton's shoulders. "I'm glad I don't have to drive anymore tonight."

"When you do that I'm pretty glad as well."

Mia confined her level of TLC to checking his cut finger for splintered glass and wrapping a plaster around it. Then she poured more wine. "You break this and you'll be onto the plastic cups Dani uses," she warned Sutton.

"If I drink that I'll be too pissed to get myself to the Lodging House. I'm still reeling from the triple brandy Tash poured into me earlier."

"Purely medicinal," said Tash unrepentantly.

This jogged Mia's conscience. "I forgot! You shouldn't be drinking when you're on painkillers."

"They'll have worn off by now. I'd rather have a drink than more pills."

108

"In that case you don't have to go anywhere. I've got three bedrooms, although the little one for my niece has got pink elephants dancing across the walls."

"Bags I have that one," exclaimed Tash. "Mia's right, Ollie. It's stupid turning out again."

"I'd like you to stay," said Mia. To hell with pride, she needed to share this fear. "The pizza wasn't the only weird thing that happened today." She told them about her two brief sightings of Dennis Plummer and the silent phone call. "But it could all be coincidence or me imagining things."

"I don't like coincidences," said Tash. "That settles it Ollie, you're on Protection Duty. I'll get your jacket and change of clothes from the car."

"No! I will." Sutton hauled himself to his feet. "You're not going out there in the dark."

Tash grinned at Mia. "Even the most liberated guy is a macho super-hero underneath." Nevertheless, she joined Mia to watch Sutton and check on his safety until he was back inside.

A few minutes later, Mia went into the kitchen to cook oven chips to soak up the alcohol. It was almost midnight and she'd abandoned the idea of talking to Sutton tonight about Bridge Road. He hadn't mentioned it and she was certain he was too tired, preoccupied and downright drunk to take anything on board.

She remembered the pizza was still on the hall table and went to retrieve it. As she picked it up she registered for the first time that the cardboard box was cold. Puzzled, she opened it. The pizza was distinctly soggy. She got out a sugar thermometer and plunged it into the centre.

Tash strolled into the room. "Wow, you are one cool cop. Hey Ollie, Mia's taking the liver temp of the abandoned pizza."

Sutton appeared in the doorway. "Okay Mia, you're the expert. How long has it been dead?"

"It's frozen. It's still not totally thawed." Mia saw the

109

joking words die on Tash's lips, but she looked puzzled, clearly taking her message from the seriousness of Mia's tone. "It suddenly hit me that the box was cold and it didn't smell of cooked pizza," she explained.

"It looks like a cut-price, supermarket pizza," said Sutton.

"You mean someone left it as a joke?" asked Tash.

"Or the person outside Mia's door brought it with them as a reason for being here, like it was some sort of quick-fix alibi."

Mia thought how close she'd come to opening the door and began to shake. It took all the self-control she could summon to say, quite naturally, "Do you want ham or eggs with your chips?"

The next morning Tash was up at six. Mia heard her in the kitchen. She got up and dressed quickly, then went down to check Tash was okay. "Have you got everything you need?"

"Yes thanks. I didn't mean to wake you."

"You didn't. I wasn't properly asleep." Fear had prevented her from going deep, despite the reassuring presence of Oliver and Tash.

She saw the shrewd look Tash gave her. "I'm okay. Just a bit jumpy."

Tash reached over and squeezed her arm. "It could still turn out your pizza delivery is some stupid joke or misunderstanding." She gulped down her coffee. "I'm so late! I meant to leave by five. Still, I'll be able to tell Tiffany I've slept in a bedroom with dancing elephants. Mia, I'd like you to come to our wedding."

"I'd love to."

"Brilliant. I'll send you an invitation." Mia opened the front door and Tash hugged her. "Thanks for having me."

Mia stood at the window, making sure Tash was safe as she drove away.

"Was that Tash leaving?" Sutton's voice from the top of

the stairs made her jump.

"Yes. Did you want to speak to her?"

"No thanks. Tash at this time in the morning is too loud and brisk for me. Do you mind me coming down like this? I could use a glass of water."

"Of course not."

There were some situations she'd never considered how she'd deal with because they were too improbable. That included having her senior officer alone with her in her house, wearing only trousers and sporting some pretty sexy designer stubble. Interesting, in a totally unreal sort of way.

He reached the hall and she smiled brightly. "Breakfast?"

"Not another disgustingly cheery first-thing-in-the-morning person. I warn you I'm a 'don't speak to me until I've had three cups of coffee' type."

"It's early. You could go back to bed for a while."

"No that's okay. You want to run your Bridge Road findings past me. I'm sorry I didn't get to it last night."

"No problem. Let's have breakfast first."

After they'd finished eating she told him about her findings and the deductions she'd made.

He said, "It sounds like it hangs together but I'd like to see everything in black and white before we act on it."

She tried not to feel snubbed. After all he was the SIO.

He stood up. "Is it okay if I grab a shower? Then I can go straight into work with you."

"Of course." Relief flooded through her. She wouldn't have to be alone. At least not until tonight. She pushed that thought away.

Sutton had a meeting with the DCI so Mia headed straight to SOCO. In the office the team was gearing up for action. At weekends the pubs and clubs provided a tidal wave of crime.

At last everyone dispersed and she was alone until Adam came in.

"Where's Trev?" she asked.

111

"Taking the morning off."

"Is he okay?"

"Chantelle's off too. They're going to play golf."

"Oh, I see." That explained why Adam sounded so unimpressed. "We'll have to hope for the best. She was okay in the pub last night. Perhaps she deserves the benefit of the doubt."

Adam groaned. "If you join the sweetness and light brigade this place will become unbearable."

With a flash of insight Mia realised the reason Adam sounded so sour had nothing to do with Chantelle or Trevor. "You're missing Jan and baby Thomas horribly, aren't you?"

"Yeah, but at least I know they're safe. Jan says she'll give it another week, and, if nothing's happened, she'll come home. Part of me wants her back but the other part's scared. They might never catch this monster and then no-one will ever feel safe again."

"They'll catch him." Mia struggled to speak confidently.

Adam forced a smile. "Of course they will. I don't know why I'm whinging. You're the one who had the fright last night. Are you okay?"

"Yeah. How did you know?"

"It's all over the Station. You had a prowler but had the sense not to open the door. I haven't heard exactly what happened, just something about pizzas."

She told him everything, finishing up with, "I don't know if I'm being paranoid."

"If so, you're not the only one. I've been checking the list of stuff sent off for processing."

"And?"

"That pizza, complete with box, was brought in this morning and sent off for fingerprinting and analysis. The request was signed by DI Sutton. It was marked urgent and the results are to go straight to the Serious Crimes Team."

She stared at him, numb with shock. She hadn't seen Sutton take the pizza. If he was involving the SCT, he must be worried.

"Why don't you go and stay with your mum for a few nights?" suggested Adam.

"No way. If I'm in danger, I could lead it to them."

"I'm working this weekend. How about I come and stay with you?"

"Shouldn't you check Jan's okay with that?"

He looked surprised, then almost angry. "No need for that. Jan trusts me. She knows I've never looked at anyone else."

"I didn't mean that! It could be dangerous."

He grinned. "I'll risk it. Your cooking's not that bad."

"My cooking's very good and I'll prove it by making you a fabulous meal. But I don't want anything to happen to you."

"It won't. If necessary we'll hide under the sofa together." He gathered up his kit. "I'd better get out on the mean streets and do some work. It's okay for you CID wannabees, lurking round the office all day."

When she was alone Mia phoned through to speak to her mum. She opened with a determinedly cheery, "Good morning."

"Good morning, darling. What's wrong?"

Mia gave up pretending and told her what had happened, although she underplayed her fear.

"Please Mia, don't let your pride stop you from being safe."

"Adam says he'll sleep at my place this weekend."

"That's good. And, before you start worrying about Rina and me, we're fine. Rina's not going out in the evenings and tomorrow a crowd of us are taking Dani and two of her friends to Paulton's Park."

"That sounds great, but don't overdo it. No rides on the Cobra."

Her mother giggled. "I wish. I'd love to go on a fast, upside-down ride again. Why don't you join us?"

"Sorry, I'll be working." Mia heard her mother's laughter and knew she'd been sussed. She had no wish to spend the day with toddlers in a theme park. The small children scene was something she'd do when she met a guy she could bear to live with for more than six months.

At ten o'clock she presented herself in Sutton's office. "Why didn't you tell me you were sending that pizza for analysis?"

He blinked at her abrasive tone but didn't point out it was inappropriate. "I didn't want to worry you."

"Thanks, but I'd prefer you kept me in the loop."

"Noted. Now kindly stop glowering at me."

"Sorry." She sat down. "Does the SCT think there's a link between my pizza delivery and the murders?"

"No more than the other incidents they're looking at. The whole town's paranoid."

"Adam was saying no-one would feel safe until this bastard was caught."

"No-one will feel safe even after we've got him. Fear's like that. It gets inside you." He stood up. "I've read your report and reviewed the evidence on the Bridge Road case. You've convinced me. Let's go."

Chapter 12

Joy Marshall turned the small evidence bag over in her hands and said, with apparent irrelevance, "I wondered if it was because of the war."

They'd struck lucky, finding Joy at home alone. She'd agreed to talk to them, unaware or indifferent to the danger of incriminating herself.

"The war?" Sutton had the same baffled look he'd worn the last time he'd dealt with Joy.

"I wondered if that made my parents the way they were."

"I'm sorry, I don't understand."

Her tired eyes seemed indulgent of his ignorance, perhaps even glad of it. "You're another generation. It would be your grandparents who fought. That makes a difference. My father and his pals joined up together, all from the same village. Most of them died. And those few that came back, there was nothing for them, no jobs or anything. It made him bitter. My parents were quite old when I was born and my mother couldn't cope."

The spate of information dwindled and then revived, "I always told myself I'd be different, a real hands on mother and grandmother. I hope you don't lock me away. My daughter's just had a baby. I want to be there for him."

"Joy, tell us about your childhood," said Mia.

"My father hated having visitors. And he didn't like Mum and me going out. I used to think that was the way everybody lived."

"Didn't you have friends?"

"Not really. They say what you don't know you don't miss, but I'm not sure that's true."

"Was that why you used to visit Lucy?" Mia felt like she was walking on eggshells, one wrong step and Joy's brittle control would splinter.

"Dear Lucy. My parents hated her but she was good to me." Joy twisted her hands together, as if physical pain was the only way to cope with the memories. "I had a kitten. At least, Lucy said he could be mine. I went over to her house to play with him. But he got too fond of me and followed me back to our garden. Dad picked him up and threw him in the pond. He held me there and made me watch while those devil fish got him." She was shuddering violently but her voice was still gentle, "How strange. I hadn't realised I'd never forgiven him."

"Is that why you chose the pond as the place to kill him?" snapped Sutton.

Sutton's sharp question had a negative effect. Joy gazed at him in clear bewilderment. Realising his mistake he gestured to Mia to take over. "Joy, tell us about your relationship with your father after your mother died," she said.

"After I got married he and Mum didn't really have much to do with us for years. He said I was bringing my children up all wrong and Mum went along with him. Then Mum got ill and he sent for me. He said bygones should be bygones, no matter how badly I'd behaved. He called me in when he wanted help with nursing her. He told me he couldn't get help to look after her. It was only afterwards I realised he'd turned down all but the essential nursing care."

"How do you mean, essential nursing care?" asked Sutton.

"The sort of care where nurses checked up on her. If he hadn't agreed to that the doctors wouldn't have let her stay at home. At the end she was under morphine all the time. But before that, one day she got a small photo out of her purse and looked at it and said, 'There's my beautiful baby girl.' It was of me when I was small." Tears poured down her face. "She told me to look after Dad and I said I would."

Mia rested her hand on Joy's writhing fingers. "What happened then, Joy?"

"Dad acted like he was the only one who was unhappy.

116

Not just the chief mourner but the only one. He was so demanding. I keep wondering what would have happened if I'd been stronger... or weaker... anything except grinding on. The trouble with trying to please everyone is you end up pleasing no-one, especially not yourself."

"I know," said Sutton gently.

"Then they decided to pull his house down and he said he was going to live with me. It sounds stupid to say I had no choice, but that's the way it felt. Cliff said it was up to me. Sometimes I wish he'd put his foot down but he wasn't that sort of man. And so Dad moved in and it was like living in hell. He was always moaning, always getting at me and Cliff and the girls. He'd got such a nasty tongue. I realised he didn't just want me to take my mother's place, he wanted me to be my mother. He was drinking very heavily. He thought I didn't know. Then Cliff had a heart attack. I got the phone call and I was rushing to the hospital when Dad told me to cook his dinner first. It sounds stupid but he made it sound so reasonable. I don't know if I'd have given in or not, but Donna, she's my eldest, hustled me out to the car. Thank God she did! Cliff died five minutes after I got there."

She took a shuddering breath and stopped speaking. There was silence then she started again. "I suppose I didn't look after Dad the way he wanted while I was mourning Cliff. Dad got angry and said he was moving away. He was going back to Wales where he belonged. He went on about the nursing home as if it was a four star hotel. I should have told him nursing homes weren't like that but I wanted him to go. And on the way back, after we'd left him there, me and my daughter were laughing at the expression on his face, then I started crying and I couldn't stop for days."

"What happened when he wanted to come back?" said Sutton.

"I came in from shopping and there was a message on my answer phone. He said he'd forgiven me and he was coming back."

"What did you do, Joy?"

"Nothing. We were going off on holiday the next day, me and my daughters. We needed some healing time after losing Cliff. I deleted the message and went." She tilted her head to one side, as if a strange thought had struck her. "It's funny, I don't believe I thought about him all the time we were away."

"What happened when you got back?" said Sutton.

"There were five messages on the answer phone. Four of them were from Dad. He said such cruel things, all in this hard, spiky voice. The last message was from Lucy. She was hysterical, screaming and sobbing that Dad had killed her cats. He'd poisoned them. He'd always threatened to. And then I knew for certain about Yen and Chang."

"Your cats? The ones buried in the garden?"

She nodded acknowledgement. "They died three weeks after Dad came to live with me. I always wondered. I knew he hated them but I couldn't bear to believe it. When I heard Lucy's message I knew it was true."

"What did you do?" asked Sutton.

"That night I slipped out of the house. I was going to tell him I'd never take him back."

"What happened, Joy? Did you quarrel? Did you push him? Or hit him with something? Are you saying it was self-defence?"

She stared at him. "He was already dead. Lying in the fishpond. It was horrible. I hardly recognised him. The fish were dead too, lying on the surface of the water. I don't know what killed them…" she shuddered to a halt.

Mia felt a spurt of understanding. Physiologically that made sense. Immersion in water for several days could speed up decomposition. It explained why a body buried for five years in a shallow grave could have gone right back to bone.

"If it was an accident, why didn't you report your father's death?" Mia wondered whether the tightness in Sutton's voice was due to pity or exasperation.

"I don't really know. It was all so unpleasant. I think I was ashamed."

118

"How did he end up in a shallow grave next door?"

"I heard Lucy next door, digging and crying, trying to make a hole to bury her cats."

"Hang on! If your father had been dead for several days, how could he have just poisoned Lucy's cats."

"I didn't say he'd just poisoned them. He'd done so several days before. Lucy couldn't dig much, it's heavy soil and she's an old lady, very frail."

"Not so frail when she loses her temper. Not too frail to crack the skull of an equally old man. So you decided to bury Daddy in the same grave as the cats?"

His abrasive tone washed over her. "It seemed the best thing to do. That must have been when I lost the stone from my ring."

"Why did you take off your father's dressing gown?"

"It was soiled, unseemly. It seemed for the best."

"And what did you do with it?"

"I burned it. We had quite a bonfire, Lucy and I. The dressing gown, the old wheelbarrow we used to move my father and lots of other things."

"Did Lucy kill your father?"

"Oh no, I'm sure she would have told me if she had." Strangely, the more vague Joy sounded, the more certain Mia felt that her mind was working fast and accurately. "She said she'd seen him lying there but, even if she'd wished to, he was too heavy for her to move."

"I'll be examining Lucy's stick for any samples I can find of blood or tissue," warned Mia. "Even after all this time it's possible something will remain." Possible but profoundly unlikely.

"That wouldn't help you. Lucy used her stick to poke the bonfire and it got badly charred. So we threw it on the fire with the other things and I bought her a new one the next day."

"Was that the same day you arranged for the fishpond to be filled in?" demanded Sutton.

119

"That was later when we were quite sure all the fish were dead. It wasn't their fault. They were following their instincts, like cats do when they chase mice."

Or as emotionally abused women do when they tidy away dead bodies.

"What about your father's money?" said Sutton.

"The money for the house? I did wonder what he'd done with that. I thought he'd probably burned it. He wouldn't have wanted me to have it." Mia knew that one of the old man's bankbooks held the whole payment for the house but Sutton didn't mention it so she kept quiet too.

"What about his pension?" demanded Sutton. "It was diverted into a savings account, and by the dates you've given us, it was done soon after he died. The account's in Lucy Logan's name."

"How extraordinary! I can't believe that's right."

Sutton sighed and gave up the questioning. "You'll have to come with us to the Station."

"Of course. But I'll need to phone Donna. I don't want my younger girls to be here alone. If I'm going to prison I'll need to make arrangements."

"We'll make sure they're okay," said Sutton.

"Thank you. I'll get my coat."

As they left the house she paused, a small wistful smile on her lips. "I keep wondering whether, if Dad had been alive, I'd have really had the courage to say no."

"So what do you reckon?" asked Sutton, when they were back in the privacy of his office. "Did Lucy kill the old boy? And does Joy know she did it?"

"Probably. Unless Joy did it and she's running a cunning double-bluff."

"Do you think that's likely?"

"It's possible."

"That's what's great about you, you're so willing to commit."

"It really doesn't matter who did what to whom, because we're never going to prove it."

Sutton's face was grim. "I could believe it was an accident if it wasn't for that bank account."

"It's hard to imagine Lucy being capable of even minor identity theft."

"She was probably a lot more with it five years ago. Maybe nothing's been taken out of it because she's forgotten it's there."

Mia wondered how Lucy knew about William's hiding place under the floorboards unless Joy had told her. "We could go and talk to Lucy? Maybe she'll confess to everything."

"More likely send us off on another false trail. Okay, I know it's got to be done."

In the car he was silent. Mia felt concerned. "Are you okay?"

"Just sick of this muck up of a case."

"There'll be plenty of other cases for you to make your mark."

"Maybe, but DCI Craig's not likely to be impressed with me so far. It'll be a miracle if we get more than a handful of minor charges for all these hours of work and expensive tests."

"But a suspicious death had to be investigated."

"I know, but I threw too many resources into it." He sighed. "I don't know what it is about Joy Marshall, but I can never find the right questions to open up what she's thinking. Interrogating her's like pushing a suet pudding up a hill."

Mia couldn't help smiling at the simile, but there was no amusement in her reply, "I think Joy told the truth about her childhood. Living under that level of control must do things to a person." She pulled into a parking space. "Here we are."

"Yeah. Tour of all the fun places in town." He stared gloomily at the red brick bulk of the mental hospital.

"She's deteriorated in the last few days. The officers who

visited her yesterday upset her. She's been very confused ever since." The ward sister looked at them reprovingly.

"Is she likely to come out of it and start making sense again?" Sutton stared back coolly, refusing to accept the proffered blame.

"With dementia it's impossible to tell. At least, last night, we managed to bath her. If you have to speak with her, please be gentle."

Cleaned up, Lucy looked a sweet old lady, with her white hair fluffed around her pouched face. Her blank gaze travelled over them as if they were part of the furniture. Mia felt a pang of pity as she remembered the wild, old termagant of four days ago.

The same thought must have hit Sutton. "This deterioration came on very suddenly, didn't it?"

"Possibly, but sometimes old people suffer from dementia for years without being diagnosed. The scans we've taken show that, over the years, she's suffered several small strokes."

"But on Monday she was active, organised and articulate in a crazy sort of way."

"It's a strange condition, sometimes manic and at other times passive."

"And when she's manic can she be violent?" asked Sutton.

"Yes."

"And there's no rational logic behind her actions?"

"Not what we'd call rational."

"And does she remember the things she's done?"

"Some of them today, some tomorrow, some not at all. And there's no relying on whether it's a true memory or false."

"That's it then." Nevertheless Sutton crouched down by her chair. "Lucy, do you remember William Davies?" The colourless eyes looked through him. "What about Joy? Do you remember Joy?"

That won a vague ripple of response. "Joy... such a kind

little girl… not like him." Her voice was as thin and frail as fraying twine. "I didn't want to leave but I had to… he told me I must. He was so violent and cruel… so sly. That poor tortoise."

Sutton sighed and gave up. "Thank you, Lucy. We won't bother you anymore."

For the first time she turned her head to look at him. "Lucy… yes, I knew someone called Lucy once… at least, I think I did."

Chapter 13

On the drive back Mia started to say, "What do you…"

"I'd rather not have any more input at the moment."

That made the gap between DI and constable unassailable. She didn't attempt to speak to him again.

Back in the Station he ordered that Joy Marshall should be brought to an interview room. The way he snapped commands made the uniformed officers exchange wary looks as they hurried to obey.

Joy entered briskly, sat down and enquired in a chatty tone, "Could you advise me? Is this the point where I should ask for a solicitor? On Law & Order, whenever people are arrested, they always annoy the police by 'lawyering up'."

Mia expected Sutton to explode but he said softly, "Joy, the way we play this is down to you. If you want a solicitor you can have one, but that's going to put the whole matter on an official treadmill that won't be easy to switch off. If you want to tough it out, that's the way it will go."

"And if I don't tough it out, I'll fall apart and end up in prison anyway." The frivolity shredded and Joy's voice was shrill with hysterical defiance.

Sutton spoke very gently, "Joy, I don't want to cause you more trouble or more pain, but I need you to convince me you weren't guilty of your father's death. I've seen Lucy Logan and there's no way anything you say can harm her. The Crown Prosecution Service isn't going to waste time and money prosecuting an old woman suffering from dementia. It's time you looked after yourself and told us what really happened."

Joy's eyes turned towards Mia, who forced a smile and nodded encouragement.

"All right."

"I have to inform you that I'll be recording this interview."

Joy nodded agreement and Sutton gave the information

that ratified the interview. "Joy, in previous statements you have claimed your father was dead when you found him?"

"Yes. I swear it's true."

"Do you think Lucy might have struck him and knocked him unconscious so that he drowned in the pond?"

"I don't know."

"But she was capable of violence?"

"Yes." She tugged a tissue from her sleeve and held it to her lips. "I didn't understand at first, but, for the last few years, there were days when she talked about me as if I was still a little girl, when I was there, a grown woman, in front of her. And sometimes she was terribly uncontrolled. Lucy had always been odd and it took a while for the truth to dawn on me. I truly don't know how my father died."

"She never told you?"

"She said a lot of things but they didn't make much sense."

"You said the fish were dead as well. Do you think Lucy killed them?" Mia slid the question in and was aware of Sutton's warning scowl.

"Oh no! Lucy would never do that." Again she dabbed her lips. "I think my father killed them."

"Why should your father kill his own fish?" Sutton allowed himself to be diverted.

"He'd finished with them. They weren't any use to him. After he moved out of the house, I used to go and feed them. He'd have left them to starve."

"Joy, could you make it clearer why you moved your father's body?" said Sutton. "You knew Lucy was mentally unstable. She needed help and treatment. If you'd spoken out she'd have received it and your father would have had a proper burial."

"I've seen the sort of help and treatment people like her get. Stuck in some vile hospital ward, more like a number than a person. Even in the best care homes the carers get impatient sometimes. And Lucy's got no-one to look out for her except for me, and I've got no power, I'm not a relative. At least this way she had a few more years living the way she wanted."

"Did you help her find her new bungalow and move into it?" said Mia.

"Oh yes. She couldn't have managed all that alone."

"And yet you claim she was capable of setting up a fraudulent bank account to divert your father's pension?" Sutton returned to the thing that rankled most.

"No, I'm not saying that. I find it hard to believe she could have done that. But I didn't, so I suppose she must have done."

"Did you know about the hiding place your father had made for his money?"

"No. What sort of hiding place?" Joy looked surprised.

"A cleverly crafted compartment in his bedroom floor."

"How strange."

"Why? Surely it would be in character for your father to have a hiding place?"

"But you said it was well made. My father was never good at DIY."

Sutton sighed and visibly gave up the questioning.

"Have you seen a lot of Lucy since she moved into the new bungalow?" asked Mia.

"I've tried to keep an eye on her and check she's okay. She was happy there. Except, of course, I couldn't let her dig up her cats and take their bodies with her. I offered to get her some new cats, just a few, but she kept saying she didn't want new ones. She wanted her precious ones back again. I used to dread she'd disinter them… and him. That he'd be lying there all white and bloated, like when we put him in." She shuddered. "It wasn't just for Lucy. It was for my father as well. He'd have hated to be seen soiled like that. That's why I took away his dressing gown." The shudder turned into full-scale shaking. "I owed him that much. I wanted so much to love him."

"You're upset. I think this interview should be ended," said Sutton.

"No, wait a moment. There's one thing I've got to say. I want to be absolutely honest. What I did wasn't just for Lucy or my dad, it was for me. I couldn't cope with any more unpleasantness. I wanted to forget about it all. And I almost did forget. I pretended it had never happened. After a while, it seemed like a nightmare and I could think Dad was still living in that home in Wales."

"Is that why you kept sending cards to him?"

"At first it was so my girls wouldn't know. But, after a while, I really believed it. Silly, isn't it?" This time she made no protest when Sutton terminated the interview.

"I'll get a female officer to bring you a cup of tea and stay with you while we decide where we go from here." He stood up and Mia followed him from the room.

As she trailed him through the Station, Mia wondered where they were going and what Sutton planned to do. She didn't ask; one snub a day was enough.

Inside his office, he shut the door and stared gloomily at her. "What a mess."

"Yes sir."

He blinked at the formality of her tone but persisted, "Have you got any thoughts about where we go from here?"

"No sir. I understood you didn't want any input from the lower ranks."

She knew that merited a reprimand but he said, "I had to think it through. I didn't want to mess things up for you as well as me."

"What do you mean?"

"Like I said, this isn't a good result."

"It's bad luck."

"I think the DCI may call it bad management."

"There was nothing you could do about it."

"Yes there was. A bit of pressure and I could have made a case against Joy for murder." She realised, throughout the

127

interview, he'd been torn between ambition and his instinct to be kind.

"Do you think she did it?"

"No. But I'm not certain. What do you reckon?"

"The same."

"Why burn the wheelbarrow? That was strange."

"I'd guess the body burst. Floaters make exceptionally vile corpses."

"Yuck!"

"Yeah. It's not surprising Joy was traumatised. I wouldn't mind betting she burned everything she was wearing when she got home and washed herself raw and still couldn't get the smell out of her nose." There was nothing positive she could say, but she tried, "It would have been a really hard case to make. The Forensic evidence has been mucked up by the chemicals in the water. Not to mention the builders scattering the bones. The CPS would have probably thrown it out before it got to court."

"I know. Well, here goes nothing, time to tell the DCI." He reached for his phone. "Sir? Sutton here. I've reached a conclusion with the Bridge Road case and I'd appreciate a chance to run it past you... Thank you. I'll be right there." He put the phone down and stood up. "Bye Mia. See you later."

As soon as he left Mia fled back to the sanctuary of SOCO. She made sure all the forensic evidence was in pristine order in case the DCI wanted to check on any of it.

Digital photography was a godsend to any forensic officer, especially with its potential for highlighting certain features of a scene. However one had to be meticulous in order to prove the original photos maintained an incontrovertible chain of evidence. She forced herself to concentrate on the protocols, but concern for Sutton kept nibbling at the edges of her mind.

She was alone in the office when he tracked her down a couple of hours later.

"How did it go?" she asked, as he spun a chair round to face her and slumped into it.

"Could have been worse. He told me to charge Joy with illegally disposing of a body and send her home.

"Do you think the CPS will take it any further."

"Probably. With her confession it's a no-brainer. She'll probably end up with community service. The pensions people will take steps to reclaim their money, but we can't link the fraud to Joy and, as far as I can see, there's no reason she shouldn't inherit the money for the house."

"Did the DCI blame you?"

"Strangely enough, he didn't seem to but I still feel a bloody failure."

She grinned at him. "As one control-freak perfectionist to another, I suggest you lighten up." That won a reluctant smile. "What now?" she asked. "Will you be able to grab a weekend off?"

"The DCI said I can look over the evidence in the major case. I'm seconded to that."

"Isn't that what you wanted?" Mia wondered why he seemed so glum.

"Yeah, but I've got a nasty insecure feeling about it."

Suddenly she understood. "Is Bycroft taking charge of CID's other work?"

"Got it in one."

"DCI Craig couldn't get rid of you and replace you with Bycroft even if he wanted to."

"I wish I had your confidence."

"I've been getting the Bridge Road evidence together. You can use it to wind up the case."

"Cheers. I've got a team meeting in half an hour. I'm not looking forward to it. I keep imagining Bycroft's gloating face."

"You're the one who's working with the SCT not him. Do you need me at this meeting?"

"No. There's no need for you to go through the aggro."

"Is it all right if I let Tim Lewis know the case is winding down?"

"The archaeologist? Why should he want to know?"

"I think it's playing on his mind."

"Over-sensitive isn't he?"

"Yeah, but I feel kind of sorry for him."

"As long as you don't say anything to pre-empt the coroner."

"Of course not." She saw he was still frowning. "Is there anything else wrong?"

"The DCI said if you were interested in continuing your secondment for a while he'd consider it. I don't know if he was worried about my arm or thinks I need a minder."

"How is your arm?" Half of Mia was eager for him to say he needed her help, the other half screamed that she should scurry back into her comfort zone.

"More or less okay. Although I haven't tried driving yet."

"Well you don't need a minder, so I guess I ought to get on with my real work."

He got up. "Thanks for everything."

"It was interesting. Thanks for giving me a taste of how the other half lives." As he left, she thought they sounded as stilted as two people winding up an unsuccessful date.

Sutton left and Mia dug out the card Tim Lewis had given her and rang his mobile. On the fifth ring a woman answered, "This is Timothy Lewis' phone. Who's that?"

"Good afternoon. My name is Mia Trent. Who am I speaking to?"

"I'm Mrs Lewis. What's your business with my son?"

Mia forgave Tim for being such a wimp, with a mother like that he didn't have a chance. "It's personal. Please tell him to phone Mia as soon as possible." She keyed off to a bombardment of questions.

She was twenty minutes into her mountain of paperwork when her phone rang. Tim demanded, "Mia? What's going on?"

130

"Nothing. I wanted to speak to you."

"That's nice." His tone warned her he'd taken this more personally than she'd intended.

"I wanted to tell you we're winding down the Bridge Road investigation. This is unofficial so don't tell anyone. The contractors will receive official notice when they can return to the site."

"Whatever you say. Mia, could I take you out for dinner?"

"Perhaps sometime. I phoned to tell you I had a word with a colleague of mine, Jason Calverleigh. He's about to lead a dig in Spain and he's willing to talk to you about joining his team. It's a short-term contract, the money will be poor, the hours long and the conditions primitive, but it should be fun." She felt a sudden longing to send in her notice and go back to her first love.

"It sounds fantastic but I don't speak Spanish."

"That's okay, necessity is a great teacher."

"Thank you so much for thinking of me. It means so much to me. I can't tell you how grateful I am." Nevertheless he spent five minutes trying until Mia contrived to end the call.

For the next three hours she put in some solid work. At four-thirty Adam returned from processing car crime in time to log-in the evidence. At five, as they were packing up to leave, Trevor and Chantelle appeared.

"What are you doing here, Trev?" demanded Mia. "I thought this was your day off?"

"Just dropped by to check you're okay. I heard about your carry-on last night."

"I'm fine. It was probably a false alarm, but Adam's sleeping over for the next couple of nights to keep me company." As she spoke Mia caught Adam's warning look and realised he still didn't trust Chantelle not to make mischief.

She was sure Chantelle had seen Adam's expression, she looked uncomfortable but said, "I'm glad you've got

131

company, Mia. Would you both come to dinner tomorrow evening? Trevor's coming too."

"That would be great, thanks," said Mia quickly. She understood Adam's cynicism but it would be stupid to waste this chance of declaring peace. She turned to grin at Trevor, who'd groaned as he sat down behind his desk. "You poor old man. You look knackered."

"Yeah. Reckon I've had more exercise today than I usually have in three months but the indigestion's been better."

"I'd guess that's because Chantelle looked after you."

"Yeah. And she plays a good game of golf. How's the Bridge Road case going?"

"It's finished and I'm all yours again. You ready to make a move, Adam?"

"Yeah."

"Me too." Trevor finished checking his messages and stood up.

As they walked towards the rear exit, Mia was hailed by Liz Murphy, "Hey Mia, where have you been hiding? Dave Bycroft wanted a word."

"What about?"

"He wanted to buy you a drink."

"Why?" Bycroft might be annoyed with her, but poisoning seemed extreme.

"To thank you for watching his back on the Bridge Road case."

"How did he know I had?" Mia searched desperately for a toehold in the conversation.

"The DI said if you'd told Dave your suspicions, he'd have had to act on them. This way the Boy Wonder had to do his own dirty work. I bet he's pissed with you?"

"He was okay."

"Well it's nice to know you're loyal to the old firm. How about coming clubbing tomorrow? Hen night in Brighton."

"Thanks but I've got a dinner engagement."

"Pity. By the way, did the front desk ring about your flowers?"

"What flowers?"

"There's an enormous bouquet down there. You've got an admirer."

She moved on and Mia turned to her companions, "I'd better go and check it out."

They all insisted on accompanying her, and she wondered if they were motivated by friendship or curiosity.

Chantelle said, "If you'd prefer clubbing in Brighton I'll understand."

"I'd much rather have dinner with you."

"Thank you." Chantelle gave a sweet smile and Mia grinned back. She'd no intention of telling Chantelle that if she hadn't had an engagement she'd have been forced to make one up.

It was an extremely large bouquet. Mia glanced at the card, 'To Mia. Thank you for everything. With love, From Tim.' She saw the amused glances of the cops manning the reception desk and felt her face heat up.

On the way home she and Adam played the car convoy game to the shops to buy food and wine, back to Adam's house to get his stuff and then to Mia's house.

They prepared dinner, fortified by glasses of red wine. Then they curled up in the sitting room and chatted while the scent of roasting meat wafted around the house.

Before she got too comfortable she did her duty and phoned Tim. "It's Mia. Thank you for the flowers, they're beautiful."

"I'm glad you like them. I hope I didn't embarrass you by sending them to the Police Station."

"Well they were quite noticeable."

"The trouble is I don't know your home address."

"No, I suppose you don't... Well thanks a lot, Tim..."

"Mia, don't go! There's something I've got to tell you. It's important."

133

"What is it?" She didn't attempt to mask her impatience.

"You're in danger. Dennis Plummer has been threatening you."

"What?" Mia took a deep breath and spoke more steadily, "What do you mean?"

"Mike says Dennis blames you for the trouble he's in. He says he knows where you live and he's going to make you pay."

Chapter 14

"Mia are you all right?" As she stood, frozen, Timothy's persistent voice kept buzzing in her ear. "Shall I come round and look after you?"

"No!... I'll be fine."

As she keyed off Adam said, "What's wrong?"

"Nothing." Tim must be playing some Great Protector game. But Mike Plummer had warned her too. The ostrich that persists in sticking its head in the sand is likely to find a predator chewing on its arse.

"Don't give me 'nothing'. What did the kid say?"

She took a gulp of wine and told him.

"So it seems likely Dennis Plummer followed you home?"

She nodded.

"And Dennis is this ugly great builder who goes crazy when he's drunk? I want reinforcements."

"You can go home if you want." Mia made the offer although she didn't mean it.

"Don't be stupid. I'm not running out on you. But you should phone DI Sutton."

"If you want him, you can phone him." Mia couldn't believe how childish that sounded.

"Okay, I will. Number please."

Sulkily she supplied it and he phoned through. "DI Sutton? Hi, it's Adam Carter. I'm with Mia." He put Sutton in the picture. "Yeah, she's here." He passed Mia the phone.

"Mia, are you okay?" Sutton's voice was sharp. Mia thought he was angry but he continued, "Mia please, tell me you're all right." She realised he was afraid for her, tears flooded her eyes and clogged her throat.

Adam took the phone back. "She's not blanking you. She's gone all emotional. Yeah, I'll tell her."

He put the phone down. "He's coming right over. Do

you want me to leave?"

This dried up Mia's tears. "Adam, stop that! He's a friend, nothing more."

He grinned at her. "Fair enough. He's a nice guy... for a cop."

Mia didn't bother to thump him. It was part of their friendship, him making lairy jokes about career cops, her retorting with insults about civilian SOCOs.

Fifteen minutes later Sutton's car screeched into Mia's driveway.

"How many speeding tickets do you think he's picked up?" asked Adam.

"None. Detective Inspectors don't get speeding tickets."

"Even ones who aren't popular with the troops?"

"Especially them. Self-preservation is an integral part of the police culture."

Mia went to the door, Adam close behind her. Sutton strode into the hall. "Mia, what the hell's going on? Why didn't you tell me you were being stalked?"

His anger was the adrenaline kick she needed. "Because I didn't know until a few minutes ago. Don't come into my house throwing your weight around."

"Seconds out, round two," said Adam, shutting and bolting the front door. "How about we sit down and pretend we're intelligent, civilised people."

Sutton glared but took off his damp coat. As he tugged it free he gave a yelp of pain.

"You claimed your arm was better," said Mia, feeling more sympathy than she showed.

"It's not up to driving full speed in answer to a desperate SOS."

"It wasn't a desperate SOS. It was a request for professional advice."

Bristling, they stalked into the sitting room and subsided onto opposite ends of the sofa.

"I'm going to check the dinner," announced Adam, and

retreated into the kitchen.

There was a smouldering silence. Mia looked sideways at Sutton and found he was also surveying her. This made her giggle and won an answering grin. "You look tired," she said.

"I am. And you look jumpy."

"I am. I'm sorry, Oliver, I didn't mean to drag you away from work."

"I was only reading case notes and forensic reports. And it wouldn't have mattered if you'd interrupted a briefing, your safety is top priority. Tell me exactly what was said."

Mia told him about her conversation with Tim. His quiet questions jogged her memory and she recalled more details. At last she stopped and said defiantly, "Now tell me I'm making a fuss about nothing."

"Don't be thick, Mia. Of course you're not." He stood up. "I'll pick up a photo of Dennis and go and check out the pub to see if any of the regulars spotted him there. Don't panic if you see car headlights, the uniformed boys are paying special attention to your place."

"You'll come back afterwards?"

"Either that or phone. Don't worry, I'll let you know."

It was ten-thirty when his car again turned into the drive. As he entered the house he looked wet and cold, his hair smoothed into a helm of dark gold. It reminded Mia of the first time they'd met. With strong self-restraint she didn't demand to be told what results he'd got. Instead she helped him with his coat and urged him into the warmth of the living room.

He leaned back in his seat with a weary sigh. "We've confirmed Dennis Plummer was outside the pub last night. Several people IDed him from his photo but no-one saw him inside. Apparently he looked shifty. A couple of our guys went over to ask him what he was playing at but he moved off when they approached."

"Is he totally stupid?" said Adam. "I mean why hang

137

round a cop pub, looking furtive, when you're already on remand for assaulting police personnel?"

"That's the weird thing," agreed Sutton. "He's loudmouthed and lairy, but he's bright enough to run his own firm. I'd guess he had good reason to be there… or one that seems good to him."

"Do you think he's dangerous?" asked Mia.

He frowned. "If, like his cousin says, he's past caring, I guess he could be. Would you like me to stay over again tonight?"

"Please." She forced a smile. "Your bed's still made up. Adam can have the dancing elephants."

"Story of my life," commented Adam. Mia knew he was trying to work out why, after less than a week, Sutton had been allocated a bedroom in her house.

"Oliver and his friend Tash spent last night here, all of us in separate bedrooms."

"I may not be Sherlock Holmes but I'd guessed that, and it's none of my business anyway. That wasn't what's worrying me."

"What is worrying you?" said Sutton.

"I was wondering if the killer got those three women to open their doors by posing as a fast-food delivery man?"

"It's not likely," said Sutton. "The SCT has checked everything like that. And even if the first woman had opened her door after dark, the second one shouldn't have and the third should have definitely had more sense."

"They all lived alone?"

"Two of them did. Angie Masters and Deirdre Anderson. Deirdre's mother died a few months ago."

"Were the women connected in any way?" said Mia.

"Not that anyone's spotted. Angie was a nurse and Deirdre worked in a supermarket, but neither Angie or Julie were known to shop there."

"What did Julie Townsend do for a living?"

"She was a teacher but she'd given up work to stay home

with her kids. She was a single mum, recently divorced. Her kids were with their dad for the weekend. He'd taken them to Euro-Disney. I gather he's feeling pretty bad about it. He hadn't told his ex-wife they were going and he didn't answer his mobile."

"Why hadn't he told her?"

"Apparently Julie had this bee in her bonnet about estranged dads running off with their kids. Although this guy isn't the cosmopolitan sort. DCI Craig told me he's a quiet man who works in a tool hire shop."

"Why the divorce? Who was screwing round?"

Sutton's swift smile lit up his face. "That was my first question. Apparently the girl had ambitions and she wanted hubby to move up the food chain. One of the team told me she'd got a dragon of a mother, who was pushing all the time. I read the husband's statement and he said the only night he could be sure of getting the kids was when mother-in-law ran a Brownie pack and his wife helped her."

Mia's brain was racing. "I'm sure Dennis Plummer had a run-in with a Brownie leader. His cousin Mike said she reported him for turning up drunk to collect his daughter."

"Did he indeed?" Sutton leaned forward, suddenly intent.

"Oliver, do you think it's possible Dennis killed those three women?" It sounded absurdly melodramatic but she had to ask.

"I don't know. It's an enormous coincidence, him appearing on our radar at this point but coincidences do happen, and it's possible he's trying to get our attention; upping the ante because he's getting bored.

"Hang on," protested Adam. "It's a big jump from drunken lout to serial killer. Even if he did have a run-in with a Brown Owl, there's no saying it was the woman who died. Did Plummer have any contact with the other victims?"

Sutton shrugged. "I don't know. And I can't contact bereaved relatives this late at night to ask. The SCT have consulted a Geographical Profiler and there's a map on the

Incident Room board." He frowned, clearly concentrating, then said, "I don't think any of the victims lived near Dennis but I'm pretty sure Deirdre worked in a small supermarket not far from where he lives."

"Do you know where Dennis is now?" asked Mia.

"No. He's not at home. I sent a team round to check."

"You mean you've put word out to look for him?"

"Of course. He broke his bail conditions. He was forbidden to visit pubs or approach you or Chantelle."

"What about Chantelle?" asked Adam. "Plummer must have a grudge against her too."

"You're right! I ought to phone her."

Mia glanced at the clock: almost eleven. Not the time to startle a nervous woman out of her first sleep and warn her she might be the target of a psychopath. But they didn't know how this predator got his victims to open their doors. Even now someone could be outside Chantelle's flat… "I'll do it."

She listened as the ringing went on and on. When Chantelle answered Mia was overwhelmed with relief. "It's Mia. I'm sorry to bother you so late but I was worried about you. I don't want to scare you but there's a possibility that Dennis Plummer could be more dangerous than we thought. I've got Adam and DI Sutton here with me. If you're afraid of being alone, we could come and get you and bring you back to my house for the night."

"You were worried about me? You'd do that for me?" Chantelle's voice was soft with wonder and, amazingly, she didn't sound afraid.

"Of course." Mia didn't add she'd do it for anyone.

"Thank you, but you don't have to worry about me. I'm not alone."

"Who's with you?" Mia spoke sharply as her mind spun into panic.

"Trevor's here." Did Chantelle sound defiant or triumphant? Mia wasn't sure.

140

"Oh… right." Mia could foresee complications leering at them from all sides. "As long as you're okay. Goodnight."

She rang off and said, "Chantelle's fine."

"So we gathered," said Adam. "Just what we need, the boss in bed with the bitch bimbo."

"Nice alliteration," said Mia, but she was thinking the same thing.

Breakfast had become crowded. As a rule Mia shared her first meal with Robinson the bear, and he wasn't much of a conversationalist. Although, to be fair, he was as chatty as Oliver. Adam was the total opposite. The lively flow of trivia was wearing and Mia was sure Oliver was fighting back caustic words.

Adam's mobile rang. He glanced at the display and abandoned his breakfast to answer it. "Hi sweetheart. How's it going? Are you okay? How's my little man?" His voice was filled with tenderness. He moved out of the kitchen and the last words they caught were, "I'm fine, but I miss you."

The door closed behind him and Oliver said ruefully, "I was about to tell him to turn off the sweetness and light."

"I know him a lot better than you and he'd got me fooled."

"I guess there's no point in emotional camouflage if people can see through it."

She giggled. "That could qualify as Thought For The Day."

When it was time to leave, Oliver double-checked everything was locked. He ushered both her and Adam into their cars and made them drive away in front of him. Mia thought it was strange that his solicitude could make her feel both reassured and hideously vulnerable.

Trevor was already in the SOCO office, giving out assignments. As always, Friday night had been prime clubbing time and the complaints about vandalism, car crime and assaults were piled high on his desk. He greeted Mia and Adam without his usual familiarity and didn't meet their eyes. She sat down at her desk feeling miserable. Chantelle was already causing trouble.

Half an hour later only she and Adam were left with Trevor in the office. Adam slid some papers into a file and stood up. "I'll go and sort that antique shop break in."

"Hold on a minute, there's something I want to say." Trevor's beefy face was dark red and his voice was rough-edged. "About last night. Me and Chantelle weren't doing anything. I mean we weren't at it. I wanted you to know."

Mia hesitated. She was tempted to say, 'Yeah, whatever,' and let it go, but Trev was a mate.

She launched into a mission statement that she hoped covered Adam's views as well. "Look, Trev, your sex life is none of our business, but Chantelle certainly gave me the impression you weren't at her place to enjoy a cup of herbal tea. We don't care if you're screwing her, as long as she isn't screwing you up."

Trevor seemed relieved at her blunt speaking. "It wasn't like that. We went out for dinner and I saw her home and I did go in for a cuppa. When you phoned, she sort of lost her head."

"As in pretending you planned to spend the night? Isn't that a bit bizarre?"

"She thought guys like Frank would make my life a misery if they knew all I was getting out of a date was a cup of funny tasting tea."

"So she was protecting your reputation as a swift moving, super stud?" enquired Adam.

Trevor chuckled. "Something like that. I told her not to be daft. You two don't judge people that way. After you phoned I did spend the night there, on the couch, to make sure she was safe. As you can imagine, she was pretty scared." Now he looked them fully in the face. "However tempting, I don't screw my staff."

Adam grinned at him. "Fine. You're not my type anyway. I'd better be going."

"I've picked your assignments to cover well-populated places. And you're to keep a uniformed officer with you all day and wear a stab vest, even if it is a pain."

Adam looked startled. "Why? This lunatic doesn't go for guys."

"I ain't taking any chances. He might turn spiteful if he thinks you're standing between him and Mia. I always thought it's out of order that you civilian SOCOs can't carry defensive weapons like us cops."

"You're just scared if I get taken out you'll have no one to protect you from Mia when she's in a bossy mood."

"What do you mean 'when'? She's always bloody bossy. Go on, get out there and earn your keep."

Trevor waited until Adam had left, then he smiled at Mia. "Thanks luv."

"What for?"

"For phoning Chantelle for one thing. She was really touched about that. And for speaking out just now. I wasn't sure how to put the record straight."

"You're welcome. I hope you're right and Chantelle isn't setting you up."

"I know you'll think I'm stupid, but I trust her. Now we've got talking, I can see she's really shy and insecure. She honestly believed we were picking on her and I guess, in some ways, in the end we were."

"Trevor, you've just crossed the boundary between nice and nauseating."

That made him laugh but he said, "Deep down she's a kind person, Mia. She spent a long while nursing her father and I think she misses having someone to look after. She's made me a packed lunch so I don't buy doughnuts and pies."

Mia thought the web of care and comfort Chantelle was weaving around Trevor could prove sweeter and stronger than the ties that came from sex. "That's great."

Trevor was looking embarrassed again. "And there's something else, but promise you won't tell anyone."

"I promise." What the hell was coming now?

"She went out with me and made me buy new trousers, four inches bigger than I'd been wearing up till now."

"You mean you've been wearing trousers much too tight for you? But why?"

"Daft ain't it? I kept telling myself I'd slim down again. Guess I didn't want to face the fact I'm a great fat slob."

"Great definitely; fat maybe; slob never."

"That's what Chantelle said, about the slob bit I mean."

"Well you'd better believe it, two bossy women can't both be wrong." Somehow, this unromantic detail about the trousers reassured Mia that Chantelle was on the level. "Where is she? Surely she didn't decide to stay home alone?"

"She's out at a scene. I'm getting grief about demanding bodyguards for my staff."

Mia hoped they'd still got a large, tough cop spare to accompany her. She didn't need sparkling conversation, just the ability to thump any stalker who came near. "Where's my assignment sheet?"

Trevor shook his head. "You ain't going anywhere, my girl. I had a phone call from DI Sutton telling me to keep you safe until he can get free to come down and look after you."

"What?"

"Laid the law down good and proper he did. I nearly told him to take a hike, but it was obvious he was wound up about your safety and I wasn't going to argue about that."

"He's a good friend."

Trevor cocked a sceptical eyebrow at her. "That all he is?"

She met his look. "No, he's also a conscientious senior officer. You haven't got a monopoly on the moral high-ground, Trev. Oliver Sutton doesn't screw his staff either."

"Fair enough. Didn't mean to be nosy. It's like you worrying about what's going on between me and Chantelle,

144

I don't want to see you come to grief."

"And instead of coming to grief, we're both in platonic, professional relationships. Boring isn't it? Have you ever been married, Trev?" She'd never asked him anything that personal before.

"Yeah, a long time ago. It didn't work out. Only lasted a few months."

"I'm sorry."

"These things happen. Especially in our line of work. I kinda steered clear of relationships after that."

"How selfish of you, that's the wanton waste of an extremely nice guy."

"That's the trouble, luv. The women all say I'm nice and go off and marry someone else."

"Plenty of women would jump at a man like you."

"That a proposal?"

She grinned back at him. "I could do a lot worse."

They returned to their paperwork until the office door opened and Oliver Sutton entered.

His first words were to Trevor. "Good morning, Inspector. Thanks for keeping her safe."

"What's wrong?" Mia's voice cut sharply across Trevor's response.

Sutton came across to her desk and perched on the edge of it. "We've had the results of the fingerprints on that pizza box and most of them are a match to Dennis Plummer's."

"What else?" He wouldn't look so stressed over something they'd foreseen.

"There were other fingerprints on the box. They belong to the second victim, Deirdre Anderson."

Chapter 15

Mia stared at Sutton. He looked like he'd been thrown into relief, as if there was a dark outline drawn all round him in marker pen. She wondered if she was about to faint and thought how embarrassing that would be. His hand closed over hers and squeezed. She took a deep breath and hauled herself back. "I'm sorry."

"Don't be. It scared the shit out of me too."

Trevor crossed the office to join them. "How sure are they? They must have put a rush on to get it back so soon."

"Yeah. They don't like cops being targets."

Mia suppressed a shudder. She pulled her hand free and asked, "What else did they find?"

"There's one or two unidentified prints, probably casual contact, employees at the manufacturers or shop, and a few smudges, like someone was wearing gloves. DCI Aron, the head of the Serious Crimes Team, wants to put you somewhere safe until it's all over."

"No way! I got into this and I want to be part of getting out of it again."

"Yeah, I guessed you'd say that, so I suggested you were seconded onto the team and you stick firmly with me all the working day."

"You reckon you can fight off this lunatic?" asked Trevor.

Sutton met his eyes. "Don't worry about that."

"No offence, but your arm's still not right."

"I can take him." There was no room for doubt or discussion in his tone.

Mia was feeling better. When scary things happened it helped to have good friends on your side. She turned to Sutton. "If I'm working this case what do you want me to do?"

"Sit there under Inspector Mayfield's eye and read this

lot. I've got you all the forensic reports and the profiler's ideas on the sort of crazy bastard we're looking for."

"Should I have these? Aren't they classified?"

"It's all stuff you'd have been told if you'd been in the briefings. I had to read it to catch up."

"As long as the SIO agreed." According to the Station gossip, DCI Aron wasn't the sort to sanction unconventional tactics.

"He did. At least he said DCI Craig could decide and Craig really rates you. I guess he knows it was you who cracked the Bridge Road case. Ring me if you spot anything earth shattering, otherwise I'll be back soon."

"What are you going to do?"

"I'm checking every detail of Dennis Plummer's life, trying to track down any connection to the three victims."

He left and Trevor eyed Mia, his curiosity clear. "What?" she said.

"Just wondering if what laddie said was true? Did you crack the Bridge Road case?"

"Only as far as the scientific evidence was the key. I don't know where DCI Craig got the idea I'd solved it."

"I'd guess from Sutton himself. He strikes me as the kind of senior officer who takes the kicks himself and makes sure the praise is passed out where it's due. It's what I'd call an old fashioned style of leadership. You don't see many cops like that nowadays."

"In that case you haven't looked in the mirror recently. You're probably right about Oliver... I mean DI Sutton... playing down his part, but I wish he hadn't. I don't need CID approval."

"I don't think it'll have done him any harm. I've known George Craig a good few years and he's no fool." He returned to his desk and opened a drawer. "I've got a taizer here. No disrespect to young Sutton but I'd feel happier if you had some protection of your own. But keep quiet about it. It's not exactly by the book."

"Thanks Trev." She took it and slid it into her pocket. Battening down her reluctance she opened the first file. As a rule she could consider horrors without flinching but this came too close to home.

The crimes were so alike. Three mirror images. There was no sign of forced entry. It seemed all three women had opened their doors to their abductor, then he'd taken them to an unknown place and done unspeakable things. The forensic reports were detailed, every procedure meticulously logged, and yet they said little, because little had been found. They still had to find the primary crimescene.

Mia read the pathologist's reports, grimly dividing intellect and emotions. They'd all been tortured, raped and strangled, then their bodies were dunked in disinfectant. All three women had been dumped, naked, in lay-bys, just outside of town. There was one piece of information in the reports that was a 'hold back,' something the investigating officers didn't reveal in order to sieve out false confessions. At some point during their abduction, their hair had been dyed blonde.

Mia turned to the psychological profile. As she read she felt increasing bewilderment. When Sutton returned she said, "I don't get it."

"What?" He resumed his perch on the corner of her desk and waved acknowledgement to Trevor as he left the room.

"The psychologist reckons we're looking for an organised and controlled sociopath. No conscience, no empathy. He's got enough knowledge of science to eradicate the evidence. And, above all he's capable of patience and planning. He watches his victims until he knows their lifestyle, possibly even gets within it."

Sutton nodded. "And?"

"It's not the Dennis Plummer we know and loathe. I can go with the no conscience, no empathy bit, but he's not clever and controlled, he's a loud-mouthed slob."

"So you reckon this player of games is more subtle than that?"

"Yeah, and so do you."

He grinned acknowledgement. "I had thought of it. And so has DCI Craig and most of the SCT, which is why they're willing to let a lowly divisional cop like me run with it."

"From what I've read those three women were quite ordinary. There's nothing special in their lifestyle or their looks, a bit like me."

"I'd guess they weren't all as fei... determined."

She glared at him. "What were you going to say?"

"I was going to say feisty, but my sisters have taught me that's a bad word, the sort that gets you thumped."

"Too right. That's my point. I felt uncomfortable when Dennis was chatting me up, which is probably why I over-reacted. I can't believe all three of them would have let him into their lives."

"Maybe the link was they all shot him down. Although probably not as ruthlessly as you."

"Thanks for the reassurance."

"Sorry, but it's got to be faced."

"But why that crazy game with the pizza box? He's left no physical evidence up to now and suddenly he's leaving incriminating fingerprints on a cop's doorstep."

"Maybe, deep down, he wants to get caught. The profiler says that's possible. The links with Dennis are coming together. I've been phoning round and Julie Townsend was the Brownie leader who reported him for being drunk when he was picking up his kid. Also he did use the supermarket where Deirdre Anderson worked. And Angie Masters was a nurse in A&E who, according to the time-sheets, was on duty when he was treated for concussion four months ago."

"You found all that out in an hour?"

"It's easy to get the answers when you know the questions to ask. It's circumstantial but it adds up to a big total."

"But where the hell is he hiding?"

"I wish I knew. He hasn't been seen since Thursday night, so perhaps he's topped himself."

"Do you think that's likely?"

"The profiler didn't think it was probable. According to her, the player of games carries on right into prison. And once they're inside they find new ways of manipulation."

"Like Myra Hindley holding out the hope she'd help find Keith Bennet's body?"

"Yeah. There's something else I don't like. I phoned Helen Plummer, Dennis' ex-wife, to arrange a meeting. As soon as I introduced myself, she demanded, 'Have you found her?'"

"Found who?"

"Ellie, their elder daughter. She's sixteen and she hasn't been home for over three weeks."

"What?" Mia stared at him. "A girl's gone missing and no alarm bells rang?"

"Oh they rang all right, but she sent two text messages and a postcard to her mum saying she was going to London. Mrs Plummer says she's sure it's Ellie's handwriting. Teenagers do run off and it didn't seem to have any connection to the murders… until now."

"So now you're interested in our Ellie. Pity you didn't care when she first went." Helen Plummer's words were belligerent but there was a tell-tale quiver in her voice.

"It wasn't we didn't care, but she's sixteen and she did contact you," said Sutton gently.

Mia felt sorry for Dennis Plummer's ex-wife and sorry for Sutton who was forced to conduct this delicate interview in front of DS Warden, who'd been assigned to accompany them. Sutton was the senior officer but Warden was a permanent member of the Serious Crimes Team. At the moment he was sitting on the sidelines listening, but Mia was sure he was taking stock of everything.

Helen Plummer lived in a homely, semi-detached

house. Mia surveyed a multi-photo frame, mainly filled with photos of two girls. One showed a young teenager standing between two men. It was easy to recognise Mike but Dennis had changed a lot. In the picture he looked fit, cheerful and approachable. Surely the photo couldn't be that old?

"Is this Ellie?" she asked.

Helen glanced across. "Yes, but that was two years ago." She pointed to another picture. "This is the latest."

Ellie was a pretty, fair-haired kid, dressed in a sparkling, white tutu. "Ellie dances?"

Helen's face softened. "Yeah. Always wanted to be a dancer. Her dad bought her the dress last Christmas. Spoils her rotten he does."

"Is she actually as fair as you? In the earlier photos she looks nearer brown than blonde," asked Sutton.

"If truth were told, we're both as brown as each other. We do each other's hair." Her lips quivered. "What's happened to my girl?"

"Nothing we know of. Dennis has got himself in trouble and when I phoned you asked about Ellie, so I thought I'd follow it up."

"What's Denny done this time? Something stupid I suppose?"

"More than stupid. He's charged with assault and it's possible the CPS will see it as attempted rape."

"Rape? Hurting a woman? Not Denny! No matter how drunk he was."

"Have you seen Dennis in the last two days, Mrs Plummer? He's broken his bail conditions by not reporting in."

"No, I ain't seen him." Mia saw the penny drop. "And now you're round here asking about our Ellie? What're you thinking? That he could have hurt her? No way! Thinks the sun shines out of his girls, he does."

"And yet you took him back to court to get his access changed after that trouble at Brownies?" said Sutton.

151

She hesitated, then said reluctantly, "I had to. That Brown Owl woman said she'd report us to the Social Services and have the girls taken into care. She said her mother used to be a Social Worker, so they'd listen to her."

"So it was the daughter, Julie Townsend, who threatened to report you?"

"Yeah, it was her who phoned me. But the mother's an old pokenose. Pair of them as bad as one another. Not that she deserved what happened to her." Her eyes widened as full understanding dawned. "You think Denny had something to do with that? You must be crazy!"

"We have to follow up anyone Julie had aggro with."

"There'll be plenty of them, the way she and her mother threw their weight around. I told our Zoe I didn't want her to go to Brownies no more and she said she was pleased to give it up. All they did was nag."

"What happened between you and Dennis when Julie Townsend threatened to report him?"

Helen shrugged. "I told Denny how it was. He understood it was his own fault for not keeping off the bottle. He'd never do anything to hurt our girls."

"Except driving them when he's drunk?"

Helen looked surprised. "He wasn't driving. His cousin Mike was with him." The anger dropped from her. "I want to know what's happened to Ellie."

"She's probably fine but we'd like to contact her and make sure. That card said she'd gone to London?"

"Yeah, that's right, same as the text messages. Said she was fed up with college and was going to London to go on the stage. Silly little muppet. It's only in storybooks that girls get famous that way. I thought she'd got more sense."

"You're sure the note was from Ellie?"

"It was her writing and her lousy spelling. Me and Denny have both been off to London hunting for her. I left Zoe with her gran, so you needn't set Children's Services onto us."

"I wouldn't do that. Could you tell me a bit more about

Dennis? His life seems to have gone out of control?"

She looked at him assessingly, then replied, "Yeah."

"Has he got a drink problem?"

"I guess he has. Mind you, he's always liked his drink. He's ex-army, you see, and those boys can put away even more than your lot can."

"Can I ask why you two split up?"

She hesitated, but when she spoke the words poured out, like pus from a sceptic wound, "I stuck with him even when he got in trouble. He's always been the only guy for me, right from when we were kids. But he got so jealous. Kept accusing me of sleeping round. Kept coming home unexpectedly and tearing the place apart looking for my boyfriends. Mike told me Denny even paid some guy to try and pick me up. It was like he was desperate to have his suspicions proved. Three years ago I told him to clear out. I couldn't live like that and it was bad for Ellie and Zoe. The divorce came through a few months ago."

"He moved out of here and into his flat? Number 22 Oakdene Mansions?"

"That's right. It's a big block of flats. Mike's got a place there and he heard there was one that might suit Denny. Mind, from what Mike's said, Denny's turned his flat into a pigsty. Denny came straight to me from his mum, he's never had to take care of himself."

"But he's been in the army hasn't he?" DS Warden spoke for the first time.

"Yeah, but, when it comes down to it, the army's just another sort of control. It doesn't leave a person free to think. His mum's a lovely lady but she makes sure she's the boss. She don't bully me 'cos I stand up to her but, between us, I don't think we did Denny any good."

Mia was surprised at how shrewd Helen Plummer was. The picture she was painting of her ex-husband was sympathetic and yet scary. It was clear Dennis was damaged but it was hard to believe such a stupid, drunken lout was a

153

cold, controlled sociopath acting out a part.

"Have you noticed any changes in Dennis lately?" asked Sutton.

"He hasn't been right for a while. A few months ago he fell off some scaffolding and hit his head. He's been worse since then."

"When that happened, did he say anything about the nurses in A&E? Did he have any aggro with them?"

She frowned, trying to think back. "Mike said about one nurse who told Denny off for swearing."

"Did Dennis say anything about it?"

"He said he didn't remember. It was a bad concussion."

"How did he take it when the Brown Owl turned him in?"

She shrugged, now on the defensive. "He was upset. I didn't like it either. I don't appreciate being told I'm a bad mother."

"Do you know if Dennis shopped at the little supermarket in Dundrell Road?"

"No idea. He lives off fast food junk." The slam of the front door made them jump. "That'll be Zoe. She's been shopping with Denny's mum. Don't say anything to upset them."

The door swung open and a young, brown-haired girl appeared, followed by a small, wrinkled woman with an amazing coil of red hair swirled around her head.

"What's goin' on, our Helen?"

"Nothing's wrong, Ma. These cops are doing a follow up visit about Ellie."

"'Bout time you lot did somethin' to find our girl." The bright, dark glare she turned upon them reminded Mia of a garden robin defending its territory.

"We wanted a word with your son, Dennis," said Sutton. "You don't happen to know where he is, do you?"

"He's not in his flat? Then I got no idea. His cousin might know. Not much Denny does that Mike don't know

154

about." She jerked her head to her granddaughter. "Go and try on that new skirt I bought yer, there's a good girl. Your mum and me need a word in private with these cops. When they've gone I'll do your nails for you, same as mine."

Instinctively Mia gazed at the old woman's blue-veined, wrinkled hand. The skin was flecked with white freckles where the pigment had given up, but her long, scarlet nails were decorated with sparkling hearts and flowers.

Old Mrs Plummer waited until the door closed behind her granddaughter then said, "I s'pose this is about Denny's latest carry-on?"

"You knew Denny was in trouble and you didn't tell me?" Helen's voice wavered between anger and hurt.

"I'm sorry, luv, but Denny begged me not to. Said you thought bad enough of him as it was." She leaned across and rested her hand on Helen's. "He's so ashamed of himself. Came to me and cried like a little kid."

"Mrs Plummer, what sort of person is Dennis?" asked Sutton quietly.

She answered without hesitation, "Loud. Always roarin' and shootin' his mouth off." There was a twinkle in the fierce eyes, "Of course, some 'ud say he takes after me."

"Impulsive," said Helen quietly.

"That's right. Does things then wishes he'd thought it through. Generous though and thinks the world of his family."

"When he and your daughter-in-law split up, why didn't he live with you?"

"I'm in one of them old people's places. I got a bad heart you see. Could drop down dead just like that." She clicked her fingers.

"Ma, you're exaggerating," protested Helen.

"Yeah, maybe. But it don't do no harm to let these cops know if they pull any bully-boy tactics they could be lumbered with a corpse."

"I don't think there's much danger of us bullying you,"

said Sutton dryly, with emphasis on the pronouns.

That made her laugh, a deep, rippling sound, much younger than her years. "Alright, I ain't that likely to drop off me perch because you talk a bit tough to me, even though I do 'ave funny turns. But I didn't want Denny lumbered with the worry of lookin' after me. And if anyone's gonna come in and find me dead in bed, I'd rather it was that warden than my boy. He's not tough about stuff like that, never was."

"Even though he was in the army?" asked Sutton, as DS Warden had said before.

"He liked the manoeuvres and the sports and stuff. And bein' one of the lads. Not too hot on killin' people though."

Mia stared at her, trying to work out if she was as shrewd a judge of her son as she appeared, or completely blind to his dark side.

"It's true," said Helen quietly. "I've known Denny ever since we started infants' school. He likes people to think he's tough but it's all show, like that stupid tattoo on his arm."

"Well it's got your name in it," grumbled her mother-in-law. Evidently this was an old bone of contention.

"Yeah. The silly devil was so proud of himself. So I thanked him for the thought and said I'd rather he didn't get any more done."

Sutton stood up. "Thank you for talking to us. We'll do everything we can to find Ellie. Are you quite sure neither of you can tell us where Dennis is now? It would be better for him if we could sort things out."

Both shook their heads. Old Mrs Plummer said, "Like I told you, it's Mike you oughta ask. If he don't know where Denny is no-one does."

"If he's gone anywhere it's to look for Ellie. The way you lot should have done." Helen's eyes filled with tears. "Why won't anyone find my girl?"

Chapter 16

"What do you reckon?" asked Sutton as they drove away from the house.

Mia didn't answer. She concentrated on driving and let the big boys talk it out.

"I reckon the wife's straight," said DS Warden. "I don't think she knows what her ex has been up to and probably doesn't know where he's hanging out. But I think she's more scared he's gone off the rails than she's letting on."

"That's my feeling too," agreed Sutton. "I think she's still fond of him but she wouldn't keep quiet if she thought Dennis had hurt their daughter."

"I'd go further than that. I don't think she'd keep quiet if she suspected he'd killed anyone."

Her interest caught, Mia inspected Warden in the rear view mirror. He was a pleasant looking, powerfully built, brown-haired guy in his mid-thirties. She had the feeling he was a lot shrewder than she'd originally given him credit for.

He caught her gaze and grinned. "Of course I could be wrong. My boss says I'm a sentimental sod and I've never been sure whether he's joking or not."

"You get on well with him?" said Sutton. Mia could understand his surprise. By all accounts DCI Aron was a peevish, by-the-book man, not the sort who joked with his troops.

"Yeah, he's the best there is." Warden picked up on their incredulity. "I don't mean Aron. I'm only on secondment to him while my own SIO's at a conference in the US. You're new to this area aren't you, sir?"

"Yeah. And the name's Oliver."

"Cheers. I'm Luke. What do you reckon to the old lady?"

"Sharp, tough and a fighter."

"Mother love, it's the scariest thing in the world. Do you reckon Plummer's our man?"

"I don't know. Certainly what Helen Plummer said about his paranoid jealousy and the way he'd gone funny after the head injury doesn't sound too good."

"Where are we off to now?"

"We're going to talk to people who knew the three dead women and see whether anyone can tie Dennis Plummer more firmly to them. It's workplace visits for the first two, they didn't have much family. Then I've made an appointment to talk to the mother of the third victim. She's the Brown Owl we've heard about. After that I'd like a chat with Dennis' cousin Mike. And I want Mia to talk to the archaeologist who did a watching brief on one of the Plummers' building sites. I think he knows more about them than he's letting on."

Mia groaned. "Do I have to? He'll think I'm encouraging him."

"Too bad," said Sutton hard-heartedly. "We need to know about Dennis Plummer from someone who isn't part of his family. Park here, Mia. That's where Deirdre Anderson worked."

It was a small supermarket and the assistants were friendly and cheerful until they spoke of Deirdre when a solemn fog enveloped them.

"You'd best ask Margery," said the girl on the checkout. "She and Deirdre were friends. She's down aisle three, putting out the breakfast cereals."

Margery proved to be a brisk, middle-aged woman, who seemed eager to talk.

"We're trying to build up a picture of Deirdre," said Sutton. "Would you tell us about her? Her lifestyle, hobbies, basically what she was like,"

"She was a nice girl. Well woman really, not a girl. But she hadn't got out much, what with her mum being ill for so long. She'd been kept pretty sheltered."

"Did she have any hobbies?"

"Quiet, homely ones. She read a lot, mainly romances, bless her. And she did a lot of needlework. She said, now

158

her mum had passed away, perhaps she'd take up some classes. She fancied watercolour painting, maybe going on a residential course to meet people. I told her to go for it and I'd look after her cat while she was away." She turned from her task, her lips quivering, "Now she'll never have the chance. It's wicked, someone taking that away from her."

"Very wicked," agreed Sutton. "We're trying to locate this man. Do you know him?" He held out a photograph of Dennis Plummer.

"Oh yes. Dennis the Menace."

"Does he come in here often?"

"All the time. He lives along the road. Booze, ciggies and microwave meals, that's what he buys, along with the odd top shelf magazine. Bit different from that chap who hangs round with him. He used to buy those series of magazines about famous composers or classic films, the sort that comes with a free DVD, but lately he's been asking for The New Scientist."

"Are you talking about Dennis' cousin, Mike?" asked Mia.

She thought for a moment then nodded. "Yes, I'm sure I heard Dennis call him Mike."

"Did Deirdre ever have any trouble with Dennis?" said Sutton.

"A couple of times. He's lairy when he's drunk. But nothing serious. No worse than we have to put up with most evenings."

"Tell me what happened, please."

"The first time he got nasty when she refused to sell him alcohol. She had no choice. He was staggering drunk and a couple of cops had just come in to pick up their sandwiches. He swore at her. That mate of his tried to quieten him down but that seemed to make him worse, and then the cops came over and hustled him outside."

"I didn't see a police report of that incident?" said Sutton.

159

"I don't know as there was one. Deirdre didn't want any fuss. She rather liked Dennis. He was always telling her how pretty she looked and how the blue of the uniform really suited her. All flannel, of course, but she lapped it up. There was no harm done and the cops probably didn't want to waste their time taking him down the police station and filling in paperwork."

"After that, did he stop coming in here?"

"Of course he didn't! This is his local shop. Next morning he was back, large as life and twice and ugly, buying stuff for his hangover. Mind you, I cured his hangover for him. Told him exactly what I thought of him for upsetting Deirdre. Lucky she was out back, sorting stock. That way she didn't have the embarrassment of hearing me tear a strip off him."

"How did he take it?" Mia saw Sutton considering whether he needed a police guard on this outspoken lady as well.

"Like a lamb. Went straight off and brought her a bunch of roses to say sorry. Lovely they were. She said she'd never had a bouquet like that in all her life."

"You said there was another incident?" This time the question was asked by Luke Warden, who was leaning casually against the stock trolley.

"Oh that was different. He came in one Sunday afternoon, as we were closing, and wanted to buy paracetemol. We couldn't sell them to him, it was past four o'clock. He knocked over the newspaper stand and I thought we were in for trouble, but then he dragged himself up and said he was sorry, his head was so bad it was making him giddy. Deirdre went all decisive on me and said she'd see him home. I waited half an hour for her to come back. I was that worried I didn't know what to do. At last she turned up again and said she'd gone into his flat with him. She'd given him some painkillers from her bag and made him a cup of tea. Then that mate of his arrived and said he'd take care of him."

"Is that all she told you about it?"

"Well she said it was a funny business, but I didn't take much notice. What she was saying didn't make sense."

"What was she saying?"

"I don't rightly know. She was flustered about keeping me waiting. It was something about someone not being where he should have been, even though she'd seen him and she'd knocked and knocked. To be honest I didn't really listen."

"How long ago was this?" said Sutton.

"About five weeks. Three weeks before she died." The woman stared at them, her face stricken. "I should have told the police about it, shouldn't I? But I forgot. He's been in here most days, like part of the furniture. And Deirdre was always doing things like that. She liked helping people. I used to tell her, 'You take things steady. It'll be the death of you, running round after people all the time.'"

She registered what she'd said and tears flooded her eyes. "Excuse me, I've got to get on." She turned her back on them and started ramming bags of Crunchy Oats onto the shelf.

The hospital interviews were productive of accurate dates and times but less useful when it came to reminiscences. The A&E staff were too used to abusive drunks to remember any particular one, but it seemed Dennis Plummer's behaviour couldn't have been too bad because his misdeeds hadn't been recorded in the security log.

When it came to Angie Masters they found plenty of people who'd worked with her but no-one seemed to know much about her. A few of her colleagues were about to finish their shift and Sutton persuaded them to give him a few minutes in the staff lounge.

"She liked walking and cycling. She spent all her holidays on cycle tours going round foreign countries," said one girl. "She didn't mix much. It's like she thought we were all airheads, not serious exploring types like her."

"Her bike was stolen a few days before she died," said

161

a male nurse. "She was really mad about that. Said it cost her over £2,000. She advertised for its return but I think she knew she hadn't got a hope."

"She kept on about the environment and how wrong it was to drive cars," said another nurse. "I told her it was funny her principles didn't stop her from going on plane journeys around the world. She didn't like that. Kept picking on me for months."

"Did she have any friends? Anyone who knew her well?" asked Sutton.

A glance rippled around the circle, then they shook their heads.

Sutton took out Dennis' photograph. "Do any of you remember treating this guy for concussion a few months ago? Or Angie having a run in with him?"

The picture travelled between them and one said doubtfully, "He looks a bit like a security guard. Angie was always having run-ins with them."

"He's a building contractor," said Sutton.

"In that case Angie would have definitely given him aggro. She hated builders. She told me she'd taken one building firm to court."

"Was this a local builder?"

"No. That was up in Scotland where she came from. But she said all builders were the same. She'd give any of them a hard time. And surveyors and council officials, she really hated them."

"And car salesmen," offered another.

"They don't count," someone protested. "They're like lawyers and bankers, everyone hates them."

"Thanks for your time." Sutton signalled to his companions and they slipped away.

"Talk about the caring profession," said Warden, as they crossed the car park.

"Yeah," agreed Mia. "I'm glad we didn't get onto what they thought of cops."

"It wasn't a lot of help," said Sutton. "Any car salesman, lawyer, council official or banker who's had the misfortune to visit A&E could have taken a contract out on Angie." He sounded discouraged and Mia saw he was cradling his arm.

"First assemble all your information, then try to make sense of it," she said.

He smiled at her. "Thank God for the scientific mind." He glanced at his watch. "We'd better hurry. Mrs Simmonds didn't sound like the sort of woman you keep waiting."

Julie Townsend's mother was plump and fair-haired, although the colour was obviously out of a bottle, as was her complexion. Foundation cream and powder pooled in the creases in her face and the waft of flowery perfume made Mia sneeze.

The drawing room matched its owner: pastel coloured and fussy, with tasselled cushions, sentimental Victorian-style pictures on the walls, and a glass cabinet full of china dolls.

"I blame him. If he hadn't been so deceitful Julie would still be alive."

"Who are you referring to, Mrs Simmonds?" Sutton's quiet voice reminded Mia that this woman had lost her daughter in hideous circumstances.

"That man who married my daughter. It was all his fault."

"It's been fully substantiated that Richard Townsend was in France at the time."

"That's what he says."

"There's no doubt he was at Disneyland. His movements are vouched for."

"You mean he'd taken my grandchildren abroad with some tart he's sleeping with?" She twisted the lace handkerchief she was clasping until it resembled a garrotte.

"No. He went with a support group who try to help divorced parents re-establish a bond with their children." The patience in Sutton's voice was growing thin.

"He had no right to. Julie would never have agreed."

The sideboard bore a framed photograph of Julie. She was round-faced and curly haired. Mia thought she looked sweet-natured and no match for her mother's dominance.

"Did your daughter have many enemies?" asked Sutton.

"Of course not! She was a dear, good girl and everybody loved her, apart from him."

"What about the people she threatened to report to the Social Services?"

For a moment Mrs Simmonds looked blank then understanding dawned, "Oh you mean that awful builder man, Zoe Plummer's father. Such a disruptive child, not surprising considering the background she comes from. I shouldn't have allowed Julie to talk me out of doing my duty. Children like that would be better off in Care."

"So it was you who wanted to have the children taken away from their mum?"

Mrs Simmonds bridled, offended by the sharpness of Sutton's tone. "It would be better for the children. To a trained eye it was obvious he was abusing Zoe."

"Did Zoe say that?"

"She's in denial. Most abused children are. And the mothers too. They're too weak to take the responsibility, you see?"

"But Julie didn't agree with you?" said Sutton.

"Julie believed the best of everyone, even that brute she married. It breaks my heart when I think how she spent her last day trying to phone her girls and getting no answer."

"What did Julie suggest you did about Dennis Plummer?"

"She said she'd phone Mrs Plummer and I agreed that if she persuaded Mrs Plummer to oppose her ex-husband's access to the girls, I wouldn't take it any further."

Mia imagined the confused conversation between Helen Plummer and Julie Townsend: Helen frightened and indignant, Julie flustered and more sympathetic than she dared admit. So that was how Julie ended up as the bad guy in the tug of power.

"Did you hear from Dennis Plummer again?" said Sutton.

"No." Mia thought she sounded regretful that she had no more grounds for complaint. "But Mrs Plummer telephoned to say Zoe didn't want to come to Brownies anymore. Not a word of thanks for all I'd done for the child and the extra time Julie spent on Zoe. Julie was a Special Needs teacher you know. Zoe's mother insists she's dyslexic, but it's the bad home environment that caused her problems. I'm trained to see it."

"Thank you for your time." Sutton rose to his feet and Mia and Luke Warden followed.

"I'm going to fight him, you know," said Mrs Simmonds as she escorted them to the door.

"Fight who?" asked Sutton.

"That man. My daughter's ex-husband. I'm going to fight him for custody of the children. Some people shouldn't be trusted with young lives."

Chapter 17

"Weird, isn't it?" said Luke as they settled round a table in the pub. "How can the villain's mum be more likeable than the victim's?"

"The terrible thing is if Dennis Plummer did target Julie, it was down to her mother giving him aggro. Julie ended as the victim in every way," said Mia.

"Yeah, I hope she doesn't get hold of her grandchildren and ruin their lives too," agreed Sutton. He glanced at his watch, "Better order our lunch."

Mia stood up. "Everyone decided what they want?" One piece of CID culture she couldn't fight was the junior officer, male or female, had to fight their way to the bar.

"I'll go," said Warden. "We can't keep an eye on you in that scrum." He took their orders and strode towards the bar.

"Nice guy," said Sutton.

"Yeah."

"Are you okay, Mia?"

She nodded. "Apart from being a bit jumpy. It's crazy to feel vulnerable when I'm with you and Luke but I do. How are you doing?"

"Like you, a bit on edge, and my arm's still sore when I do too much with it." He read her thoughts. "But if I see any bastard coming for you I'll floor him and suffer for it later."

"I've been trained in self-defence. I'm not totally helpless you know." If you started to lean on people it was hard to stand alone.

He grinned at her. "I'd noticed." His mobile rang. He glanced at the display and there was a perceptible hesitation before he answered. "Tash? What's wrong?" He listened, then said, "There's nothing I can do about that."

Mia could hear the crackle of Tash's emphatic voice though not the words.

"I'm sorry, Tash, but that's the way it is. I told you I can't keep putting my life on hold for Gail. I'm working on an important case. I'll try to call you later."

He keyed off. Mia felt daunted by his grim expression but she asked, "Trouble, Oliver?"

"Gail made another suicide attempt. She's asking for me, so her parents got onto Tash."

"At least they didn't ring directly."

His smile was bitter. "I changed my phone and won't give Gail or her parents my new number. She used to ring me at all hours, day and night, threatening to kill herself unless I stopped her. You know that saying about how if you save somebody's life that life belongs to you? Well that got twisted so my life belongs to Gail."

Mia wasn't sure what to say. By taking this stand he was gambling not just with Gail's life but his own overwhelming guilt if she killed herself. "If you're worried about me, take that out of the equation. Do what you need to. I've got lots of people looking out for me."

"No Mia. Thanks, but this isn't about you. The one thing I know I shouldn't do is go to see Gail. I shouldn't have gone to her the first time, when she slit her wrists. Or the second, when she took an overdose. Or the third, another overdose. Or the fourth, fifth sixth… after a while the details tend to merge but I know we're into double figures now. Every time it's like she jerks a string to bring me back. And so I go to sit by her bedside and listen to her cry and swear she won't do it again. Last week, when I saw her, I told her I couldn't come to see her again if she tried to kill herself. I don't think she believed me. For that matter I don't know if I believed it myself."

Mia moved round to sit next to him on the padded bench. Concealed by the table she sought his right hand and gripped it sustainingly. She tried to send all the sympathy and support she was feeling through that slight contact.

"Thanks Mia."

"You're welcome." Amazing how much could be said by

a few oblique words.

"I told Gail if she kept herself okay for six months I'd take her somewhere nice to celebrate. She smiled and said, 'That's a date.' I guess she didn't mean it even then."

"I don't know, Ollie."

"Tash expected me to go to her. She thought I should."

"Then maybe Tash doesn't know you as well as she thinks she does."

"You mean I'm not as strong as she expects?"

"I mean you're a lot stronger. Gail hasn't got over it all these years when you've kept running to pick her up. Maybe she needs the space to get her life together by herself." She prayed Gail didn't counter Oliver's refusal by a successful suicide.

Obviously he was thinking the same thing. "If she succeeds in killing herself everybody will blame me and I'll blame myself."

"I won't. But I'm scared you might blame me for giving you the wrong advice."

"Don't worry about that. The thing about advice is no-one takes it unless it's what they want."

Luke approached the table, carrying a tray of drinks. Mia gave Oliver's hand a final squeeze and released it. If Luke had noticed anything he gave no sign, merely passed out two glasses of orange juice and kept the third for himself. Mia was surprised. Few detectives stuck to the soft stuff and she'd expected Luke to be a beer man.

He interpreted her look and grinned. "I've been well trained. My boss doesn't let anyone booze at lunchtime." He lowered his voice, "There are two guys who seem interested in you, Mia. Over in the corner."

Sutton put his drink down and casually turned his head. "That's Mike Plummer and Tim Lewis, Mia's admirer. How convenient, now we don't have to track them down."

"Too convenient," said Mia.

"That's what makes it interesting. Smile at them Mia

168

and encourage them over here."

Mia glared at him, then she looked towards Tim, turned on a dazzling smile and waved him over.

"Beautiful," murmured Sutton. "Anyone would think you'd been picking up men in pubs all your life."

Yet again Mia abandoned the respect due to a senior officer. She kept her smile in place but kicked Sutton hard enough to make him wince. "Hi Tim," she said. "Won't you join us?"

Tim took this literally, squashing onto the seat beside her. "I wanted to say hello but Mike said not to, in case you were talking police business."

"We are," said Sutton. "But that's okay. You can help with our enquiries."

Tim looked uncertain, "Help with enquiries? Isn't that what the police say when they suspect someone?"

"He's joking, Tim," said Mike quietly.

"Nice pub this. Do you come here often?" Luke directed the question to Mike.

"No, but Tim fancied having a pint here today." Mike smiled at Mia meaningfully.

"I didn't realise you two were such good friends," she said.

"Mike's my best friend," said Tim. "Apart from you, Mia."

Again Mike's eyes met Mia's and she felt the mutual understanding of two adults embarrassed by a socially inept child.

"I've made Mike realise he can't waste his life as a builder," continued Tim. "He's started his A-levels and he's going to University next year."

"Assuming I can get the grades," said Mike.

"You'll get them. You're really bright." Tim's patronage was ludicrous.

"What are you planning to study?" asked Sutton.

Mike glanced towards Tim. "I've always been keen on history."

169

"Are you thinking of archaeology, like Tim?"

"More likely teaching, but there's a long way to go before I have to decide."

"It's a big step, going back to study after you've been out of school for years."

"Over twenty years. I left school at sixteen."

"He was brought up by Dennis' mother. You can imagine how culturally aware she is," sneered Tim.

Mike shrugged. "Aunt Gwen means well. It was good of her to take me in when my own mum died. Life wasn't easy for her, a widow bringing up two boys."

"I noticed you don't have the same accent as Dennis and his mum," said Sutton.

"No. My mother worked hard to learn to talk nicely and she wanted the same for me. She was very proud of me. Dennis used to call me a snob for trying to improve myself, but that's Dennis for you, always going head-to-head with the system."

"This time Dennis pushed his luck too far," said Sutton. "He's broken the terms of his bail. Don't tell me he wasn't outside this pub on Thursday night. He was seen."

"No use denying it if you already know. It was my fault. I shouldn't have let slip what Tim had told me about this pub. As soon as I saw him, I told him to go home."

"Why was he here?" snapped Sutton.

"I don't know. He was crazy drunk, not making any sense."

"Have you got proof he went home?"

"No, but where else would he go?"

"We believe he followed Constable Trent home and left something upon her doorstep."

Mike's gaze swivelled to Mia. "You mean something dead?"

Silently she shook her head. Tim gripped her hand. "I'll protect you, Mia."

"I'm being looked after." She pulled her hand away.

"Why did you think it would be something dead, Mr

170

Plummer?" Sutton's voice was like ice.

"I thought it might be Dennis' idea of a joke. What did he leave?"

"Where's Dennis now?" Sutton didn't say he was the one asking the questions but it was implicit in his manner.

"I don't know where he is. I haven't seen him since yesterday morning. Work's pretty slack since you closed us down."

"And he's angry with Mike about him going to University," put in Tim.

"You can't expect him to like it. We've been working together since he got out the army."

"For all his big talk he knows he'll go under without you. He's more or less illiterate."

"He would have managed," said Mike. "He's a lot brighter than he lets on."

"Why the past tense?" asked Luke.

Mia thought that Mike hesitated but, if so, it was only for a moment before he replied, "I thought he might end up in prison because of what he did the other day."

"Do you remember where Dennis was on the evenings when three young women were abducted? Was he with you?" Sutton reeled off the days and dates and Mia was surprised he'd show his hand so openly.

"Sorry, I don't know where he was. But you can't think Dennis had anything to do with that?" Mia was unconvinced by Mike's display of shock.

"We're trying to cover as many bases as we can. You're certain you weren't with Dennis on any of those dates?"

"They're my evening class days, so I wouldn't be with Denn. I remember the first date you mentioned was when I was taking tests."

"Do you remember when Dennis had concussion, he had a run-in with a nurse in A&E?"

"Yeah, Scottish girl. You mean it was her who got killed?"

"What about the other people Dennis had trouble with?

171

The shop assistant he was abusive to? And the daughter of that Brown Owl?"

"Denn might have had a grudge against that Brown Owl woman but he liked the shop assistant. He was upset when she got killed. He said how he'd given her a…"

"Given her what?" demanded Sutton.

Mike hesitated, then muttered sullenly, "He'd given her a lift home a few times."

"How about the day before she was abducted?"

"I don't remember." His stubborn expression told them he didn't plan to conquer this amnesia.

"Yes he did!" said Tim. "You must remember? You said he…"

"I don't remember!" For once Mike's voice was loud.

"Said what, Tim?" asked Sutton.

"Nothing."

There was a brittle silence until Mike spoke, "You're wrong about Dennis."

"Then why's he done a runner?" said Luke.

"I don't know. I'm worried about him, but that doesn't mean I think he's killed anyone."

"His ex-wife told us he's probably off looking for his daughter," suggested Sutton.

"Maybe she's right." Mike didn't sound convinced. "We'll leave you to get on with your business." He stood up and walked away. Tim followed like a well-trained pup.

"But you don't think he's looking for Ellie?" Sutton's voice cut across the distance between them.

Mike turned back to look at him. "I don't reckon he needs to look. If anyone knows where Ellie is it'll be Denn. The truth is, he was obsessed with her."

"So what do you reckon?" asked Sutton, as they ate lunch.

Luke shrugged. "We've got grounds for search warrants for Dennis' flat and their builders' yard."

"I've already applied for the warrants. They'll be waiting for us at the station. Are you okay, Mia? You're very quiet."

"I'm thinking."

He grinned at her. "You're a woman, you can multi-task, that means thinking and talking at the same time."

"Actually, I was enjoying listening to two experts at work."

"Thank you kindly, ma'am." Still seated, Luke bowed to her. "What do you reckon, Oliver? Is Dennis our man?"

"There's plenty of evidence pointing that way. He had dealings with all three women and aggro with all of them, even if he did make it up with Deirdre."

Luke nodded. "There's no saying Deirdre didn't wind him up again."

"Yeah. Angie was a tough, independent woman, used to travelling the world alone. There was no reason she wouldn't open her door. But Deirdre was timid and there'd already been one murder in the town. If her caller was Dennis, we've got a reason why she'd let him in."

"Yeah, she wouldn't be wary of someone she knew who gave her lifts," agreed Luke.

"But what about Julie?" protested Mia. "By that time the whole town was paranoid. And she wasn't on friendly terms with Dennis Plummer."

"Unless he'd made an appointment with her," said Luke. "She was a Special Needs teacher. Perhaps he said he wanted her to give Zoe some out of school lessons. Cash-in-hand comes in useful to a single-parent, but if she didn't want her Benefits cut she'd keep quiet. Her mother's the sort that'd turn anybody in, even her own daughter. The thing I find hard to swallow is the coincidence of you encountering him on your last case."

"Yeah," agreed Sutton. "Coincidences do happen but I don't like it when they get as big as that. What worries me more is the profiler's report. It emphasised this is an organised, controlled killer with forensic knowledge. Dennis

Plummer doesn't fit that profile."

"Profilers don't always get it right but they're not usually that far wrong," agreed Luke. "But Mike did say Dennis was a lot brighter than he seemed."

"Yeah, he made rather a point of it, didn't he?"

"It's odd he didn't mention he was with Dennis when he had the run-in at Brownies," said Mia. "Do you think he suspects Dennis and wants to steer us towards him without actually putting himself on the line?"

"Or Cousin Mike's not squeaky clean himself. It wouldn't do any harm to check out his alibis for the evenings of the abductions," suggested Luke.

"Could we check out Tim Lewis' too?" That thought came to Mia without any reason she could pin down.

Sutton nodded and phoned through to the Incident Room to order a check on both Mike Plummer's and Tim Lewis' whereabouts at the relevant times.

"So what do we do now?" asked Luke when he keyed off.

Sutton stood up. "We go with the evidence and search Dennis Plummer's flat."

"The DI said to give them a minute to make sure the coast's clear." Luke's hand on Mia's arm prevented her from following Sutton and the two uniformed officers into the flat.

"Okay." She shifted uncomfortably, the weight and bulk of the stab jacket dragging her down. She knew Sutton was cross with her. He'd wanted her to stay safely at the Station but she'd argued that her forensic skills would be invaluable, and eventually he'd agreed.

Luke Warden glanced down and grinned at her. "Don't look so miserable. He's not really mad at you, just stressed about keeping you safe, and about not mucking up. They're all the same, the ambitious, driven ones, Superintendent at forty or heart-attack at thirty-nine."

"Don't!"

"You really rate him, don't you?"

She glared at him defiantly. "Yes. He's a good cop and a really decent guy." The best form of defence is attack and she demanded, "How come you're not the ambitious sort?"

"I've only got three years 'til I'm thirty-nine. I'm not going to make it to Superintendent so I might as well steer clear of the heart attack."

"All clear!" Sutton's shout came from the flat.

"Coming." Warden ushered Mia inside. He looked around and gave a low whistle. "The biggest danger here's from Bubonic Plague. This guy takes the word slob and gives it a whole new meaning."

Mia stared at the squalor and sighed. This was going to be hard work to process. She raised her camera and started recording before they shifted anything.

"Tell me when you're ready and they'll bag the videos and DVDs," said Sutton.

"I'll record everything individually if that's okay with you." So far all the labelled DVDs were top shelf porn, distasteful but not illegal, and the magazines were in the same league. However there were a few home-recorded videos that could prove more interesting.

Sutton nodded. "Treat it as if a defence lawyer's sitting on your shoulder." He hesitated. "Now I think about it, with your connection to Dennis, you probably shouldn't be here working at all."

"Now if only you'd thought of that earlier you'd have been able to sideline me," said Mia. "Trev's sending a SOCO to process this lot as soon as possible. They can take over as CSM."

"Fair enough. By the way there's evidence he got takeaways from your pizza place."

"I'd be more suspicious if there wasn't. It looks like he got stuff from every fast food joint in town." Mia surveyed the debris of empty boxes, half-eaten, mouldy food and stickily festering beer cans.

As they went through the flat they discovered no evidence that Dennis Plummer was a killer but plenty about the squalor of his life.

"What are you thinking?" asked Sutton, catching her unawares.

"How hard it is to be unprejudiced sometimes."

He smiled. "You have to try to separate off what you want to find and put it in a box to one side. It must be similar when you're doing archaeological work. You might be longing to prove some site holds a fantastic Roman villa but a good scientist doesn't twist the evidence."

"True, but the archaeological evidence isn't tied to a guy who's threatening me."

"The personal factor does make a difference," he agreed. His voice was solemn but there was mischief below the surface.

She was glad he'd forgiven her for being so stubborn. "I'm sorry if I added to your problems by insisting on coming here."

"That's okay. But I don't understand why you were determined to come when you're scared."

"It's because I am scared. There's one thing I'm more afraid of than some lunatic targeting me, and that's being too afraid to do my job."

"Yeah, I can relate to that."

"It was only when I was standing outside the flat I realised I'd fallen into another trap. I was afraid I'd compromise your safety because you were preoccupied with worrying about me."

"In that case would you bite my head off if I suggested you went back to the Station rather than accompany us to the builders' yard?"

"No. I'll go back if you want."

"Could I suggest you both go back to the Station and leave the search to me?" Luke chimed in.

"Sir!" an uniformed officer broke into the conversation. He sounded excited.

"Yeah?" Sutton was beside him in the kitchen in two strides.

176

"These sir, stuffed down behind a drawer." He held out a wad of photographs.

Sutton looked through them. Mia came to join him. They were of the first three victims, obviously caught unawares, most of them entering or exiting their homes. Apart from the last photo. That was of Mia, at night, outside her front door.

Chapter 18

DCI Aron was a thin, anxious man in his mid-forties, with sparse fair hair that was fading into grey. The Incident Room was crammed and as Aron led the briefing, Mia could tell he was pleased they'd identified a prime suspect, although peevish that they hadn't caught him. However, he congratulated DI Sutton for providing the breakthrough in this case.

"Thank you, sir," said Sutton, "But we can't be certain Dennis Plummer is our man."

Sitting beside him, still quaking from the shock of seeing her photograph in Dennis Plummer's collection, Mia was impressed at Sutton's integrity and courage in speaking out.

"Certain?" repeated Aron. "What more do you want?"

"He doesn't fit the psychological profile, sir."

Aron glanced at a quiet woman sitting in the back corner of the room. "With all due respect to our distinguished consultant, I must point out, Inspector, that when you've been working Serious Crimes as long as I have, you'll realise theorists rarely get things a hundred-per-cent right. There's no doubt Plummer is our man. Apart from those photographs we have other evidence."

He nodded to a detective constable on his team, who said, "I sent Dennis Plummer's description round the whole of the district. Ten weeks ago, a few miles outside of town, a schoolgirl, walking home one evening, was grabbed by a man wearing a balaclava. He tried to drag her into the bushes but she fought him off and ran. She described him as tall and strong, with a tattoo on his arm with the name 'Helen' in it."

"I've been checking on Plummer's lifestyle," said another officer. "He goes with pros several times a week."

"Any violence?" asked Sutton swiftly.

"Bit lairy when he's drunk, but nothing much."

"DI Sutton told me to check out the alibi of Dennis Plummer's cousin, Michael Plummer," weighed in another constable. "What he said was true. He was in college every time a woman was abducted. The class times don't quite cover the last two abductions but when Angie Masters was taken he was doing exams all evening."

"Well done for ordering that, Inspector," approved Aron. "It's wise to tie up loose ends."

"Yes sir," said Sutton, wooden faced. "I'm still worried about the psychological aspects…"

"Well don't be. Evidence is what we're concerned with and we've got plenty of that."

"What now, sir?" asked DCI Craig, who'd been sitting silently at the edge of the room.

"Now I talk to the wife. If I can convince her that Dennis was responsible for the disappearance of their daughter I'm sure I'll get her co-operation." He turned back to the team. "You know what you've got to do. I want this man caught as soon as possible and I want the case against him watertight."

Most of the officers dispersed. DCI Aron beckoned to Mia. "I understand from DI Sutton that you're anxious about your family. I sent two officers to the theme park to meet them and escort them home and I'm pleased to inform you they are safe."

"Thank you, sir." Mia felt tears of relief prickling her eyes.

Aron turned back to Sutton, "I want you to accompany me to interview Mrs Plummer."

"Yes sir." Sutton spoke softly to Mia, "Go down to SOCO and stick with your inspector and Adam. Let me know all your movements. I'll phone as soon as I can."

"Yes sir." Mia saluted cheekily.

"Don't play the fool, Mia. I'm scared for you."

"Me too. That's why I'm playing the fool. I promise I'll stay safe. You be careful too."

As soon as she left the Incident Room she phoned

179

through to her mother. She believed DCI Aron's assurances but she wanted to hear Mum's voice.

"I'm fine, sweetheart. We all are. Are you okay?" The anxiety in her mother's voice twisted at Mia's heart.

"Yes. Everyone's taking good care of me. I'm sorry to have let you in for this."

"It's not your fault. Don't worry about it, love."

"This must be upsetting you horribly."

"I admit there was one heart-stopping moment in Paultons when I saw the policemen coming towards us and I was terrified something had happened to you. But the moment passed and you're all right, so it's fine." She continued in a determinedly light tone, "We've got a policeman in the hall and Dani thinks he's lovely. Both she and Rina are sitting on the stairs with him and he's reading Dani a Little Red Train story."

"Shouldn't he be on surveillance outside?"

"Poor boy, it's so cold and miserable in the car. Anyway, what better observation place could there be than sitting in the hall? That way he can make sure we're all completely safe."

"Well don't offer him alcohol when you give him dinner." She knew the constable would be well fed.

"Of course not. Are you coming back here tonight?"

"Thanks Mum, but Adam's still looking after me. We're probably going to dinner with Chantelle." She'd been walking through the corridors as she talked and had reached the SOCO offices. "I ought to go. Bye. Love you."

Adam, Trevor and Chantelle were all in the office. "Everyone okay?" she asked.

"I'm having a wonderful time," said Adam sarcastically. "Oliver Sutton threatened my uniformed escort so well they followed me closer than a strip of sealing tape. They were so on my heels I could hardly gather evidence before they stood on it."

"Is it true Dennis Plummer's the killer?" said Chantelle.

"There's a lot of evidence pointing that way."

"That's so scary!"

Chantelle's desk phone rang and Trevor, who was nearest, reached across to answer it. "Hello?… Yeah, she's here." A scowl appeared. "It's that Human Resources woman for you."

As Chantelle listened to her caller her pretty face grew stubborn. "I've told you already I've got no complaints. There's no reason for you to ring me. I was being stupid before, taking offence where none was intended… No, my office manager's totally supportive. You don't need to phone again. If I've any problems I'll contact you."

She slammed the phone down and smiled when they gave her a round of applause.

"Are we still on for dinner?" enquired Mia.

"Of course."

"We'll have to stay on call," said Trevor. "But we shouldn't complain. Liz Murphy's crowd are whinging they've got to work rather than go clubbing in Brighton."

"I'd forgotten about that hen night." Mia felt sorry for the bride-to-be.

"If you think you're missing out we could dress Trev in pink tassels and get him to give you a lap dance," suggested Adam.

"Do you have to!" said Mia. "No offence, Trev, but that's an image I could have lived without."

"Me too," agreed Trevor. "It'd be like something out of that Disney movie, the one where those hippos are dressed up as ballet dancers."

"Fantasia. Cheers Trev, you've just corrupted one of my favourite cartoon films."

Trevor gave his deep chuckle and suddenly the tension broke and they all started laughing.

At last, Trevor said, "Now settle down you lot. I don't know what this place is coming to."

Mia nodded, grateful for the strong voice that had hauled

her back from the edge of hysteria. She moved clumsily to her desk and sat down, aware how fragile her self-control was. She listened to Trevor handing over to Steve, the evening supervisor, and thought that Trev might be physically flabby but mentally and emotionally he was strong.

Trevor stood up. "Everybody fit?"

"Yes, said Chantelle. "But I've got to stop off and buy some ice cream." She captured Pixie who'd been curled up asleep in Trevor's correspondence tray.

"Ice cream? I didn't think you'd approve of that," teased Adam.

"It's organic," explained Chantelle and looked surprised when everybody laughed.

"I promised DI Sutton I'd stay here until he phoned," said Mia.

"No problem," said Adam. "Trev, you and Chantelle go and get dinner sorted. I'll wait with Mia. It's quite handy, I've got some stuff to finish."

"If DI Sutton would like to come to dinner he's more than welcome," said Chantelle.

"Okay, thanks." There was no real reason she couldn't leave a message for Oliver but she wanted to make sure he was okay. She knew her fear for him was illogical but it felt very real.

Sutton arrived fifteen minutes after Trevor and Chantelle had left. "Sorry I didn't phone. I got caught up and it seemed easier to come straight back."

"No problem. Are you finished for tonight?"

"Yeah. DCI Craig told me to take you home and keep an eye on you. Are you ready?"

"Five minutes," said Adam.

"We'll wait for you in my office," said Sutton. "I want to brief Mia about that last interview."

Mia knew he wouldn't discuss the case in the corridor, which gave her a brief window to sort out their eating arrangements. "Chantelle has invited us all back to her place for dinner, but say if you'd rather not."

"You're going?"

"I ought to. It matters to Chantelle and she's making a lot of effort to fit in."

"In that case I'll come with you. I hope Chantelle's cooking isn't too repulsively wholegrain."

"At least there's going to be ice cream, although I admit it's organic." They entered his office and she switched to business. "How was the interview with Helen Plummer?"

"Hellish. How do you tell a woman you think her ex is a monster who's killed three women and probably murdered their daughter as well?"

"How did she take it?"

"Half didn't believe it, half totally terrified. Then, to make matters worse, Dennis' mum turned up, escorted by the ever-present Cousin Mike. Of course he had to add to the fun by winding the old girl up until she got breathless and blue round the lips and we had to phone for an ambulance."

"Poor woman. And poor Helen. I can't imagine what she's feeling."

"I think she's beyond feeling. She looked numb. Cousin Mike offered to stay with Zoe, so Helen could go to the hospital with old Mrs Plummer." He hesitated. "Mia, this is totally confidential, but Aron needs a new DI and he's suggested I apply."

"That's good isn't it?" She wondered why he sounded so subdued. DI on a Serious Crimes Team must be a high-flyer's dream.

"So you think I should go for it?"

"Why not?" She blanked out the thought of how much she'd miss him and whether he'd want to keep in touch.

"Aron and I don't approach things in the same way, but then neither does Craig."

"A lot of older cops aren't comfortable with things like psychological profiling."

"Oh Aron has his psychological moments, when it suits him."

"How do you mean?"

"He's insisting Dennis Plummer has a fixation about women in uniform. You know, nurse, shop assistant, guider. It's a sort of pick-and-mix psychological approach. The profiler wasn't thrilled with it."

"How did DCI Aron find out that Dennis liked women in uniform?"

"Cousin Mike told him, but not until Dennis' mum and Helen had gone off to hospital."

"Mike doesn't seem that loyal to Dennis, or grateful to Dennis' mum."

"Not by the way he spoke to her this evening. A regular rant about how Dennis had brought it all on himself. He raked up just about every stupid thing Dennis had ever done, going right back to primary school, and finished by saying how he'd shamed them all."

"How did old Mrs Plummer take it?"

"She was furious and so was Helen. Mike was moaning they'd all have to change their names and move away and Mrs Plummer ripped back at him about how he had no right to the name Plummer anyway."

"I suppose he took his aunt's name when his mum died," said Mia.

"I guess so. Then she really lost her temper and slapped him round the face. With those rings she wears she actually drew blood. God knows what he'd have done after that but the old lady's heart started playing up and he went back to being the dutiful nephew."

He picked up a report from his desk and skimmed its contents. "This is the preliminary report on the DVDs. Just run of the mill porn, nothing sinister."

"What about the home videos?"

"They seem to be the most innocent things of all. They're home movies of his daughters. The only nude shot

184

is the younger one, aged about two, in her paddling pool. Three of the videos are of his eldest daughter when she was little, dancing in various shows. They're the sort of videos any family man might have." He stared out into the dark, dismal evening. "Where the hell is he hiding?"

"You're sure he's not in Helen's house?"

"We checked. She gave permission and so did the old girl to search her place, then Mike Plummer got in on the act and insisted on handing over his keys."

"Without being asked?"

"Yeah, he was playing the good citizen for all it's worth." He shrugged. "Aron seemed impressed." There was a tap on the door and he yelled, "Come in."

Adam entered. "Ready when you are."

They trooped down to the car park. "I'll drive," said Sutton.

Mia thought of saying he should rest his arm but she realised he was so wired up he needed to be active or he might explode.

As they approached Chantelle's block of flats Mia got out her phone. "I'll ring through and tell Chantelle we're on our way."

As soon as Chantelle answered she knew by her voice that something was wrong. "Chantelle, what's the matter?"

"It's Pixie. He's lost."

"Lost? How?" Chantelle rarely let him out of her sight.

"I don't know. I can't have fastened his basket properly. He was very quiet when we were driving home but I thought he was sulking because we stopped at the shops."

"But didn't you notice the difference in weight when you were carrying the basket?"

"No. We were carrying a lot of shopping and the lift wasn't working."

"Where's Trev now?"

"He's gone to look for him. He wouldn't let me, although I wanted to. I'm certain Pixie was in the basket when we left

185

the office but I phoned through to Steve, just in case. He hunted round and said he wasn't there. He must have got out while we were in the shops."

"In that case he's probably in the car and Trev will find him."

"That's what Trevor says. He'll call me as soon as he's got him. He said it will take him a while to walk upstairs again."

"Would you rather we didn't come round tonight?" Mia was ashamed of her desire to avoid the cat hunt and Chantelle's lamentations.

"Oh no, please come. Hold on! I can hear something outside my door."

"Is it Trevor?"

"It's Pixie! I can hear him meowing. He must have found his way home."

"No, Chantelle!" Mia had no idea where the fear came from but it was there, fierce and consuming. "Don't open the door!"

"I must. But it's okay, I've got the chain on."

"No wait!"

Mia heard the click of the door catch and Chantelle's cooing voice, "Pixie, where are you?..." There was a crash. Then a terrified scream echoed down the phone.

Chapter 19

"Chantelle?" Mia heard another more muffled scream followed by a scuffling sound.

"Oliver, he's got her! It's Chantelle he's after! She opened the door and he's got her." Fear made her almost incoherent.

"Stay on your mobile, Mia." Sutton hurled the car along the crowded streets, calling emergency services from his phone as he went. "Where's Trevor?"

"Out looking for her cat."

"Phone him, Adam. Mia, you keep monitoring what's going on."

Mia went into another dimension, somewhere strange, remote and terrible, where she was a powerless listener: she heard the muffled sounds on her phone; Adam shouting his warning to Trevor; Sutton yelling details to the control room. She tried to monitor out the last two and concentrate on the terrifying action that was coming down her phone. She heard, "Struggle and I'll kill you." It was a crackling, sexless, whisper.

More bumps and rustles. A voice shouting. Then a scream and thump and groan, all the sounds of nightmare intermingled. When the phone clicked back to its dialling tone she hardly registered it.

The car lurched to a halt. As Sutton leapt out he grabbed a folding baton from the side pocket and cracked it to full length. "Come on, Mia. I'm not letting you out my sight."

That feeling was entirely mutual. And she wouldn't slow him down. The front doors of the building were open. She matched him, step for step, through the lobby and up the stairs. Up and up, heart pounding fit to burst. Sutton in front of her, Adam on her heels.

"Sixth floor." She barely had breath to gasp the words.

Sutton gave no sign he'd heard but, at the next landing,

he diverged to the left and along a corridor.

"Oh God!" One swift glance round to check the coast was clear and he'd skidded to his knees beside Chantelle. She was crouching next to Trevor, who was lying, eyes closed, face deathly white. Her hands were pressed to his stomach. Blood was welling through her fingers. The stain on his white shirt was growing larger all the time.

"Which way did he go?" snapped Sutton.

"Out there." Chantelle's voice sounded small and distant. She nodded to a fire exit at the end of the corridor.

"Have you dialled triple nine?"

"Yes, they're on their way."

"Good girl. Adam, grab this and take a swing at anyone you don't like the look of." Sutton tossed Adam his baton "Mia, take over here."

"Ollie, be careful!" The words were wrenched from her.

He sprinted away. Mia tore off her jacket and cotton tee-shirt and wadded the latter into a firm pad. "Chantelle, let me do that. You talk to him. He may be able to hear you. Tell him you're okay and he's going to be fine."

Chantelle moved sideways and allowed Mia to take her place. Pressing onto the wound was like pushing into a sodden sponge. She could hear the urgent reassurance of Chantelle's voice. All the time she kept on pressing and all the time the blood kept seeping through.

There was a swirl of activity: cops and paramedics. "Okay, love, let us get there." She shuffled to one side and, with the end of responsibility, came a feeling of dizziness and a trembling that ran through all her limbs. Then Oliver was beside her, helping her to her feet, and she felt a rush of relief he'd not been hurt.

"No sign of the bastard. He had his escape route planned." The breathless voice rustled in her ear.

She became aware of Chantelle, sobbing in Adam's arms. She gave Oliver a wavering smile and released herself from his grip. She stumbled towards Chantelle and Adam and put her arms around them, but all the time her eyes were fixed on the paramedics who were working on Trev.

"Chantelle." Oliver's voice was low-pitched but compelling. "I know you'll want to go in the ambulance with Trevor but I need to know what happened here. I'm going to catch this bastard but I need your help. Can you answer some questions?"

"Yes." She spoke in a shuddering whisper.

"What happened when you opened the door?"

"There was a man out there. He cut the door-chain. It only took one cut."

"Did you see his face?"

"No he was wearing a balaclava. But I saw his arm, he had a tattoo... I recognised it... it was Dennis Plummer."

"Then what happened?"

"He grabbed me and said if I struggled he'd kill me. He said he'd break my neck."

Her eyes were on Trevor, who was being lifted onto a stretcher. Sutton gripped her forearm. "Concentrate, Chantelle. Just for a minute, love. You say you were being held close to him. What did he smell of?"

She paused. "Cigarettes and alcohol and deodorant, but it was all sort of stale."

"How tall was he?"

"Tall... taller than you... and strong."

"You're doing great. What happened then?"

"I didn't know whether to struggle. I knew he'd probably kill me anyway. Then Trevor came pounding up and I tried to scream to warn him but the man had his arm against my throat and I clawed at it, trying to get free but I couldn't. He swore at me."

"What was his voice like?"

"Just a whisper. Then Trevor grabbed his arm and forced it away from me and I fell down. I didn't really see what happened next but I think Trevor hit him and then he stabbed Trevor. I didn't even know he'd got a knife."

189

"Chantelle, I know this is hard, but I need you to tell me what happened then."

"Trevor looked so surprised. When he pulled the knife out he gave a sort of groan, but he was still holding onto him. Then he pushed free and Trevor fell. I couldn't even reach him to break his fall." She gave a retching sob. "It's all my fault."

"It's not your fault. Could I just clarify something? It was the man who attacked you who pulled the knife out of Trevor?"

She looked at him blankly. "Yes."

"And Trevor was holding onto the man until the man broke free?"

"Yes."

"What happened after that?"

"He grabbed my arm, like he was going to drag me away, but I went for him. I was screaming and scratching and kicking. Trevor was groaning, trying to get up and help me. That monster shoved me away and ran."

"Good girl. You probably saved your own and Trevor's lives. Now there's one more thing I need you to do. As soon as you get to the hospital with Trevor, I want you to strip off those clothes and put them in sealed evidence bags. And I want a swab of your nails. If you scratched the bastard there may be trace evidence."

She stared down at her shaking hands. "They're covered with blood."

"I know, but the forensics could still make the difference between catching this guy or not."

"I'll come with you," offered Adam. "I'll see to it."

With part of her mind Mia wanted to go with them. That way she could wait by Trevor's bedside, but another angrier part wanted to be out there, tracking down this animal.

The paramedics moved off, Chantelle and Adam with them. When they were out of sight Mia pulled on her jacket and buttoned it. Then she sent one of the constables down to the car to fetch her camera and set to work, methodically recording the scene. She forced her brain past the fact that this was Trevor's blood, and photographed a partial shoeprint.

Around her there was the routine of police procedure: the questioning of neighbours, although those living closest to Chantelle's flat were out. She directed the cops in a cautious hunt for material clues, making sure no-one's size elevens destroyed any vital traces. The official SOCO team arrived. She handed over to the Crime Scene Manager and saw how shaken everybody was when they realised the identity of the victim.

When the new team was in place, Mia stood out of the way, watching Sutton direct operations. Within her jacket pocket, her hand caressed the surface of her phone; Adam had promised to contact as soon as he had news of Trevor.

Between giving orders Sutton gravitated back to her, anxious and watchful, and she forced herself to smile at him. A false smile, pretending she was okay. He was standing with her when a constable approached. "Sir, SOCO found these in the side road, beside the fire exit."

He held out two evidence bags, one contained a knife. Its blade was about four inches long but the end had broken off. It was coated up to its hilt in blood.

"Thank you." Sutton's face grew even grimmer. "Phone through to the hospital to warn them the tip may still be in Inspector Mayfield. What's that?" He pointed to the second evidence bag.

"This was near it, sir." The bag contained a heavy, old-fashioned key.

Mia stared at it. "Oliver, that looks like the conservatory key from 2, Bridge Road… William Davies' house."

Sutton frowned. "All the Plummers' development properties were checked earlier, but I guess it's worth another look." He turned back to the constable. "I want two patrol cars ready to accompany me to Bridge Road. That's four officers, all dressed in stab vests and armed with batons. And

191

I need another car to take DC Trent back to the Station."

"No," said Mia, "Please, I want to go with you."

He stared at her and, for a horrible moment, she thought he'd refuse. "Okay. But you stay with me all the time. You could still be this lunatic's target."

Within five minutes they were driving across town. Again Sutton had claimed the driver's seat, although from the jerkiness of his gear changes Mia suspected it was costing him. She breached the tense silence, "Oliver, I'm sorry to be a nuisance."

"You're not." Full marks for good manners, rather less for sincerity.

"I've been thinking about Chantelle and her cat."

"Mia, we've got more to worry about than the fate of a cat."

"I know. I didn't mean that. I was thinking that Chantelle was scared but she opened her door because she thought she heard her cat."

She didn't need to say more. "You mean anyone will open the door if something they care about is whimpering outside?"

"Or someone. Julie Townsend was worried about her kids. If she'd heard a child crying outside…"

"She'd open up. What about the others?"

"Deirdre had a cat. Her friend in the shop mentioned it. It's easy to get a recording of a cat meowing or a child crying, and when people are worried they don't stop to think." Mia remembered how she'd nearly opened her door when she thought Oliver had collapsed outside.

"The bastard's cheap, he can even repeat his effects… Here we are again." They screeched to a halt in a familiar road.

The world seemed quiet, cold and deserted. Not driving rain this time but a soaking drizzle. The cops moved quietly, keeping a tight formation, uncertain what they might find. The ground was rutted and slimy. Mia stumbled and was sustained by Oliver's firm grip.

There was a crackle and flare of flames. Sutton sprinted towards 2 Bridge Road and Mia followed him. Within the conservatory something was on fire.

Sutton flung open the door and Mia flinched at the brightness. The fumes of smoke and petrol tore at her throat. And something else, the stench of burning meat. A burning body.

Sutton dragged off his coat and she did likewise, but someone was there already, beating at the flames with his bare hands. A uniformed guy pulled the rescuer away. Sutton and Mia wrapped the burning figure in their coats. At the same time, Sutton yelled, "Cuff that bastard!"

The flames died away and Sutton shone his torchbeam onto the victim. Still swaddled in their coats, all that was visible of the inert figure was a smashed and charred face and a swathe of flaxen hair.

Sutton switched the light towards their captive. Dennis Plummer, arms secured behind him, was struggling to get loose. He had no coat and the front of his shirt was sodden with blood.

He wrenched free and flung himself on his knees beside the girl.

"Ellie!" His scream echoed through the darkness.

Chapter 20

"Six impossible things before breakfast," said Mia, as she watched the hard-pressed SOCOs move quietly around the garden processing yet another scene.

"Pardon?" said Sutton. He draped a coat around her shoulders. He must have scrounged it from a male uniformed officer, it was too big but she was grateful for its warmth.

"The White Queen. Through the Looking-Glass."

"I know, but this isn't the time to start throwing literary quotes."

"I'm not the White Queen and I can't believe impossible things. I don't believe Dennis Plummer killed his daughter." Dennis had been taken, under guard, to the hospital, for treatment on his burned hands.

"I know where you're coming from but, like DCI Aron said, there are plenty of killers who've been overwhelmed with remorse when it's too late. Especially when they're caught."

"I'm not convinced."

"Why not? He had the tip of that broken knife in his pocket and his clothes were covered in blood." She winced at the image his words conjured. "Sorry."

"No, you're right. Facts are facts. I want the bastard who stabbed Trev to burn in hell. But I want to be sure it's the right bastard. Dennis Plummer's a wreck, not capable of all that clever planning."

"Maybe killing his daughter sent him over the edge."

"I suppose." She didn't ask why, if he'd set fire to Ellie's body, Dennis had tried to beat out the flames. She could predict the answer, that Dennis had been overwhelmed with regret. Anyway, Sutton was turning away to greet DCI Aron.

Her phone rang. The display read: ADAM- MOBILE.

"How is he?" Dread was suffocating her.

"In surgery."

"Still?"

"It took a while to stabilise his condition before they could operate. Even though there's no knife tip in him the way we first thought, he's lost a lot of blood."

"They can put more blood in him. What the hell do we donate blood for?"

"They're doing that."

"I'm sorry. I feel so helpless."

"Tell me about it."

"Is Chantelle okay?"

"Bearing up. I've bagged her clothes and done the hand swabs and everything and I've got Trev's stuff bagged as well, although the chain of custody isn't as clear."

"I'll tell Oliver that's sorted."

"I'd better get back now."

"Of course. Thanks for phoning. Adam, please, keep me informed."

"I will. Take care of yourself, Mia."

The phone went dead and she was left, isolated amongst the torchlight and the darkness, between the busy, bustling people and the silence of the night. If she listened carefully she thought she could hear the shush of the sea, across the scrubland. It was as if she was alone in the world with her despair and overwhelming guilt. If on that first day in Bridge Road she hadn't called Dennis down, maybe he wouldn't have focused on her and Chantelle, and Trevor wouldn't be close to death.

"Detective Constable Trent are you all right?" DCI Aron was beside her.

"Yes thank you, sir." With an effort she hauled back.

"A dreadful evening, but we've got the fellow now."

She didn't deny it. Everyone kept saying so.

"DCI Craig will keep us informed about your inspector. He's gone straight to the hospital. As soon as he contacts me I'll let you know."

195

"I've just heard. Trevor's in surgery. He's pretty bad." She saw the SIO stiffen and realised she wasn't supposed to know more than him. She threw in a placatory, "Thank you, sir."

The ice thawed. "It's been a difficult day for you." He glanced at his watch. "DI Sutton and I are about to attend the post-mortem examination of the latest victim."

"The pathologist's doing it in the middle of the night, sir?" Because of the nature of they crime they would need a Home Office pathologist.

"In the extraordinary circumstances of this case that seemed necessary. Of course DI Sutton exceeded his brief, allowing the pathologist to move the body before I'd attended, but I can understand his eagerness to get things underway. He suggested your input might prove useful, but if you don't feel up to it I'll understand."

"I'm fine, sir. I'll come."

"Selling tickets?" The pathologist glared as Sutton and Mia followed Aron into her office.

DCI Aron cleared his throat. "This is a complex and serious case and Detective Constable Trent has excellent forensic knowledge."

"We have a bit of forensic knowledge here as well."

Wonderful! Mia felt sure the post-mortem would be punctuated by Dr Danvers' sharp questions, designed to display Mia's lack of expertise. Her phone rang.

"Excuse me." She fled from the room, fumbling under the protective clothes to get it out.

"Mia? It's Adam."

"How is he?"

"Out of surgery and hanging on."

"That's good, isn't it?" She wondered why he sounded so subdued.

"Yeah, but he's not out the woods yet. The next few hours are critical. I guess I'm scared to be too hopeful."

196

"I know what you mean. How's Chantelle?"

"Incredible. She won't allow any thoughts that Trevor won't make it, something to do with not admitting negative energy. She's like a different person to the pain who used to drive us crazy. She hasn't even whinged about her cat."

"Yes, I guess poor old Pixie's gone for good. I'd better go back in. The pathologist's not too keen on me as it is." She was aware of a dragging reluctance to go back into that room.

"I heard there'd been another death. And Dennis Plummer's here in A&E. Mind you there's plenty of cops who'd like to help him have a nasty accident."

"They'd better not. He's got too many questions to answer."

"Who's the dead girl? Word is it's Plummer's daughter."

"There's no identification yet because the body's been badly burned but he was yelling 'Ellie' when we dragged him away from her."

"How could anyone do that to any kid, much less their own?"

"I don't know. I must go. Let me know as soon as there's any news."

In the pathologist's office, Aron and Sutton were standing, waiting, like two naughty boys in front of the headmistress' desk. It seemed Dr Danvers had gained the upper hand and, as it was due to Mia's phone call, she knew Aron would make her pay.

"If you've finished arranging your social life, Constable, perhaps we could proceed?" snapped Dr Danvers.

"I'm sorry. I didn't intend you to wait for me. One of my colleagues has been seriously injured." Mia felt angry at the pathologist's insensitivity. She saw Oliver's anxious face and, turning to him and Aron, gave them the update on Trevor's condition.

Dr Danvers said, "I'm sorry I was sharp with you. I'd heard an officer had been hurt but I didn't realise how badly.

Is he a friend of yours?"

"My boss, Inspector Mayfield."

"Trevor Mayfield! I'm sorry to hear that. I know him well. He's a fine man."

Mia nodded, too choked up to speak.

"Please keep me informed how he's going on." She surveyed the two men standing rigidly at the other side of the table and smiled, a mischievous grin that deepened the wrinkles around her mouth and eyes. "I know I'm a cantankerous old bat but there's no need to stand to attention."

She looked down at the notes in front of her. "A very nasty case. Identification will be difficult. Before the body was set on fire, she'd been submerged in bleach."

"Bleach? Not disinfectant like our other victims?" queried Sutton.

"Bleach," confirmed the pathologist. "And, unlike the previous victims, she was dressed and her face was smashed in after she died and her hands were badly burnt before the fire, probably on some sort of hot plate. With these deviations from the other cases it's hard to tell whether this is the work of the same man or a copy cat killer. Levidity indicates she was killed elsewhere. DNA will be the only way to make a foolproof identification, although some of her left hand fingertips may be in a condition to produce fingerprints."

"We have a probable ID," said Aron.

"Indeed?"

"It may be a sixteen year old girl called Ellie Plummer, who has been missing from home for three weeks."

The pathologist frowned. "I'd have thought she's younger than sixteen but that may be because she's malnourished. The older age would tie in with the fact she's been sexually active for some time."

"You're sure of that, Doctor?"

"Quite sure and she'd endured some very violent sex judging by the damage. I'll be able to tell you more when

I've taken a detailed look. We've bagged her clothing ready for forensic tests but this may help identification." She picked out an evidence bag containing a discoloured charm bracelet.

Sutton took it from her and held it under a light. "That confirms it. A silver charm bracelet was listed as one of the things Ellie Plummer had with her and I'm sure the little heart has Ellie engraved on it."

"I took X-rays, which I'd like to show you before we look at the body." Dr Danvers put the X-rays on screen for them to view. "As well as the sexual activity, she's been badly abused. Severe physical trauma over several years, resulting in many broken bones."

"That's crazy!" Sutton bit back the words. "I'm sorry, that wasn't what I expected."

"Indeed? And yet you have the father in custody?"

"Yes but the mother seems a caring sort of mum and there's no medical or social services records flagging up abuse."

"From the rough nature of the mends I'd guess she'd not been taken to the hospital. The injuries were left to heal themselves. There were three breaks in the right arm. In my judgement the first one occurred when she was very young, it has damaged the proper development of the bone. There's no way a mother, living in the same house, could have been unaware of this scale of injuries."

"I'll get straight on to Social Services," said Aron. "The younger girl must be removed immediately."

The door opened and Luke Warden entered, an apology on his lips. "I'm sorry to interrupt, doctor. I need a word with the DCI."

"More spectators! Just what I need. Well come in, don't stand there dithering." Dr Danvers' air of ferocious jollity dropped from her as she recognised the intruder. "You're off your usual patch aren't you, Sergeant? I thought you knew better than to interrupt me."

"Yes ma'am." Warden grinned at her, apparently

uncowed. "I'm sorry, this couldn't wait." He turned back to Aron, "We've brought Dennis Plummer back at the Station, sir. He discharged himself from hospital. He insists the only officers he'll talk to are DI Sutton and DC Trent. I know it's out of the question when he's been stalking DC Trent but it's up to you to veto it."

"I'm not sure." Aron looked thoughtful. "A confession would be the quickest way out of this. What sort of state's he in?"

"Crying and disorientated. It might be some clever trick but he looks wrecked."

"Inspector, I'd like you to conduct this interview."

"Of course, sir, but Mia mustn't be there. Letting him anywhere near her is a bad idea."

"I'll decide whether ideas are good or bad, thank you, Inspector. Constable Trent, do you feel unable to cope with this?"

"I'll manage, sir." She was wandering through a surreal nightmare.

"Before I left the hospital I went up to check on your boss and he's hanging on pretty well," said Luke.

"I know, but thanks for checking."

"You should go before the prisoner changes his mind," said Aron. "Sergeant, you'd better stay here and observe the post-mortem with me."

"If you'd asked, I'd have had revolving doors fitted," commented the pathologist acidly as Mia and Sutton left.

Slumped over the interview room table, Dennis Plummer seemed to have shrunk. His white face was the same colour as the dressings covering his burnt hands, but his eyes were red-rimmed and bloodshot with a maze of broken red veins marring the bilious yellow. Mia wondered if this disintegration was common in psychopaths when they'd been caught.

Sutton gave the information to the tape and said, "Mr Plummer, I know you've been informed of your rights but, before we begin, I have to remind you that you have the right to legal representation."

Dennis gave no sign of having heard. "My little girl, my Ellie, where have they taken her?"

"The pathologist is looking at her. How do you know it's Ellie? Her face was badly disfigured."

"I recognised her outfit… that skirt and top."

"Can you be sure they're hers?"

"I bought 'em for her. She likes the posh labels. She always talks me into payin' for 'em, even though her mum says I'm too soft." His face crumpled. "I'm never gonna see her again. She ain't ever gonna say 'Oh go on Daddy, please.'"

"What were you doing at 2 Bridge Road this evening?" said Sutton.

"I dunno."

"How did you get there?"

"I dunno." To Mia his confusion seemed genuine.

"Do you remember how your clothing became stained with blood?"

Plummer shook his head. He peered down at his ill-fitting, police-provided clothes as if uncertain how he'd acquired them.

"What about the tip of a knife that was found in your trousers' pocket?"

"What?… What knife?"

"What can you tell us about the attempted abduction of this woman and the stabbing of this police officer?" Sutton slid pictures of Chantelle and Trevor across the table.

"I dunno what you're talking about. What's this gotta do with my Ellie?" He focused on Mia. "For God's sake tell me what happened to my little girl?"

"That's what we're trying to work out, Dennis, but we need you to answer our questions." She found it no effort to speak moderately to him. The man was an animal and she used the same tone she'd adopt to calm a savage dog.

"Okay. But I don't know nothin' about stabbin'

201

anyone." He wiped his nose on his sleeve, leaving a slimy trail. Repulsed, Mia handed him a tissue. "Ta." He cleaned himself up, clumsy because of his heavily bandaged hands. "You accusin' me of knifin' this cop?"

"You're certainly in the frame," said Sutton.

"I been sick all day… had this bug. I bin throwin' up… totally out of it."

"What's the last thing you remember before this evening, Dennis?" said Mia.

He frowned with the effort to concentrate. "Outside that pub. Standin' in the car park in the rain."

"What were you doing there, Dennis?" Sutton took over the questioning, voice low and smooth, not breaking the flow.

"Waitin'."

"Who were you waiting for?"

"Ellie."

"Why did you think Ellie would be there?"

"She sent me this message… text message it was… said she was in trouble and asked me to come alone. I rang her number, rang and bloody rang, but she didn't answer. So I had to go to find out what was wrong. All I wanted was to get her home safely with her mum." He ended on a sob.

"And did Ellie turn up?" asked Sutton.

"No. I waited there for hours. I was soaked through and the cops kept givin' me funny looks, but there wasn't nothin' else I could do."

Sutton gestured towards Mia. "Did you see Constable Trent leave?"

"Yeah."

"Did you follow Constable Trent home?"

"No."

"Did you take photographs of her without her knowledge or consent?"

"No."

"Did you leave a pizza outside her door?"

This jolted him out of monosyllables. "Why the hell

should I do that?"

"You tell us, Dennis. Your fingerprints are all over the box. And, while you're at it, you can explain why it's also got the fingerprints on it of a woman who was murdered."

"That's crazy! You're settin' me up." He was sweating.

"Why were you loitering near Bridge Road on Thursday afternoon?"

Plummer hesitated. At last he said, "I'd lost somethin'."

"What?"

"Some pills. They must have fallen out me pocket." He nodded towards Mia. "When I saw she was there I didn't go over and look."

Sutton changed track. "What did you do when you'd finished standing in the pub car park?"

"Mike turned up and told me to clear off."

"Then where did you go?"

"Home o' course. Me flat."

"Dennis, where have you been for the last three days?" Sutton's tone was crisp.

"Three days? What you talkin' about? What day is it?"

"Saturday night."

"Saturday? Nah, that must be wrong. I can't have lost three days."

"Are you claiming you don't know where you've been?"

"I bin at my place. In me bedroom, 'cept when I was in the bathroom throwin' up."

"Dennis, we know you weren't at your flat today. We got a warrant and searched it. How about you tell us the truth?"

Plummer stared at him, or tried to, but his focusing kept veering off. "What you playin' at? You're tryin' to trick me. Of course I was in me flat."

"There are no tricks, Dennis, apart from the one you're trying to pull. You weren't in your flat this afternoon."

Plummer shook his head, slowly, jerkily, wincing at each move. Mia thought he looked scared but he also seemed bewildered.

"What do you claim to remember about the last three days?" Sutton's voice was sharp.

"I can't remember nothin' 'cept our Ellie's voice, but might be I dreamed that."

"What was Ellie saying?"

"'Dad wake up.' But it was like it was in the darkness, sort of danglin'."

"Then what?"

"Then I woke up and there was this bright light and this bloody awful smell…" He retched and pressed his wrist against his mouth.

"Dennis, Ellie's body shows evidence of long-term, physical abuse."

"What?"

"Evidence of a lot of broken bones."

"There can't be! She broke her arm last year, skatin', but that's the only time." Mia thought he was either the best actor in the world or his bewilderment was genuine.

"We're talking about long-term physical abuse since early childhood," said Sutton. "And she wasn't taken for medical treatment."

"Ellie's been hurt all through her childhood? You mean that bitch has had some bastard in beatin' up my girls? I'll bloody kill her!" He slammed to his feet and stood there swaying, his face grey-yellow, then he retched again and acid yellow bile dribbled down his front.

"Mr Plummer has been taken ill. I am suspending this interview and summoning medical aid." Sutton recorded the required information and switched off. "We'll get a doctor."

"I don't need no doctor. I told yer, I bin doin' this all weekend. You look in me en-suite and you'll see it's true. All I need's a shower. After bein' so sick it's a while since I've bin clean." He looked down distastefully. The clothes supplied by the police were on the skimpy side and his bile spattered beer gut protruded where the buttons had come adrift.

"Didn't you have a shower at the hospital?" asked Mia.

"No. I changed me clothes like they told me but I didn't get a chance to wash. I'd need someone to help me with me bloody hands like this."

'Bloody.' The word rang through Mia's brain. She said something she'd never envisaged asking Dennis Plummer, not in her darkest nightmares. "Mr Plummer, would you take your shirt off for me, please?"

Chapter 21

"So where does that get us?" said Sutton, half an hour later, as he slumped into his chair.

"You must admit it's weird," said Mia. She hovered in the doorway of his office, uncertain if he wished her to stay or go.

"Weird! It's totally crazy."

"What's weird and crazy?" Luke Warden's arrival behind her made her jump. He didn't wait for an answer, "If you mean the conduct of this case, I agree. But I'd advise you to keep your voice down, Oliver. DCI Aron's on the prowl."

"That doesn't seem to worry you," snapped Sutton.

Luke grinned. "It doesn't." He ushered Mia into the office and shut the door. "But I'm not the one in line for DI on Aron's team."

"How the…? Did DCI Aron tell you?" demanded Sutton.

"No. I heard it from that loud-mouthed DS. What's her name? Liz something or other."

"Oh great! If she's heard it'll be all over the station by now."

"You must know you can't keep secrets in a cop shop." Luke swung a chair from the edge of the room, placed it beside Mia's and sat down.

"I'd rather make my mind up before Liz Murphy spreads the word."

"So you haven't jumped at it? Good for you." Mia saw a quickening of interest as Luke looked at Oliver, then he yawned. "At least we've got the bastard."

"No we haven't!" Mia and Sutton spoke in unison.

Luke stared at them. "Why not?"

Sutton answered, beating Mia by a breath, "Because Dennis Plummer doesn't have any blood upon his chest."

"Is that supposed to mean something?" Mia couldn't

blame Luke for sounding annoyed.

"Dennis Plummer was wearing clothes stiff with dried blood but there was hardly a trace of it on his chest," she explained.

She saw Luke's irritation transform into understanding. "He didn't clean up at the hospital. He just changed his clothes into the stuff the SOCOs provided, and he was closely watched."

"I'd already checked that out," said Sutton.

"So I got them to examine his clothes." Mia continued the story. "His shirt's covered in blood. If he'd been wearing it to stab Trevor it would have soaked through to his chest, but he'd only got a few smears, like he'd put the shirt on when the blood was almost dry. And, even more significant, his trousers haven't got any bloodstains, except a faint smear in the pocket where they found the tip of the knife."

"Then Mia got them to examine his trainers and compare the tread with the half-print Trev's attacker made in his blood," said Sutton as she paused for dramatic effect.

"No blood on the tread and a different pattern." Mia wrested the narrative back. "Then the most significant thing of all hit me. The knife was dropped in the alley but the tip was in Dennis' pocket. So I got the SOCOs to check the area outside the flat. There are marks indicating someone broke the knife against the wall."

"So he was set up and didn't attack Inspector Mayfield," said Luke. "I should have noticed the inconsistencies with the blood when he was in A&E. But it doesn't prove he didn't kill his daughter and the other women."

"No," agreed Sutton. "But his lighter, with his fingerprints and only his fingerprints, and a petrol can, with his fingerprints and only his fingerprints, were found next to the body in Bridge Road. For an organised killer he's been ludicrously careless. If he's been set up for one crime, I'd like to be certain he hasn't been set up for everything before we wrap it up."

"No argument here, though Aron's liable to spontaneously combust. He's even more uptight than usual. He loathed the post-mortem on Ellie Plummer. He's got daughters himself."

"Are we sure it is Ellie Plummer?" asked Mia.

Warden groaned. "You're on a mission to complicate life for the SCT, aren't you?"

"Get used to it," said Sutton. "Thinking outside the box is her speciality. Although, in this case, I was also set to query an ID based solely on what the victim was wearing."

"There'll be other checks," said Luke defensively. "We have to start somewhere."

"I know. And, while we're following a false trail the killer gets an even bigger head start."

"Exactly," said Mia. "It's all circumstantial evidence. Like Dennis' clothes being covered in blood, and the knifepoint in his pocket, and that pizza box and lighter and petrol can all being covered with his fingerprints."

"Yeah," said Luke. "You're right."

"Yes," agreed Sutton. "But he's lying about one thing. He says he's been in his flat for the last few days and we know that's not true. Still I've asked the police doctor to do a full blood check on him. If he's innocent I want to know what he's been drugged with and if he's guilty I don't plan to give him any loopholes."

"But you both think he's innocent, don't you?" said Luke.

Sutton shrugged. "Maybe I'm soft, but that scream he gave when he saw the body seemed for real, and the injuries he sustained trying to put out the fire definitely are quite bad. And his grief and anger when I told him Ellie had been abused seemed totally genuine."

"I wondered about that," said Mia. "How come no-one noticed Ellie was being hurt? Her school attendance record seems okay, and there's the dancing, apparently she did a lot of that?"

"From what I saw on those videos she was pretty good," said Luke.

"Dance is a tough form of exercise, much harder than most sports. If she'd been injured that frequently she'd never have been able to dance."

Sutton nodded agreement. "My middle stepsister used to do ballet and she'd got incredible leg muscles. That girl could kick! Probably still can if I was thick enough to get in range."

"Do you know where Ellie learned dance?" asked Mia.

"The Audrey Something Dance School," said Luke.

"The Audrey Borrowdale School of Dance? Audrey would have noticed any unusual injuries. She's a friend of my mother and I had lessons there."

"You did?" Luke looked unflatteringly surprised.

"Why not?"

"No reason. Just didn't think it would be your thing."

Mia remembered Audrey's assessment of her talent as, 'a very dogged little dancer,' and decided not to blag it. "I gave up when I was twelve, most of us did who weren't that good. If Ellie stayed on she must have been pretty good or desperately keen, let's find out which."

She leaned over, grabbed the phone directory from Sutton's bookcase and leafed through. "Audrey works from her house, so the number's the same, day or night." She picked up the phone on Sutton's desk and switched to the speaker-phone.

"You can't phone her at midnight," protested Sutton.

"It's okay. Mum told me Audrey makes her overseas calls at night. She always said she prefers to sneak up on dawn from the rear." That sort of comment had made Audrey seem exotic to the middle-class little girls who'd flocked to her lessons.

Audrey answered on the third ring. "Hello?" The crisp voice sounded fully alert.

"Audrey, it's Mia Trent. Do you remember me?"

"Of course I do. Is something wrong?"

"Not exactly. You know I'm a police officer? I'm speaking

209

from work. We'd like to ask you for some information."

"Indeed? Who is the 'we' you're referring to?"

"Detective Inspector Sutton and Detective Sergeant Warden are with me. We're on the speaker phone." Mia felt uncomfortable. She hadn't seen Audrey for many years and the gap between inept pupil and acerbic teacher had never been adjusted.

"I must watch my words then. What do you wish to know?"

"We're concerned about a girl called Ellie Plummer. I understand she's a pupil of yours?"

"Yes, since she was a small child. Her mother told me she'd run away from home. Is there bad news?"

"We're not sure. You said Ellie's mother told you she'd run away?"

"Yes. She asked if Ellie had said anything to indicate where she'd gone. But a day or so later she telephoned to say she'd received a postcard from Ellie, posted in London. Mrs Plummer asked me to keep Ellie's place open for her and I agreed."

"Was her mother keen for her to dance?"

"Very keen when Ellie was little but she wasn't happy about her taking up dance as a career. She thinks it's a hard life and, of course, she's right. Anyway, Ellie didn't have the talent or the toughness to make a career in ballet."

"Did she diet a lot or show any signs of anorexia?" The pathologist had said the dead girl was malnourished.

"Certainly not. Her mother would never allow that, and I always keep an eye out for eating disorders. Now will you tell me why Ellie's dance ability is of interest to the police?"

"We're trying to get an over-all picture of the family. Did Ellie keep it up as a hobby?"

"Not exactly. I persuaded her to go for a more all-round performance career. She left school in July and went to Sixth Form College to study dance and music. What has…?"

"Did you see anything of her father?"

"Quite a bit. He no longer lives with his family but he has always been actively involved. He wanted Ellie to follow her dreams. He said most people don't get a chance to do that."

That sounded totally out of character for Dennis Plummer. Mia looked towards Sutton, who nodded and mouthed, 'Ask about their relationship.'

"Audrey, I know this is a delicate question, but did you ever notice anything untoward in the relationship between Ellie and her father?"

"No." She sounded startled. "I'm not naïve and I've seen many families where I thought that was a possibility, and one where I reported my concerns, but not with Ellie's family."

"What did you make of Dennis Plummer?"

"A rough, loudmouthed man, but devoted to his daughters."

Again Mia followed Sutton's mime. "Did he ever turn up drunk to collect Ellie?"

"Yes, several times in the last few years, but Ellie always dealt with it."

"How?"

"She'd take his car keys away and tell him they were walking or getting a taxi home. Quite often his brother would accompany him, and try to stop him offending the other parents."

"His brother? Do you mean his cousin, Mike Plummer?"

"Quite possibly. Ellie called him Uncle Mike. What has…?"

"Just one more question. Throughout the time you've known her, has Ellie had a lot of injuries or ill-health?"

"No, she's a very robust girl. Apart from that broken arm last year. I warned her professional performers shouldn't risk their safety by ice-skating. However, it healed quickly and no lasting harm was done. Now, will you please tell me about Ellie? Has something terrible happened to her? Are you saying her father has harmed her?"

Mia looked at Sutton, he smiled at her, half-rueful, half-relieved, then said, "Miss Borrowdale, it's DI Sutton. I'm grateful for your co-operation and I'm pleased to inform you that we are not aware of Ellie Plummer being harmed."

"I see," she said. "I gather that means harm has come to some other poor girl"

Sutton kept his voice carefully non-committal. "I'm afraid I can't answer that. I'd be grateful if you didn't mention this conversation."

"I'm not in the habit of gossiping."

"Thank you for your assistance. I apologise for disturbing you. Good night."

"So now what?" said Mia, as she put down the phone.

"We put the Plummers out of their misery," said Sutton.

"And we stop the DCI from setting Children's Services on them," said Luke. "The last thing we need is the fall out from Zoe being taken into Care. Apart from that, we move back to square one and begin again."

"We've moved on to a different game," said Sutton. "We have to work out who's in a position to set up Dennis Plummer and who wants to make him suffer."

"His cousin Mike," suggested Luke.

"Not unless we're separating what happened tonight from the other three murders. Mike Plummer's got an alibi for them. Come to think of it, this evening he was baby-sitting Zoe. I'll have someone check what time Helen got home and whether Cousin Mike was still there."

"That's easily done," said Luke. "Helen's downstairs, demanding to know what we're doing to her ex. No-one's told her about the girl's body but I guess she'll have picked up rumours."

"I'll go down and speak to her, but first I must bring DCI Aron up to speed," said Sutton.

"Want me to do it? He's not going to be happy."

Sutton's blue eyes were like ice. "Thanks, but I'll do my own dirty work."

He left. Luke grinned at Mia. "Good kid, isn't he?"

"Luke, he's so not a kid," said Mia, then wondered if he'd take her words out of context, she hadn't been talking about Sutton's undeniable sexiness.

"No, he's a good cop. He could go a long way, assuming he doesn't make too many bad career choices."

"Like becoming DCI Aron's DI? Or not going for it?"

Luke's grin widened. "You're a smart girl, you work it out."

When Sutton rejoined them, he looked tired but not as strained as when he was entering the lion's den.

"How did Aron take it?" asked Luke.

"Not happy but reasonably resigned. DCI Craig helped. He pointed out how bad it would have been if we'd IDed the victim as Ellie and charged her dad with murder and then been proved wrong. Especially when the real killer's still out there." He flexed his shoulders, trying to ease stiff muscles. "The SIO's going to speak to Helen Plummer and I asked him to check on Mike Plummer's whereabouts this evening. I'm sure Helen will have phoned home."

"What's happening about IDing the dead girl?" said Luke.

"They're still working on getting a useable fingerprint. Now they're saying this is a smaller built girl than Ellie and the eye colour is wrong. Amazing they didn't spot that before."

Mia thought that was what happened when you ran ahead of the evidence but she stayed silent. She was pretty sure Sutton knew what she was thinking anyway.

He glanced at his watch. "DCI Aron's called a team meeting for two a.m. and he wants our local CID as well. We'd better rally the troops."

In the CID office the air was heavy with warm food and eager chatter. The newcomers were welcomed and Mia noticed Luke had ingratiated himself more thoroughly than she and Sutton had.

"How's DI Mayfield?" That question was on most lips as they entered.

"I phoned through a few minutes ago and he's holding his own." To her dismay, Mia heard her voice wobble.

Liz Murphy hugged her. "He'll make it. He's tough."

"I hope so."

"You hungry? We ordered in Chinese. It's still warm."

"Please." Mia realised she was starving.

Liz served her chow mein and rice. It was lukewarm but still tasty.

"I hear you've set a cat among the pigeons, Guv?" Liz didn't try to mask her curiosity.

"Not me, it was Mia's doing. She spotted several inconsistencies."

Mia saw them staring but she was too tired to feel embarrassed.

What sort of inconsistencies?"

Between mouthfuls, Sutton listed them.

"The thing is, I've got an idea." Liz sounded uncharacteristically hesitant.

"What sort of idea?" asked Sutton.

"About the dead girl. But this lot say I'm obsessed."

"Try me then." He moved to sit on the edge of her desk.

"I wondered if she could be connected to those travellers I told you about."

"The non-Romany, scum-of-the-earth lot? Why do you think that?" Sutton gave a quelling look at the rest of the CID team.

"I've been keeping an eye on them. Like I told you before, I'm sure they're involved in child prostitution and pornography. It isn't easy sorting the kids but I got to recognise some of them. There's a girl I haven't seen for the last week, a red-haired kid. I think her first name was Day."

"You got any pictures of her?"

"Yes Guv." Liz rummaged through a file and held one out.

Mia moved to stand beside Sutton. The girl in the photograph was a thin child with wary eyes and a knowing face.

"I'll send this over to the pathologist," said Sutton. "There's no way I can be sure. You said the travellers were camped on the Bridge Road wasteland recently?"

"Yeah."

"That's interesting. Where are they now?"

"Ash Park. That's on the edge of town, Guv. Word is they're due to be moved on soon."

"Perhaps we can get them a stay of execution, at least until our SOCO teams have taken their camp apart. Look at the time! Come on you lot, don't keep the SIO waiting."

"It makes me mad," said Liz. "If it's her, she never had a chance. Used all her life, then used again by this sick bastard to jerk us round."

"We'll get them," promised Sutton. "The sods who made her childhood hell might take some time to nail, but the bastard who killed her and burned her body has got our attention now.

Chapter 22

They filed into the Incident Room and sat down. Mia noted that most of Aron's team stayed aloof but Luke Warden stuck with the local CID.

DCI Aron looked harassed and peevish but he acknowledged it was a good thing the identity of the victim had been discovered before it was too late. "We've just had the results of the substance tests on Dennis Plummer you ordered, DI Sutton."

"Yes sir?"

"In this case ordering such fast-track tests has proved justified, but I trust you'll remember such things are expensive."

"Yes sir. And the results of the tests, sir?"

Aron handed the report to him and he scanned it. "He had benzodiazephene and senna and ipecac syrup in his system. That's a sedative, laxative and a syrup that makes you throw up. No wonder he thought he'd got a stomach bug."

"He could be malingering," said Aron.

"There's no proof he didn't take it himself," said Sutton, "But if he did, there's no way he could have run round stabbing people and setting bodies on fire. He'd hardly be able to stay on his feet." There was a note of repressed irritation in Sutton's voice and Mia saw Aron frown.

"We've got a possible identification for the victim, sir," said Luke. "DS Murphy came up with a possibility."

DCI Aron turned to Liz, who wriggled her skirt down until it was within hailing distance of her knees, sat to attention, and outlined her theory.

"Good thinking, Sergeant. We'll send a SOCO team round there at first light."

"It'll need more than one SOCO team, sir," said Liz. "There's a lot of stuff to go through."

"And they'll need a large police presence as back-up," warned Sutton.

Aron frowned. "I can't put in a lot of personnel. I'm already over-budget on this case."

"With respect, sir…"

Sutton's angry words were halted by a gesture from DCI Craig, who took up the protest, quietly but implacably, "With respect, sir, we'll need to bring in more SOCOs. We're already down several personnel. And we'll find suitable uniformed back-up. SOCOs aren't going out there unprotected."

There was a moment's pause while everyone waited for the bomb to drop, then the tension was split by a jangly tune. Mia felt a hysterical desire to giggle, the 1812 Overture didn't sound good as a mobile phone ring-tone.

DCI Aron got out his mobile. "It's the ACC. DCI Craig, carry on with the briefing, please."

He left and Craig spoke to the assembled officers. "Liz, you know these travellers. You work on getting an ID for this poor girl. Dave, you keep the Station running for us, okay? Oliver, have you got any thoughts where to take the investigation from here?"

"We've got to work out who had the opportunity to set up Dennis Plummer."

"And who had reason to," said Craig.

"Actually, sir, I think it's more relevant to decide who could do it. This killer's reasons could be so crazy they'd make no sense to us at all."

"What do we actually know?" asked Craig.

"If it's the same man who stabbed Trevor Mayfield he's tall and strong, and has access to Dennis Plummer's life. And he's got a distinctive tattoo like Dennis' on his forearm."

"I think it's more likely to be a transfer of a tattoo like Dennis Plummer's," said Mia apologetically. "Chantelle scratched the man when he was holding her. I just phoned Adam. He's the one who scraped Chantelle's fingernails. He's dealt with tattoos before and he said the ink was wrong.

217

We'll have to wait for the official verdict, but it seems likely it was another scam to set up Dennis."

"And Dennis Plummer's got no scratch marks on his arms?" asked Craig.

"It's hard to tell, sir. He's got scorch marks on his forearms."

"So we've got nothing. All we know is the man we're looking for is about Dennis Plummer's height and build."

"What about Mike Plummer, sir?" asked Sutton.

"Is he as big as Dennis?"

"Not as hefty, but he's a big guy. It's his quiet manner that makes him seem smaller."

"DCI Aron told me he'd checked with Mrs Plummer and she said Mike Plummer answered the phone both times she'd called him from the hospital," growled Craig. "Anyone got anymore suspects to offer me?"

"Sort of, sir." Mia spoke hesitantly. "I wondered about Tim Lewis. He hasn't got an alibi for any of the murders. He says he was home alone."

Craig frowned. "The archaeologist? Why should he set up Plummer?"

"I'm not sure. Tim dislikes and despises Dennis, but he's scared of him as well."

"That makes psychological sense, sir," said Sutton. "If you're going to destroy someone it makes it easier if you can degrade them first."

"I'll take your word for it," said Craig. "Is there any sign this kid's a psychopath?"

"He's rather odd and very immature."

"What do you mean by immature? How old is he?" asked Craig testily.

"Hang on, sir, I'll check." Mia rummaged through her bag and found a copy of the c.v. Tim had given her. She stared at it in disbelief. "He's twenty-nine!"

"Now that's immature," agreed Luke. "I'd have put him around twenty-one."

"I'd usually recognise a contemporary," said Sutton.

There was a brief silence. Mia thought everyone who'd encountered Tim Lewis must be comparing him to the high-flying, responsible, socially adept DI.

"That's upped the weirdness stakes," said Luke.

"He still lives at home with a dominant mother," said Mia.

"And goes around with a builder fifteen years older than himself," said Sutton.

"Odd but not criminal. Have you got anything else with more substance?" asked Craig.

Sutton cast an apologetic look towards Mia. "He's got a sort of thing about Mia."

"Is that true?" demanded Craig.

She felt her colour rising. "He can't have delivered the pizza. He sent me flowers to the Station because he didn't know where I lived."

"Or he sent them here to pretend he didn't know," said Craig.

"Or to establish a relationship with you in the eyes of your colleagues," suggested Sutton.

"It's flimsy," said Craig. "Not enough to give us grounds for an arrest."

"I'd like another word with Dennis Plummer," said Sutton. "Perhaps he can make some suggestions about who hates him enough to set him up."

"Leave that to Mia and Liz. You take DS Warden and go and ask Tim Lewis to come in for questioning. Two-thirty's a nasty, cold hour to be dragged out of bed. It may unsettle him."

"What if he refuses to come?"

"Arrest him, flimsy evidence or not. We'll deal with the fall-out later."

Craig turned as a young cop entered the room and handed him a report. "They managed to get a partial print off that poor girl's hand and compared it to Ellie Plummer's fingerprints. They're definitely not a match." He leaned across his desk, his clipped tones suddenly urgent, "The dead girl was dressed in Ellie Plummer's clothes. That means the killer probably has Ellie. Finding her is our top priority."

The meeting dispersed soon after that. As Mia, Sutton, Liz and Luke walked along the corridor, Liz asked, "What exactly are the SCT going to do for the rest of the night?"

"Good question," said Luke. "If you find out what that lot do most of their time you'll qualify as super-detective of the year. Their last DI was good and kept them on their toes. Aron didn't want her to leave. Word is she had to practically tunnel out, Colditz style, to get clear."

Although he was answering Liz, Mia thought he was aiming his words at Sutton. Giving him some oblique career advice.

Liz grinned at Mia. "You ready to interview Dennis Plummer?"

"Are you sure you'll be okay with him?" asked Sutton.

Liz grinned. "Don't be so sexist, Guv. I got the sort of judo qualifications that could break him in two before he got anywhere near us."

"And if that didn't work she'd boast him into submission," said Luke. "How about you stop bragging and go and put the poor guy out of his misery."

"You mean…? Surely he's been told the victim's not Ellie?" exclaimed Mia.

"No. Aron let the mother know, but he said it wouldn't do Dennis any harm to stew."

"Bad idea, that. It's hard to explain away prisoners topping themselves," commented Liz.

Mia remembered the despair in Dennis' eyes. "Especially the innocent ones," she said.

Dennis had been cleaned up but he still looked terrible. His grey-shaded face was puffy and his bloodshot eyes were haunted.

Mia spoke swiftly, "The girl whose body we found isn't your daughter."

He stared at her, although it was clear focusing was difficult. "What you tryin' to pull? I saw her. It was my girl. I recognised her clothes."

"No Dennis. The clothes were Ellie's but it wasn't her body. It was a smaller girl, different in lots of ways. This girl had been abused all her life. The pathologist managed to take a fingerprint and it isn't Ellie. I wish I could tell you Ellie's safe, but the truth is we don't know where she is."

She saw him process what she'd said. His face quivered and he began to cry, great rending sobs that tore at his body. Mia stood up and rested her hand on his shoulder. After a while the sobs calmed to hiccuping gulps.

"Would you like some water?" He nodded and she filled a glass from the jug on the table. "You need to keep drinking. You must be dehydrated."

Obediently he drank, then belched. "Pardon. This bug's taking forever to clear."

"It's not a bug. Someone's been feeding you a mixture of sedative, laxative and a syrup that induces vomiting. Have you any idea who did that to you?"

"No." He seemed totally bemused. "There was this jug of squash by me bed. I didn't think about how it got there. I was just glad to have a drink." He shivered. "Any chance of a cup of tea? This water chills me guts."

"I don't suppose tea will do you any harm." Presumably the worst that could happen was he'd throw up again.

Liz, who was being remarkably self-effacing, opened the door and gave the order.

"So that wasn't our Ellie?" Dennis shook his head. "Funny, I reckoned I'd know my own little girl anywhere."

"It was cunningly staged and you were still half-drugged. Have you got any enemies?"

"Not that'd do a thing like that. There's plenty of people don't like me. I'd have put you and your mates high on the list."

221

"We've got good reason," said Liz.

"Yeah, I guess. I dunno how things got so crazy. I wouldn't really have hurt that other Crime Scene girl."

"How about threatening to carve up the DI with a broken bottle?" Mia wondered how many enemies this guy could have made without even noticing.

"I know it was wrong. It was just the way he looked at me like dirt."

The answer was obviously quite a few enemies if he attacked people who gave him a snide answer or a contemptuous look.

"DI Sutton and DC Trent have gone all out to establish your innocence, so you'd better start thinking who else hates you," said Liz.

There was a knock on the door and she opened it and took the tea tray.

"I dunno," said Dennis. "I got people who hate my guts but it's one thing to take a swing at me, another to set me up for this. I mean that kid was dead and the bastard must have my Ellie. Do you think he's killed her too?" His voice broke on a sob.

"We're doing everything we can to find her. What can you tell us about Tim Lewis?" Mia was reluctant to put ideas into his head but subtle questioning was going nowhere.

"That little prat? I don't like him and he don't like me, but he wouldn't have the balls to kill someone."

"Why don't you like him?"

"Always showin' off. Goin' on about education and makin' me look thick. He keeps on at Mike, puttin' ideas in his head."

"So you and your workmen made Tim's life difficult? Played a few tricks on him?"

"Nothin' he didn't deserve." Suddenly his expression became sharper. "Hang on, I've just remembered. Mike told me how the kid fancied our Ellie and he was a weirdo and I'd better warn him off. So I told him to stay clear of her."

222

"Did you threaten him in front of people? Humiliate him?" asked Mia.

"Yeah. In the pub. Why the hell haven't you pulled the bugger in?"

"DI Sutton has gone to bring him in for questioning."

"Let me get me hands on him. He'll tell me fast enough." He half-rose from his chair, then doubled over, his bandaged fist clenched against his belly, obviously fighting pain.

"Sit down, Dennis. You know we're not going to let you anywhere near him." Mia surveyed his bleached, sweat drenched face with concern. "You ought to be in hospital."

He managed a contorted smile. "Nice of you to care."

"I don't, but prisoners dying in custody makes a lot of paperwork."

To her surprise that made him laugh. "Good for you, darlin'. I deserved that. I don't wanna go to the hospital. I'd rather stay 'ere. That way I might find out what's happenin'. After all I'm still in trouble for breakin' me police bail, ain't I?"

"Okay, if that's the way you want it." It occurred to her that if anything else happened, having one of their suspects locked in a police cell would give him an unbreakable alibi.

As Liz summoned an officer to escort Dennis back to the cells, Mia turned impulsively to him, "Dennis, won't you tell us where you've been for the past three days?"

He stared at her, his face expressionless. "I told you, I was in me flat."

Chapter 23

"I've arrested Tim Lewis," said Sutton, entering his office with the harried air of a man who has too much to do and too little time to do it in.

"Wouldn't he agree to come in voluntarily?" Mia felt surprised; she'd have pegged Tim as the ostentatiously cooperative type.

"His mother told him not to."

"I see. In a way that's handy, arresting him gave you the right to look around."

"Yeah."

She gathered Sutton was in one of his less forthcoming moods. "What's Tim got to say?"

"Nothing. Mummy told him to keep quiet until his lawyer arrived, so he's keeping shtum."

"Shall I have a go at him?"

"No!"

"There's no need to shout."

"Sorry. But I'm not exposing you to anymore lunatics."

"What's got you so rattled?"

He looked at her warily, took a deep breath and said, "In his room we found a locked drawer full of pictures of you, including a duplicate of the one we found in Dennis' flat."

"So that's Dennis off the hook." She saw Sutton looked embarrassed. "What's wrong?"

"There were some pictures taken with a telescopic lens, of you in your bedroom, naked."

"Oh!" She shivered. So this was what it felt like to be stalked.

She pulled herself together, "I might be able to make him talk. My feelings don't matter when Ellie's life's on the line."

"There's no reason to assume she's still alive."

"If she isn't why dump the other girl's body?"

"I've been talking to the profiler. If Tim Lewis is our killer, she thinks it's unlikely Ellie's still alive."

"Why?" She saw the stubborn look upon his face. "Tell me or I'll ask the profiler myself."

His reluctance was obvious. "She thinks Tim Lewis could fit the profile of a killer. Someone who needs the boost of dominating and destroying. He'd keep Ellie while she was the focus of his desires but he'd dispose of her once his interest focused elsewhere."

"You mean on me?" It was irrational to be swamped with guilt.

"Mia, it's not your fault."

"I know but it feels like it. If Ellie's dead, why didn't he leave her body for Dennis to find?"

"I asked that too. If it's about punishing Dennis, it could be to prolong the torture. Submit him to the trauma of finding the body. Then that period of waiting until the DNA came in. Followed by hope when we discover it isn't Ellie. Then the long wait, torn between hope and grief. Perhaps never having closure."

She shuddered. "What a price to pay for humiliating a guy who fancied your daughter."

"Is that what he did?"

"Yeah."

She described her interview with Dennis. As she was finishing, her mobile rang. She snatched it up, saw Adam's name in the display panel and fumbled to key it on. She was shaking with dread. It was only twenty minutes since she'd last checked on Trevor. "What's wrong?"

"Don't panic, he's doing okay. They reckon he could regain consciousness in the next hour."

"Oh thank God! I'll be there straightaway." She keyed off and met Sutton's sardonic eyes. "I forgot! I can't disappear in the middle of a case."

He grinned. "Nice of you to remember. You can go but

225

you need an escort to the hospital."

She was trying to rustle up a constable to act as her escort when she spotted an ambulance parked close to the back doors.

"What's happening?" she asked as Dennis Plummer was escorted through by a paramedic and two uniformed cops. He was on his feet, but only just.

"His gut ache's got worse," explained one of the constables. "The custody sergeant said he wouldn't take responsibility for keeping him here, so he's off to hospital."

"Are you staying with him there?"

"Yeah."

Can I have a lift to the hospital?" She'd work out later how to get safely back.

"Sure. How's your inspector?"

She gave the latest news of Trevor and climbed into the ambulance. Dennis greeted her with a wan smile and she sat down opposite him.

"You okay?" asked Dennis.

"Yeah. I'm going to see a colleague who was injured."

"The cop who'd been stabbed? Hope he does okay."

"I thought for you the only good cop's a dead cop." Her strained nerves snapped and she rapped out the words.

He shrugged. "I get mad when people bad-mouth me."

"What do you mean?"

"You and that DI, talking about me, sayin' how thick I am."

Mia thought back. "We called you a wanker when you wasted our time with that fishpond."

He frowned. "I could have sworn Mike said… maybe I got it wrong. I should have told you about the fishpond. Everyone said it'd be a real good laugh. I know what you're goin' to say, it ain't so funny when it's your own kid missin' and the cops are followin' false leads."

"I don't need to say it, you know it anyway."

"You'll let me know if there's any news?"

226

"Of course. You're better off in hospital. I should have insisted you went there."

"No you shouldn't. You paid me the respect of listenin' to what I wanted. That custody sergeant just didn't want me gettin' sick in his cells."

She shrugged. "It lowers our reputation."

"You're a spiky one, I'll give you that."

"Spiky?" Mia knew she probably shouldn't ask.

"Sharp as a needle, that's what my old mum used to say. Always got a smart answer. That's what my ex-wife's like."

"I've met Helen."

"Yeah, I s'pose you would have. She alright?"

"Hanging in."

"Does she believe I hurt our Ellie?"

"No. She said you could be an idiot sometimes but she didn't believe you'd kill anyone and she knew you'd never hurt Ellie."

"Hurt her!" He choked on the words. "I'd bloody die for her."

It was strange to see Trevor so still and pale. And scary to see all the tubes and drips and machines attached to him. Mia and Adam stood at the end of the bed but Chantelle was seated, her hand resting on Trevor's. She welcomed Mia with a strained smile, then her gaze pivoted back to Trevor's face.

His eyelids fluttered and closed again, then they opened fully.

"It's all right, Trevor, we're all here with you. Mia, Adam and me. You'll soon be well again." Chantelle's voice was soft and soothing as warm honey.

Trevor's gaze sharpened. "You okay?" His voice was a croaky whisper.

"Yes, darling, you saved my life."

It was clear she was unaware of the endearment but a smile twitched the corners of his grey lips. "I'm glad." He lingered on her face for a moment then moved slowly on to

Mia and Adam. "What're you two skivers doing here?"

"Waiting to claim my lap dance," said Mia huskily.

"'Afraid I'll have to take a raincheck on that." A spasm of pain clenched his features.

A nurse hurried in. "Only two people round a bed. You'll tire him."

Obediently Mia and Adam moved towards the door but Trevor said, "No wait… the DCI 'll want to know… I didn't see the bastard's face… but I got a good punch in… might have marked him."

Mia nodded. "I'll tell the DCI. See you later, Trev."

Chantelle didn't move from Trevor's bedside. "Please Nurse, may I stay with him until the doctor comes? I won't talk to him anymore."

The nurse nodded agreement, checked the monitors, and joined Mia and Adam outside the room. "We need the name of his next-of-kin. I understand that lady isn't a relative?"

"He's got no close relatives," said DCI Craig, arriving in time to hear the question. "Just an ex-wife he hasn't spoken with for years." He showed his identification and asked, "Is he going to make it?"

"It's looking hopeful but he's very weak. You can't question him now."

"I'm not here to question him. He's an old friend. I'm here to check how he's doing." The words were civil but there was an edge to his voice and his eyes were fierce.

Mia feared the nurse might take offence but she smiled and said, "I'm glad he's got good friends to stand by him. It's amazing how much difference that makes to people getting well." She bustled away.

"I've spoken to him, sir." Mia relayed Trevor's message.

"Thanks Constable. Have any of our suspects got a bruised face?"

"Dennis Plummer's pretty battered, sir. It would be hard to be certain. I don't know about the rest, but DI Sutton said that Dennis' mother lashed out at his cousin, Mike and cut his face."

"I'll check that out. Are you coping okay?"

"Yes sir. I must get back to the Station soon." Briefly she told him the latest developments.

"Thanks for keeping me in the loop. If DI Sutton needs clearance for anything tell him he can get me on my mobile."

A nod was as good as a wink but it amazed Mia that Craig would encourage them to bypass DCI Aron. "Yes sir."

Craig turned to Adam, "Keep me informed on Trevor's progress." He left, having given a lot of information by what he didn't actually say.

As she left ITU Mia felt lightheaded with exhaustion and relief. She bought a giant Mars Bar from a vending machine and ate it as she walked through the empty corridors. This was the first time for a long while she'd been alone outside the safety of the police station.

Licking the last traces of chocolate from her lips, she decided to head to A&E. Perhaps one of the cops assigned to Dennis Plummer would agree to accompany her back to the Station.

"Excuse me, officer." Startled, she swung round to confront Helen Plummer.

"Hello, Mrs Plummer. How's your mother-in-law?"

"Okay. She has these turns quite often."

"I'm sorry about what you've had to go through."

"It doesn't matter about me. It's Denny I'm worried about. I'm going back to the police station now and staying there until they let me see him. And if any reporters are hanging round I'll tell them the way he's been treated."

"Please, don't do that! You could endanger Ellie. Anyway, Dennis isn't at the police station, he's back here at A&E. I don't see why you shouldn't speak to him, but I'll have to stay with you." She was exceeding her authority but the rulebook seemed irrelevant tonight.

It was late and, to Mia's dismay, the indoors connection

between A&E and the main hospital was shut. Helen headed purposefully out of the main doors and along the edge of the building. Mia followed her, inwardly quaking.

"Is your little girl being looked after okay?" She chatted to fend off the demons of fear.

"Oh yes. I phoned earlier and Mike said she was fast asleep."

"It's good of Mike to stay with her."

"I guess. But it's only right he should rally round when Denny's mum needs help. Anyway, we're old mates, all at school together, Denny, Mike and me." Her tone was wryly apologetic. "Mike's always had a soft spot for me and I'm afraid I take advantage of him sometimes."

"Perhaps he hopes you'll turn to him now you and Dennis are divorced."

"I've told him that's not going to happen. I might not be able to live with Denny but I don't want anyone else." They continued for a while in silence, then Helen said, "It's funny really, Mike's so steady, rather dull really, and Denny's so wild. It's like they were switched over when they were babies."

"How do you mean?"

"Denny's ma's always been respectable and hardworking. Mike's mum was a good-time girl and a lousy mother. Denny's ma used to say Lydia was the typical peroxide blonde."

"Mike said his mother died when he was a baby."

"That's just one of his tales. She dumped him with Denny's mum when he was two. Asked Gwen to look after him while she went shopping and that was it, straight round the corner, into her new bloke's car and off. She'd got herself a rich boyfriend who didn't want to be lumbered with a kid. Gwen did her duty but she told me she could never take to Mike."

"Poor little boy."

"Faults on both sides, I guess. It wasn't easy for Gwen. She adopted him, but when he was a kid he kept insisting he wanted to use his real mum's name. Gwen didn't like that.

She told me she was afraid everyone would think he was her bastard, seeing as it was her maiden name."

"What was his original surname?" asked Mia, casually curious.

Helen frowned thoughtfully. "I can't remember… something to do with carts. Isn't that odd, me not remembering, when Mike went on about it all the time?"

"Was Mike a difficult kid?" Mia began to see where this was leading and it looked like a scary place.

"Yeah, not wild like Denny but in his own way he was a right pain. He went on about his mum like she was a cross between Marilyn Monroe and a saint. Never a word of affection for Gwen, who was slaving to bring him up. Not that he wasn't always polite to her, just like he is to everyone, but she said that made him sly, just like his mum."

"In what way sly?"

Helen shrugged. "She used to say he was never there when anything bad went down but he was always around just before and just after… Someone's in a hurry."

There was the sound of running feet, pounding towards them along the ill-lit path. Mia felt her inside curdle with fear.

Chapter 24

A young man brushed past with a muttered apology and sped on towards A&E.

"What did he say?" asked Helen.

"That he was late for shift." Mia slid the taizer back into her pocket.

"Can I ask you something?" Helen sounded nervous.

"What do you want to know?"

"It's about what Denny did the other day. Did he really try and rape your colleague?"

"I don't know what he intended but he certainly scared her and he threatened to carve up my DI with a broken bottle."

"Bloody fool! He never used to be so touchy and jealous and certain people were getting at him. But I still don't see him hurting a woman and certainly not rape."

Mia had her own ideas about Dennis' change of personality. She took the conversation back, "Is Mike's mother still alive?"

"No, she died when he was in his teens. Drunk driving. Drove into a bus queue of school kids before she hit a wall and killed herself. Miracle none of the kids was killed as well. Mike took what everyone said about her pretty hard. He started failing at school. That's when he decided to call himself Plummer. Then he started doing a Denny and bunking off. Before that he was really smart and brilliant at science."

The doors to A&E slid open and Mia felt a surge of relief as she stepped into its well-lit interior. She showed her ID and was directed to a long room, lined with curtained cubicles. Dennis' space was easily identified by the two uniformed cops staring into the cubicle.

Mia put a hand on Helen's arm. "Wait a minute. I'll tell him you're here."

As she got closer she saw Dennis was sitting on the bed,

clumsily trying to drink clear liquid from a pint glass. It had been placed on a trolley that kept shifting and steadying the glass with his injured hands was obviously agony.

"Let me help." She shoved past the sadist cops and held the glass for him.

He drained it and said, "Ta."

"Do you want any more?" She refilled the glass from the water jug.

"In a minute mebbe. The doctor said I had to keep drinkin' or they'd put me on a drip."

"You should have asked one of the officers for help."

Dennis stared sullenly at his guards. "They'd rather see me turn to dust."

Mia wondered whether to explain yet again to the cops that Dennis was a victim, but she was pretty sure she couldn't get through to them. "Your ex-wife's here to see you."

"Helen?"

"How many ex-wives have you got?" demanded Helen, appearing in the cubicle.

"I'll supervise this." Mia pulled the curtains, shutting off vision if not sound. To her surprise the cops didn't protest.

Dennis stared at Helen beseechingly. "Hello, Helen luv."

"Don't you 'Helen luv' me. What you been up to now?"

"He burnt his hands trying to save the girl he thought was Ellie." Mia decided to help him out. She saw Helen's expression soften briefly, then the cold mask clamped back in place.

She didn't think Dennis had spotted the moment of gentleness. His voice was rough, "I'd have done it even if I hadn't thought it was Ellie. You don't leave kids to burn."

Perhaps he did deserve the odd kind gesture after all.

He lay down again, arms folded across his stomach. Helen moved nearer to stand next to his bed. Mia lurked in the background.

"I thought you'd had your hands seen to, so why're you back here?" said Helen.

"I got gut ache."

"Been drinking too much like usual?"

"No, I was bloody poisoned."

"What?"

Mia intervened. "A bit melodramatic but basically the truth." She explained about the cocktail of drugs and their effects.

"But who'd do that? And why? Can you buy them things over the counter?"

"Not the sedative," said Mia.

"Dennis, why are you looking so shifty?" demanded Helen, spotting what Mia had missed.

"The Temazepam's mine." Dennis sounded sullen. He glanced towards Mia. "I told you I lost me pills at Bridge Road the other day."

"I see." There'd been no record of any such pills being recovered at Bridge Road and Mia wondered who'd made them disappear. The blood tests had shown that Dennis had taken… or been given… far more than the recommended therapeutic dose.

"Temazepam? That's for depression, isn't it?" said Helen.

"Don't go on, luv. I don't wanna talk about it."

"Well I do."

Dennis groaned. "Please luv, leave it. I feel really rough."

"We'll talk about it later." Helen's quiet determination made it clear this was postponement rather than escape. "How bad are your hands burned?"

He shrugged. "Bit of a mess. Gonna be a while before I can do much with 'em."

"They given you anything to help the pain?"

"Nah. I don't want nothing to knock me out, not when our Ellie's missing." Tears glimmered on his unshaven cheeks. "How did I make such a mess of everything? Helen luv, the cops reckon Ellie's dead."

Helen's face blanched. She stared at Mia. "Do you?"

234

"We don't know. We're worried about her safety."

"I can't believe she's dead. I won't believe it." Helen shook herself, like a dog clearing its coat of water and glared at Dennis. "What the hell have you been playing at, getting the cops against you like this?"

"I made a bloody idiot of meself." He turned to Mia. "Would you tell your mate I'm sorry. I wouldn't really have hurt her."

"I'll tell her." Something stirred in Mia's memory. "Someone said you like girls in uniform."

Dennis looked surprised but not guilty. "That's a joke."

"A joke?"

Helen explained, "When Denny joined the army I said it was because he fancied girls in uniform. So he used to tease me, describing how sexy soldier-girls looked when they were doing manoeuvres. He was kidding, everyone knew that."

"I see." That was a different story from the one Mike Plummer had supplied.

Helen seemed softened by this memory. She perched beside Dennis on the bed and made no protest when he leaned against her.

He turned to look at Mia. "I've been thinking. Your boss said something about fingerprints on a pizza box? Were they Deirdre's prints?"

"Yes." Mia saw no point in denying it.

"I gave her a lift sometimes if I saw her walking home. Last time was the day before she died. She was in a state because she'd lost her cat and I drove her round to look for it."

"What's that got to do with the pizza?" asked Mia, determined to get things straight.

"It was on the front seat and she held it for me."

A plausible explanation. Mia believed him but made a mental note to check whether the fingerprints were compatible with Deirdre holding the box.

"Did you tell anyone about this?"

He thought for a moment. "Yeah, I said to Mike how funny it was that Deirdre had never had a take-away. I said to her to open the box and pull a chunk off to try it but she wouldn't." He leaned back against Helen's cradling arm.

"If they don't keep you in hospital you'd better come home with me, Denny. You can't look after yourself with your hands like that."

"Get real, Helen luv, I can't look after meself at all."

He sounded humble and miserable and Mia saw Helen melt. "We'll look after each other, Denny. We need to stick together 'til we get our girl back."

"Yeah. Earlier on, when they were saying I'd hurt Ellie, I needed to talk to you. I tried to phone you when the cops said I could make a call, but it was engaged all the time."

"I'm sorry, Denny, the house phone's out of order. Apparently it sounds like it's engaged but it isn't ringing at our end. Otherwise Mike would have answered. He was babysitting Zoe."

"Why're you here, luv? Did the cops tell you I was hurt?"

"No. Your mum's had one of her turns."

Dennis swore. "That's my fault, worryin' her."

"She's on the mend now. She'll be…"

Mia interrupted, "Helen, if your phone's out of order, how come you told us Mike answered when you phoned?"

"I rang his mobile when I couldn't get through on the house phone. He told me to try the house phone again, and then he said it was probably an intermittent fault and he'd ring the telephone people to get it fixed. I don't like it being out of order, not when Ellie could ring. I tried to tell that cop about it, the really important one, but he was too busy to listen."

"He should have done." That was half of Mike Plummer's alibi exploded and DCI Aron could have known hours ago if he hadn't been so set on his own agenda.

"Helen, should you be getting home? Is Mike still looking after your little girl?"

She must have spoken casually enough because Helen shook her head and replied calmly, "Oh no. I phoned my sister. She went in an hour ago and collected Zoe and took her home with her. She said Zoe didn't wake up, even when my brother-in-law carried her to the car."

"Bet your sister blamed me for havin' to turn out," said Dennis. "She always hated me."

"No she doesn't."

"She wanted you to marry Mike."

"Well I didn't marry Mike, I married you. And it wasn't Mike's fault you were such a prat we got unmarried again."

Mia was beginning to feel certain that it was very much Mike's fault. "I think you ought to phone your sister and ask her to bring Zoe here to be checked out."

"What?" Helen jumped up and Dennis swung his feet clear of the bed to go to Zoe's aid.

"Please don't panic. I'm probably way off target."

Helen got out her mobile and made the call. "They'll be here in ten minutes. My sister was still up. She said she was worried that Zoe was sleeping much too sound."

"I know you'll want to be with her as soon as she arrives but I need to ask you some more questions. They'll seem strange, and I don't want to be intrusive, but this is important."

She read doubt on both their faces. She couldn't blame them, neither of them had enjoyed positive experiences with the cops. Then Helen said, "I guess she's on the level, Denny. She's been pretty decent. I think we should trust her."

He shrugged wearily. "Do what you think's best, luv. It don't matter much for me. I've screwed up every chance I ever had and I can't see no way back. All that matters is you get our Ellie home with you, and keep our girls safe."

"That's our priority too, whether you answer my questions or not," said Mia, balancing carefully between keeping up the pressure and not alienating them.

Helen nodded agreement. "What do you want to know?"

Mia made record time back to the police station. "I want to talk to Tim Lewis." She demanded as soon as she was through Sutton's office door.

"We've been through this. We're not exposing you to this lunatic. Anyway we're still waiting for his lawyer to turn up." He yawned. "Not that he's likely to at four in the morning."

"Oliver, please. Order him to be brought to an interview room. Give me five minutes with him, that's all I ask. How about you trust me on this one? I've trusted you all along the line."

"That's because you didn't have any choice, I'm your superior officer." Nevertheless he phoned through and gave the order. "You planning to tell me what this is about?" he asked as he put the phone down. "Or is this trust you're asking for like a piece of elastic, keep pulling and see how far it'll stretch before it snaps?"

She gave him a dazzling smile. "Of course I'm going to tell you. Like you said you're my superior officer."

Tim looked scared and bewildered as he sat at the interview table. When he saw Mia he blushed, a boiling tide that engulfed his pale face and prominent ears.

"Hi Tim." She sat down opposite him and Sutton took the chair beside her.

"I'm sorry, I can't talk to you. Mother said I mustn't say anything"

"All I'm asking is five minutes, Tim. I thought we were friends. Don't you trust me?"

"I'm sorry. I'd like to help you but I can't."

Mia pushed her personal feelings aside and leaned forward, speaking with professional intimacy, "Tim, you know how it is in archaeology? You can have lots of bits of information about a site but they don't make any sense until you get the one small bit that links everything and then it all falls into place."

He nodded. "But I don't know anything."

"You know about the exams Mike had to do at college before he could start his A-Levels." She saw his stricken look and knew she'd scored.

"No I don't." The words of denial were belied by his shrill voice and shaking hands.

"You didn't mean any harm, Tim. You were just helping a friend."

"I don't know what you're talking about."

"Did he say he was worried about the tests? Did he ask you to help him out?"

"No. I didn't do anything."

"We can get the test papers and do handwriting analysis."

"No you can't, they gave the test papers back… I mean, Mike said they had."

"Tim. It's very important you tell the truth, otherwise more people will be hurt."

He shook his head, tears welling in his eyes.

Sutton spoke for the first time. "Tim, there's no shame in having been fooled. This man's an expert at using people. He set his own cousin up for three murders. When he asked you to take his place he gave himself an alibi and left you without one. If his scheme to destroy Dennis fell apart, he'd have you as a second fall guy."

Tim dashed away his tears. "He's my friend."

"Friends don't set each other up. You're better off without a friend like that."

"You wouldn't think so if you'd never had any friends."

Mia saw an opening, "I wanted to be your friend but you weren't fair to me. You used our friendship to tell me lies and to frighten me. Dennis wasn't stalking me but you were. I'd guess it was you who made that silent phone call on Thursday night."

Tim looked sulky. "I wasn't stalking you. I wanted to talk to you. Before I could work out what to say you said, 'Is that you, Oliver?' and I knew you'd been two-timing me."

Mia bit back the indignant words that were sizzling on

her tongue. Instead she said, "Was Mike with you when you phoned?"

Tim didn't answer but his expression was admission enough.

Sutton opened a file and took out a wad of photographs. "You claim you haven't stalked Mia but our search of your room revealed these. They're all of Mia, taken without her knowledge. This one is the duplicate of a photograph we found concealed in Dennis Plummer's flat, along with pictures of the three women who were murdered recently."

"There you are! That proves it was Dennis who was doing the stalking."

Sutton laughed. "Give up on that. We've cleared Dennis." He opened another file and took out more photographs. "You remember these people? You met them in the pub. Chantelle and Trevor. This is a picture of the hallway outside Chantelle's flat. The blood is Trevor's, after they'd rushed him to hospital. Of course, Mike Plummer has a convenient alibi. Have you?"

"I haven't hurt anyone!" Mia believed him. He was a total coward.

Sutton got out another photograph. "This is an unknown victim, a young girl. She'd been raped, strangled and had her face smashed in. Her body was doused in bleach, then petrol and set on fire. At the moment you're the only person we've got in the frame for all these crimes. If you co-operate you may get yourself out of the mess Mike's landed you in."

"Okay."

For a moment they were silent. His sudden capitulation came as an anti-climax.

"Do you waive your demand to wait for a solicitor?" asked Sutton.

"Yes."

"We're going to record this interview." Tim nodded sullen agreement and Sutton set up the recording. "Now, Tim, tell us about what happened when Mike Plummer had to take some tests at College six weeks ago."

"Mike was worried he might fail, so I offered to take his place."

"Whose idea was this?"

"Mine. Mike didn't want me to do it. I had to persuade him."

"What A-Levels is Mike Plummer studying for?"

Tim hesitated, then replied, "Maths, Biology and Chemistry."

"And what does he plan to study at university?"

"Bio-Chemistry."

"You were present when Mike Plummer told us he was going to study history?"

"Yes. But Mike doesn't like it when people contradict him." Resentfulness shifted into fear.

"Is that why didn't you admit to his piece of minor cheating before it came to this?"

"Mike said you'd realise I was innocent but if anyone found out about the cheating, I might be prosecuted."

"Tell us about Mike's relationship with his cousin, Dennis."

"Mike tries to look after him but Dennis is jealous of him because his mother adopted Mike. And Mike's own mother was wonderful. Dennis always resented that."

"Tell us about Mike's mother," said Mia, aware she hadn't had time to brief Sutton on this.

"She was an actress. Very beautiful. She had to travel a lot for her work but she used to send Mike wonderful presents and take him on fabulous holidays. She was killed in a horse-riding accident on the ranch she owned in Texas."

Mia wondered how even Tim could have swallowed this load of garbage.

"What about Ellie Plummer?" asked Sutton.

Tim scowled. "Ellie likes making trouble. One minute she really fancied me, the next she claimed I was pestering her and her oaf of a father threatened me."

"Did Ellie ever say she fancied you?" said Mia.

"No, but Mike told me she was keen."

"What about stalking DC Trent? Was that your idea or Mike's?" snapped Sutton.

"That's not stalking!... Mia, I wanted the pictures because you're so beautiful. When this is over I'd like to marry you."

Chapter 25

"How about that? Not every girl gets a proposal of marriage in the interview room," said Sutton, as they walked wearily back towards his office.

Mia pulled a face. "Are you sure he's not our guy? He's crazy enough."

"Maybe he is. We've had so many suspects in the last twelve hours my brain won't expand enough to fit them in."

"What now?"

"Now I tell DCI Aron you've changed your mind again and selected another prime suspect."

She laid a hand upon his arm. "I don't mean to be a pain."

"I know. The trouble is that some people think outside the box, you think outside the universe. Ow!" The slight pressure of her fingers on his arm made him gasp with pain.

"I'm sorry! I forgot about your arm. Is it still bad?"

"It's a lot better, just a bit tender."

"Shouldn't you be wearing your sling?"

"Only if you reckon it'll stop the DCI from throwing things. I suppose I could remind him of the Disability Discrimination Legislation. Wish me luck."

He left and Mia lingered in Sutton's office for a while, then, feeling restless, she went along to the main CID office but it was deserted. She followed the sound of voices to the Incident Room set aside for the murder investigation and found Liz Murphy and Dave Bycroft standing by the boards, looking over the information about the victims.

"What are you doing?" she asked.

"The Serious Crimes lot have gone off duty so we thought we'd have a nosy, see if anything hit us about the case," explained Liz.

"But Serious Crimes can't have gone off, not at this stage of the case."

"They can, you know. DCI Aron doesn't run a tight ship, especially when he's sulking about DCI Craig stepping on his toes," said Luke Warden, entering with Sutton in time to hear her protest.

"Then how come you're still here?" demanded Bycroft. He was obviously embarrassed at being caught prying into the big case and his tone was aggressive.

Luke refused to rise to the aggro. "I'm only on secondment to Aron's team." He grinned at Sutton. "And I thought your guv'nor might need the pieces picking up."

"How did it go?" asked Mia.

Sutton shrugged. "DCI Aron's gone off duty but I caught DCI Craig. I can't say he's happy but he was reasonable about it."

"About what?" asked Dave Bycroft.

Sutton sketched out the state of play. "The trouble is we've got three suspects and all the physical evidence points to the one we're pretty sure has been set up. There's nothing pointing to Mike Plummer, not even Tim Lewis' word. Mike's convinced Tim that Tim's the one who has all the good ideas."

"Maybe it's true," said Bycroft. "They could be working together, egging each other on."

"I know. They're both egotistical. And they both fill the psychologist's profile. At the moment Tim's convinced us Mike's manipulating him, but when we talk to Mike maybe he'll make it sound like it's the other way around. The only thing we can be reasonably sure of is that it was Mike who manipulated Dennis. In fact, from what Dennis and Helen Plummer told Mia, I'd think he's been doing it most of their lives."

"I wouldn't be surprised if he hadn't wrecked their marriage," chimed in Mia. "Helen said how jealous Dennis had become. Dennis couldn't remember exactly what Mike had said to him, but as Helen and I asked him questions it became clear Mike had warned Dennis she was playing round and suggested ways of testing her."

"Very Othello," commented Liz. "What's up?" She met their amazed looks with a grin.

"Didn't think you'd know a Shakespeare play if it got up and bit you on the arse," said Luke, venturing where her longer-term colleagues wouldn't dare.

"I used to date an actor. Come to think of it he was pretty good at arse-biting."

"Thanks for sharing that," said Sutton.

"You're welcome. What's your next move, Guv?"

"We'll haul in Mike Plummer. Not that we've got anything resembling evidence."

"At least with all three of them under raps no more bodies should turn up on country bus stops," said Dave Bycroft.

"What?" Sutton strode nearer to the boards and peered at the crime scene photos. "They were all dumped in lay-bys, but I can't see bus stop signs."

"They're not really official bus stops but the school kids always wait there and the bus picks them up. I'm sorry, I wasn't holding out on you. I never thought about it before."

"No problem," said Sutton. "It doesn't prove anything but it might give me a lever when I'm questioning the bastard."

"I know I'm only a thick regional cop, but I don't get it," complained Liz.

"Mike Plummer's mother was killed in a car accident after she drove into a bus queue of school kids," explained Mia. Another thought struck her although she didn't say it aloud. She remembered the 'hold back' about the murdered women's dyed hair and that Mike's mother had been a peroxide blonde.

"The bastard's going to stonewall until we run out of time," said Sutton.

Mia searched for something positive to say and came up empty. They'd had Mike Plummer in custody for nine hours. It was early afternoon and weary determination was dissolving into exhaustion and despair. Relays of officers had taken turns interrogating him. They'd pushed him to the limit PACE would allow and got nowhere. He'd not asked for a solicitor, he'd answered all their questions with patronising patience and he'd given nothing away.

Mia hadn't been allowed to interview, which she found frustrating, although it meant she'd achieved a few hours' restless sleep.

Soon they'd have to charge him or let him go and they had no grounds to charge him. Once this lunatic was loose again no-one would be safe, especially Mia who'd pissed him off big time. She'd spend the rest of her life looking over her shoulder, afraid to be alone.

"Nothing in his flat?" asked Sutton.

"Nothing. It's abnormally clean, practically sterile."

"Where the hell is Ellie? Dead or alive she's got to be somewhere."

The search teams had gone through every house Mike had access to and visited every spot Dennis and Helen could suggest.

"We haven't got enough to keep him," he continued. "All we've got is that bruise on his face and those scratches on his arm. We may be certain Trevor and Chantelle gave them to him but we can't prove it until we get the DNA results from the skin under Chantelle's nails." Science results couldn't be rushed or they'd become unreliable and inadmissible in Court.

"I'll see if there's any word from the lab." She got out her mobile and checked her answer service. "That's strange. Joy Marshall wants me to ring her as soon as possible."

She was halfway through keying in the number when Luke put his head round the door. "Our turn again, Guv. Though I don't know what we're supposed to say that we haven't already said."

"I've got one card left," said Sutton. "He doesn't know we've worked out his method yet."

"Let me have a go." Mia cancelled the call and put her phone away.

"No. It's too big a risk."

"I got the truth out of Tim Lewis, didn't I?"

"He was a soft option compared to this bastard."

"Oliver, what have I got to lose? He's already got me in his sights. The only way I'll be safe is by nailing him."

He hesitated, obviously swayed by her logic. "Okay, if the SIO agrees."

"He'll agree to anything that sorts this case," said Luke.

Ten minutes later she slid into place in the interview room again and surveyed Mike Plummer across the table. Last night, when Dennis had sat in that seat, his grief and sickness had made him pitifully human. Mike was invulnerable. A softly spoken monster. A beast who thinks.

"Was it fun?" asked Mia.

"I beg your pardon?"

"Being so clever. Manipulating people. Was it fun?"

"I'm afraid I don't know what you're talking about."

"That's the latest game is it? Playing thick. The thing is, Mike, manipulating is like a conjuring trick. It's only impressive when you don't know how it's done. You were too impatient. You wanted to get our attention. We were going too slowly for you. Well the pace has hotted up now, so get your running shoes on." She smiled at him. "We're arranging for Dennis and Helen to have counselling to repair the damage you've done and get them back on track."

Sutton moved in to claim the questioning, "I suppose it was inevitable you should hate Dennis. I mean look at him, a loud-mouthed, brawling, drunkard, and so stupid."

Mia watched Mike's hands stretch out, the fingers strong and taut. 'A strangler's hands.' The thought slithered through her mind.

"Of course you hate him," continued Sutton. "Because, with all those bad qualities, he's still loveable. So many people

247

care about him and only tolerate you."

"That's not true." But the hands tensed.

"Of course it's true." Mia picked up the ball and ran with it. "Last night Helen said how dull you were. She always felt sorry for you, having to make up all those stories about your glamorous mum when everyone knew she was a selfish slag who dumped you without a second thought. A peroxide blonde already past her sell-by date. And a drunk driver who hit a crowd of kids and topped herself."

She saw the hands twist, as if they were clenched on a woman's neck but the face stayed as motionless as a mask.

"Of course, Helen's angry about what you did to her daughter," said Sutton.

She saw Plummer relax. "I haven't done anything to Ellie and you can't prove I have."

"Oh no, not Ellie," agreed Sutton. "Zoe. Helen was worried about her, so we arranged a blood test that showed she'd been drugged with Temazepam. The same drug you used on Dennis. Of course you needed her asleep so you could slip out with your cat recording to attack Chantelle and set up Dennis. Face it, Mike, you've got no cards left to deal."

For the first time Plummer smiled. "Then I'm afraid Ellie won't have any left as well."

"Where is Ellie?" Mia was impressed by Sutton's quiet voice.

"If you release me I'll look for her. I'm good at locating lost objects."

"Interview terminated at 14.13 hours." Sutton turned off the recorder.

"Don't you want to hear about Ellie?" Anger and outrage twisted his face.

"Not from you." Sutton stood back to let Mia precede him from the room.

"Give you two credit, you're good," said Luke, emerging

248

from the next door room to join them in the corridor.

"You were watching us?" asked Mia.

"Yeah. The SIO wanted the psychologist to observe."

"What do you reckon, Doctor?" asked Sutton as the psychologist also appeared.

"I agree with the sergeant, you work remarkably well together."

"Do you think Ellie's still alive?"

"He certainly implied that, but it could be another move in his power game. You played it perfectly. By not asking about her you've unsettled him."

"It doesn't get us nearer to finding Ellie."

"If you'd played his game, he wouldn't have told you the truth. Sociopaths get off on power games. I've no doubt you've got the right man."

"The question is whether we can get the evidence to keep him," said Luke.

"I'd like to spend some time talking to Dennis and Helen Plummer," said the psychologist.

"I'm sure they'll co-operate," said Mia. "They'll do anything to find Ellie."

"You did well in there. Your allusion to the conjuring trick was particularly apt."

"It was, wasn't it?" The rapt note in Sutton's voice made them all stare. "Come with me, Mia, I need to talk something through."

He led the way to his office at top speed, leaving her to trot after him, which she did.

"What's wrong?" She shut the door and turned to face him.

"Mike Plummer's a conjurer. He creates illusions. He was fed up with waiting for us to latch onto Dennis, so he decided to hurry things along. He's been orchestrating everything right from the start. Even Bridge Road and finding the body and digging out the fishpond, everything."

"Aren't you being paranoid?"

"I don't think so. What was it old Lucy said, 'I didn't

249

want to leave but I had to do what he told me. He was always so violent and cruel and devious.' Perhaps it wasn't William Davies she was talking about. I think Mike Plummer forced her to go. Didn't Dennis say something like that?"

Mia thought back. "Yes, but it's one hell of a stretch. And how did William's pension get diverted into an account with Lucy's name on it?"

"I don't know, but Lucy moved out straight after William's death. What if Mike blackmailed her into leaving?"

"And what if we'll never know and it doesn't matter anyway? It's getting him on murder that matters."

"It shows the way his mind works and the way he prepares the ground. There's another conjuring trick. Dennis swears he was in his flat when we know he wasn't. And that woman who worked with Deirdre said something about Deirdre seeing someone going into Dennis' building but not being there when she knocked. It must have been Mike she was talking about."

Mia stared at him blankly, then understanding dawned. "You think he's got another flat in the same building?"

"It's the only thing that makes sense. Have you got that list of tenants?"

She unburied it from the pile of paperwork and they both stared blankly at the meaningless names. "We'll never get search warrants for them all," said Sutton.

"Hang on." Mia grabbed the phone and rang through "Helen? It's Mia Trent. Is Dennis there?... I know it's a funny question but could you ask him his mother's maiden name?"

The answer made her feel like a gambler whose long-shot has come in.

She rang off and pointed to Number Two, "Wheelwright. Helen said it was something to do with carts. It's Mike's mother's surname."

"Got him!" said Oliver. "I'll fix up a warrant, you get together a team to search the place."

250

"Michael Plummer, welcome to his world," said Luke, staring around the immaculate and terrifying front room.

"Yeah, this is where the real Mike Plummer has his being," said Sutton. "Always assuming there is a real Mike Plummer."

"No," said Mia, "This is Michael Wheelwright's place."

Silently they all stared at the tall, freestanding frame of pictures. There was a blonde woman, holding a small child. The same woman appeared with a boy. So it continued, until the boy was a young teenager and easily recognisable as Mike. The age of the child altered but the woman did not change in looks or fashion.

"Rewriting the history of his relationship with his mother," said Sutton. "I'd like the psychologist to see this in situ."

"It's not the only relationship he's rewritten," said Mia, pointing to another frame. In it were pictures of Helen, Zoe and Ellie, but Dennis' image had been digitally replaced by Mike's.

Sutton pressed on briskly through the flat, followed by Mia, Luke and Liz Murphy. The SOCO team were already recording everything. The master bedroom proved that Dennis had not knowingly lied. The room and en suite were a perfect replica of his own, although his recent sickness had rendered this one even more sordid.

"How did you figure it out, Guv?" asked Luke.

Sutton shrugged. "A while ago, Mia was talking about, 'Through the Looking-Glass,' and it hit me this is the sort of game Mike Plummer likes to play."

The second bedroom was as bare as a monk's cell. There was no trace of the person who'd existed there. In the kitchen the washing machine was full of wet clothes. "Bag them," Mia ordered the SOCO, "And check the filter and drain." In the bathroom there was a lingering smell of bleach, and several bleached hairs were caught in the plughole. SOCOs would be working here for days.

Back in the living room, they forced open a deep, wall cupboard and unearthed the programme of events that orchestrated Mike Plummer's grisly campaign. A detailed diary of each victim, photographs, maps, timetable of their routines, patterned paper with which Mike had faked the tattoo. There was a pocket tape recorder. Careful not to smudge any prints, Sutton pushed 'Play' and the plaintive meowing of a cat echoed through the room.

"So the method was like we thought," said Sutton.

"Good result, Guv," said Liz.

"Could be better. We haven't found Ellie."

"We can use this lot to pressure him into telling us where he's dumped her body."

"I doubt it. Knowing Ellie's whereabouts is the only power he's got left. And he'll use it to carry on putting her parents through hell." He nodded to Luke and Liz, "You two start canvassing the neighbours. If he's got another hideaway in this building I want to know about it. I'll call the profiler. Seeing this might tell her where we should search."

Luke and Liz left quickly and Sutton moved towards the centre of the room to make his call. Renewed meowing made him snap, "Stop fiddling with that tape."

"It wasn't the tape." Mia spoke hesitantly, "I think there's a cat under the floor."

Chapter 26

Sutton was beside her. He fell to his knees, prying at the floorboards with no thought of preserving evidence. They came up in a panel, like a makeshift coffin lid.

Mia screamed, "We need help here!" and straddled Oliver's crouched form to shine her torch into the dark hole.

There was a body down there, huddled and unmoving. Sutton glanced up at her. She saw his agony and knew he was reliving a nightmare. "Oliver, let me get there. I'll do it."

He shook his head. "No." He grasped the body and hauled. He banged his bad elbow, not a hard blow but enough to make him gasp. Mia ditched the torch and helped him support the inert weight as he shuffled backwards. Her call had brought help and eager hands were there to assist them. Sutton knelt, both arms around the girl, supporting her.

She was fully dressed, in a high necked jumper and stained jeans. From the marks and the smell it was clear she'd soiled herself. She was still breathing, although the rise and fall of her chest was shallow. Her blue eyes were open but their gaze was blank and unfocused. Mia peeled back the duct tape that sealed the girl's mouth. Someone supplied scissors and she cut free her hands and feet.

All the time, Sutton's voice was in her ears, "It's okay Ellie. You're safe now. We're the police. We'll look after you. My name's Oliver. Speak to me, sweetheart."

Mia could feel his dark despair as he assessed how much air there was in her under-the-floor coffin and his growing conviction this girl was brain dead like the one he'd rescued years ago.

There was a scrabbling sound from the hole and an indignant meow. A ginger cat scrambled out and wound itself around Mia, purring like he'd regained a long-lost friend.

"Pixie!"

Still purring, he approached Ellie. Mia grabbed at him but he evaded her and nuzzled Ellie's face. Waveringly, Ellie smiled. "Pixie," she whispered. "That's a funny name for a cat."

Miraculously, Ellie didn't seem to be physically damaged, apart from stiff, cramped limbs and slight dehydration. The tape that had bound her arms wasn't tight enough to have cut off her circulation. With relief they realised she'd been tied up in the dark for nearly twenty-four hours, but not for days or weeks. He'd told her he was sorry but it was for her own good. It was because of those bastard cops.

Sutton and Mia accompanied her to hospital in the ambulance. She was still clutching Pixie. The paramedics had objected, then backtracked when Sutton pointed out in a savage whisper that the poor kid was traumatised enough.

"Then you shouldn't be questioning her," muttered the paramedic.

He spoke loud enough for Ellie to hear. "No, I want to tell."

"Thank you, Ellie. Could you start at the beginning?" said Sutton. "And may we record this? So we can get everything straight."

She nodded agreement and he asked, "How did Uncle Mike get hold of you, sweetheart?"

"He asked me to come and see him... after my dance class."

"Why didn't you tell your mum you were going there?"

"He told me not to. He said he wanted to talk about my dad."

"What happened when you got to Uncle Mike's flat?"

"He was going on and on about things that happened years ago and how Mum should have married him not Dad. And about his mother, and how she'd been so wonderful, when everyone knows what she was like. I knew I should be angry about the stuff he was saying about Dad but I felt so tired and I must have gone to sleep."

"Did he give you anything to drink?" asked Mia.

"Orange squash. It tasted horrible but I was thirsty. I wanted to ask for water, but, somehow, you can't tell Uncle Mike you don't like something, not like Dad." She buried her face in Pixie's fur and the next words were muffled, "Is my dad dead?"

"No, he's fine," said Mia.

"That the truth?"

"I swear it is. He's burnt his hands and he's had a bad stomach upset but he's okay. As soon as he sees you, he'll feel wonderful."

"Why did you think he might be dead?" asked Sutton.

"I saw him." For the first time she wouldn't meet their eyes.

"Saw him where, Ellie?"

"In that place. That awful place where I woke up. That flat, with all those crazy photos. Uncle Mike kept calling me his little girl. And I said, 'I'm not your little girl. You're not my dad.' And he got mad and he said he'd show me my dad and he opened this room he always kept locked and dragged me over there. Dad was lying on the bed, and the room stank. Dad was snoring and he'd been sick on the floor... it was gross. Uncle Mike said, 'That drunken slob's your dad. You proud of him? Perhaps you'd like to rethink who you want as a father. You'd better get used to it. Your mother prefers me.'" She said each word as if they'd been etched into her mind.

"Your mum doesn't prefer him," said Mia. "It was another of Uncle Mike's lies."

"I'm so ashamed." Again her face was deep in Pixie's fur.

"Try not to be ashamed of your dad. He's made some bad mistakes but that's because of what Uncle Mike's been doing to him," said Sutton. "And he couldn't help what happened the other day. Your uncle had drugged him."

She raised her face, sparkling with indignation. "I'm not ashamed of Dad! I'm ashamed of me. I wanted to tell Uncle Mike how he'd never be my dad but I was scared to.

255

He had this white, tight look around his mouth and he felt so… cruel."

"You did right, Ellie. If you'd provoked him he could have hurt you or your dad even more. What happened before that? In those three weeks he kept you prisoner?"

"Nothing. He just kept me there." She glared at them with childish bravado. "He didn't rape me, if that's what you mean."

"I didn't think he did," said Sutton gently.

"Why not?" She sounded ridiculously insulted.

"Because he wanted you as a daughter. Were you drugged, Ellie?"

"I guess so. I slept a lot. I'm so out of training. It'll take ages to get my fitness back."

"Did you try to get out of the flat at all?"

Her lips quivered. "I couldn't. He had me on a leash, like I was a dog. He wouldn't even let me into the bathroom. He made me use this pot in a chair. That was so gross. And he brought a bowl of water for me to wash. When he wanted to move me he hauled me on the collar. She fingered the chafed line on her neck. "Do you think it'll scar?"

"No, I'm sure not," said Mia.

"Ellie, your mum received a letter, saying you'd run away to London," said Sutton. "Do you know anything about that?"

"He made me write it. I didn't want to but I was scared."

The ambulance was turning into the hospital gateway. "What happened last night, Ellie? Before he put you under the floor?"

"He came in all covered in blood. He had the cat… Pixie… in a box and it clawed its way out and scratched him. He went crazy. He picked up a chair and tried to kill the cat but it ran to me. I picked it up and said, 'Please Daddy, don't hurt it.' And he stopped swearing and said, "If Daddy's little girl wants a pet she can have it, but she must be good.' Then, before I knew what was happening, he put tape round my

256

arms and legs and on my mouth. Then he pulled up this trapdoor and shoved me down the hole. And he threw the cat in on top of me."

"What happened then, Ellie?" Sutton's voice was soft.

"I was there so long. And I was thirsty and I needed the loo. Then I heard you up there moving round. It was torture. I tried to bang my feet but I couldn't move enough to make you hear. Then a cat meowed and Pixie meowed back."

"And we found you," Sutton finished for her.

"Thanks to Pixie," she said, and suddenly she sounded like a little girl.

Sutton arranged for Ellie's parents to meet them at the hospital, timing it so the medical and forensic tests were done before they arrived. Mia thought wryly that he was showing himself to be the consummate professional. Now Ellie was safe his priority had switched back to preserving the integrity of his evidence.

Mia had never considered herself sentimental, but the joy on Helen's face when she saw her daughter reminded her of a shaft of sunlight. Helen let go of Zoe's hand and ran across the room to pounce on Ellie, patting her all over, as if to convince herself she was real. Dennis looked blank, as if his feelings were too intense to express.

Helen saw this and said, "Your dad's been worried sick about you, Baby."

Ellie thrust Pixie into her mother's arms, ran to her father and hugged him fiercely. His face crumpled and he put his arms around her, rocking her gently. "Are you all right, Dad?"

"I am now. Are you?"

"The doctor says there's no great physical damage," said Sutton. "But there might be a few kick-backs in other ways."

"We'll get through that," said Helen. "I'm just grateful… well you know." She turned back to Ellie and spoke with mock severity, "Will you tell me, young lady, why you've given me a cat to hold?"

"His name's Pixie and he saved my life, so can I keep him, please Mum?"

Helen looked dismayed. "Oh sweetheart, you know we can't have a cat. Zoe's allergic to them."

Mia intervened, "I'm sorry, Ellie, but you couldn't keep Pixie anyway. He's got an owner and she loves him very much."

"I tell you what," said Dennis. "They may send me to prison for something stupid I did but when I get out I'll get a cat and you can play with it when you come to visit me. I know I can't see Zoe but you're sixteen, you can come to see me sometimes."

"From what I've heard you'd lose a cat under all the garbage in your flat," said Helen.

He glared at her. "I'm moving. I couldn't stand livin' back there and I ain't havin' Ellie near that place again."

"I'll ask the CPS to reduce your charges," offered Sutton.

Dennis looked surprised. "Thanks," he said gruffly.

"Mum, there's something I want more than a cat." Ellie put on a little girl, beguiling tone.

"What's that then?"

"I want Dad to come home and live with us again."

"You do, do you? You think we're in some slushy feel-good film?"

"Please Mum," repeated Ellie.

"Please Mum," echoed Zoe, sidling across to join her sister.

"What about the social workers? They're set against your dad."

"Don't worry about that," said Sutton. "Our case against Mike will show how he's been drugging and manipulating Dennis."

Mia thought that, for once, Dennis showed wisdom. He said nothing but looked hopeful. Helen surveyed the three pairs of eyes gazing at her beseechingly. "You look like you're posing for one of those pet adverts: 'Will you give this loser a good home?'"

Dennis ventured to speak, "Please luv, I won't mess up this time."

"Says you." She put Pixie down and held her arms wide for a family hug..

"Quick Mia, take a shot." Sutton indicated her camera and the family.

She obeyed, although it felt intrusive and not what a SOCO camera was intended for.

Dennis said, "I'd like a print of that."

"Sure," said Sutton. "With your permission, I intend to show a copy to your cousin Mike the next time I get him in the interview room."

"If you want to make him suffer, show him this," said Helen. She twined her arms around Dennis' neck and pressed herself against him, kissing hard. Somewhat embarrassed, Mia photographed the scene.

Helen stepped clear. "Tell Mike, while he's in prison, I'll send him a photo like that every month."

Mia turned to Dennis. "When all the legal stuff is sorted will you go back to being a builder?"

"I reckon so. I'll try to salvage the contracts and start again. It's funny, when we was kids in Bridge Road we dug up some old bones. The bloke from the museum said they was hundreds of years old." He gave a wry grin and continued with more wit than Mia had thought him capable of, "I never thought the nastiest skeletons buried there were ours."

"Do you think they'll stay together this time?" asked Mia, as they walked slowly back through reception. Pixie clambered up from her arms to lean his head on her shoulder.

Sutton shrugged. "Who knows? They're survivors."

"I can't believe that kid went through an ordeal like that and bounced back so fast."

"Trauma can be like that. You go along on adrenaline, thinking you're coping fine, and then it hits as soon as you relax."

She wondered whether he knew this from his own experience.

Luke Warden sprinted up, carrying a cardboard box labelled 'Medical Supplies'. "You'd better put that cat in here. You can't walk around a hospital with it on open display. I'll dump the box in my car while you go and tell Chantelle."

She blew him a kiss. "You are a diamond guy."

"I know," he agreed. "Make the most of me. I'm going back to my own team tomorrow. Although I suppose I'll be seeing you over at Headquarters pretty soon, Oliver?"

"Maybe. I'll see you later, Luke. I want to buy you a drink before you leave."

Luke headed off and Mia looked quizzically at Oliver. "Or maybe he won't be seeing you at Headquarters?" she said.

"Maybe not," he agreed. "It's not a good career move to keep chopping and changing."

"And I thought it was because you were getting to like us."

He grinned at her. "That too. At least a few of you. I'd better get back to the Station."

"And I'll tell Chantelle the glad news about her cat."

Mia went straight up to ITU and delivered her message. The joy on Chantelle's face lifted her mood. Some things had survived Mike Plummer's holocaust.

As she left Intensive Care she was surprised to encounter Joy Marshall. "Hello Joy. Were you looking for me?"

"No." Joy shook her head. "When I saw you I thought you must be looking for me."

Mia drew her across to a waiting area. "You phoned. You wanted to speak to me?"

"About the cat bones, but it's too late now."

"I beg your pardon?" Mia wasn't in the mood to apologise for delay in returning the remains of dead cats.

"I didn't want to be a nuisance but Lucy was fretting about them and I wanted to sort it out before she went."

"Went? Went where?" The significance of Joy's presence

260

in ITU hit Mia. "Do you mean…?"

"She died an hour ago. She just seemed to give up. It's strange she was quite lucid towards the end."

"I'm sorry. I wish I'd got back to you before."

"It doesn't matter. I lied to her. I told her the casket I'd brought in to show her was lined with lead and sealed, so she couldn't look inside. I promised to bury them in my garden and honour their memory."

"I'll get the cat bones to you as soon as possible."

"Thank you. I would like to keep that promise."

It occurred to Mia that, while she had Joy here, she could try out Oliver's theory about Mike Plummer orchestrating the discovery of the bones at Bridge Road. "Joy, do you remember two cousins called Mike and Dennis Plummer?"

"Yes, of course, although they were a lot younger than me. My father hated Dennis."

"Why was that?" She prayed Joy wasn't going to turn their case upside down.

"My father called him a lout and I suppose he was, but there was no real harm in him. Big, soft and loud, and much too easily led, that's what Lucy used to say when he did something daft. It was the other one Lucy said was bad."

"Do you remember what Lucy said about him?" Although it would be of no value as evidence, just hearsay from a deranged old woman.

"After her cats died, she kept saying someone had put my dad up to it. It took me a while to work out it was Mike Plummer she meant and that she was scared of him."

"Do you know why?"

"She said he liked to hurt things. He liked to watch things suffer."

"What else did Lucy say about him?"

"When he was five, she'd caught him torturing a tortoise belonging to two old ladies who lived down our road. He hurt it so badly the poor thing died."

Mia felt her skin crawl. "Did Lucy punish him for it?"

"Yes, she smacked him. She said he'd never forgiven her."

And forty years after that childhood smack, Mike had still felt enough malice to set up that bank account to frame Lucy. He'd probably made that secret hiding place for William Davies' documents, maybe even suggested it. All carefully planned. Just as he'd watched, waited and plotted to destroy Dennis. His abyss of jealous rage was so dark and deep.

"Lucy said a child who enjoyed hurting animals would grow up to hurt people," said Joy.

"That's true." Mia wished they'd known the right questions to ask a week ago.

It felt strange to walk out of the hospital alone. She reminded herself there was no need to be afraid. The nightmare was over.

She thought about the resumption of development at Bridge Road and what Dennis had said about finding old scattered bones. The archaeologist in her stirred. She knew that she should never want to go near Bridge Road again but instead she felt possessive. If there was new archaeology underneath the soil it was hers to uncover. She could find out who was taking over the archaeological watching brief and put in a bid for the osteoarchaeology.

The beep of her mobile recalled her from her thoughts. It was Trevor's stand-in. He sounded harassed. "Mia, we're really shorthanded. I know you're still officially on secondment but is there any chance you could cover a scene for me?"

She stiffened, instinctively worried. Fear is a nasty, clinging thing. It doesn't just disappear when danger is past. She was tempted to say she was too tired. And it was true, she was exhausted. But tomorrow it would be even harder to force herself out onto the streets.

"I'll need to pick up my kit and change into uniform."

"That's okay. There's no panic. It's a break in at the

Margrave Shopping Centre. Uniformed are already there."

That meant plenty of people on the Scene. Relief flooded through her. Time to be brave another day. "Okay, I'll cover it."

Look out for other books by the same author

About the Children

Prologue

"People died here. Hundreds of them." The boy's voice holds an exulting note. "The Druids killed them."

He reaches out and strokes the gnarled bark of the ancient oak, once a giant, now cut off at six-foot and pinioned in place to support the Play Area zip wire. "They tortured them first. That man who's written a book about it came into our class and told us."

He finds a roughly carved heart encircling initials. He wishes he had a knife with him. He'd carve out his own message.

"Don't keep talking about death." His brother's voice is shrill. He turns away. "I don't want to think about it."

"You're pathetic." He knows what he wants to write, stabbing through to the tree's core. "It's awesome."

Chapter 1

The two boys lay sprawled and broken, like fledglings that had tumbled from the nest. Tyler looked, and carried on looking until he could process the details of their deaths.

They were young… under twelve years old… both had brown hair and both wore tracksuits. One child had fallen into shallow, muddy water. A knitted hat lay near to his right hand, its red wool mottled with a darker stain. The other boy must have tried to get away, marks of blood trailed for several feet.

Both boys had been shot.

Sheltered by the Scene of Crimes tent, they lay close to the stump of the ancient oak, Stone Park's last link to its dark history.

"Superintendent Tyler?" A slim, fair-haired woman entered the tent. "I'm Gill Martin, your replacement DI."

"Yeah, the ACC told me." He couldn't manage welcoming but he thought he'd hit neutral. It wasn't her fault his regular second-in-command was on sick leave. "This is a nasty one."

"Yes, sir. SOCO's processed this area and the pathologist should be here to move the bodies soon," said DI Martin. Her voice was brisk and Tyler didn't know if she felt more than she was letting show. "It's lucky you got here in time to see them."

He wondered what sort of luck that was, good, bad, or totally lousy. "Yeah."

"Are you okay, sir?" She must have picked up on the sarcasm in his voice.

"Of course." That was a lie. After a gruelling conference in America, his plane had been diverted because of freak weather conditions, tripling the travel time. He'd dropped in at the Station with some paperwork and found himself catapulted into becoming SIO in a child-murder case. "Tell me exactly what we've got."

"Five victims. Three dead; a woman and these children. Two wounded, a man and a young woman. The adults were in the garden, quite a way from the kids. The emergency call was logged in at 13.55. It was anonymous, a male voice said, 'Park… all shot.' We've got the phone. It was lying next to the bodies. It belonged to one of the victims… the dead woman."

"Any connection between the two sets of victims?"

"Not that we've found, sir. The shootings were in two different locations in the park. They've taken the survivors to hospital but we left the dead in place for you to see."

Tyler thought, at some point, his life had taken a wrong turn. Normal people didn't get a mini-massacre as their welcome home package after a conference. "Any witnesses?"

"Only the two wounded and they're not fit to talk. We've secured the park and we're doing house-to-house in the area. We've got armed units available in case more trouble breaks and we've warned the public to stay indoors."

"Right. So are we looking for a gunman who was targeting one of the people in the park or a random killer who ran out of bullets?" Tyler was thinking aloud, not expecting a response.

"I don't know, sir."

"No, of course not." Great! Just what he needed, they'd given him a DI who answered his rhetorical questions. "Have we got the weapon?"

"No sir," her tone was apologetic.

He sighed. "You got any more good news for me?"

"We've got IDs for the adult victims but not these boys yet, sir."

"What do you mean you haven't got IDs? The whole case could rest on what we find out about these children."

"It might not be about the children." Gill Martin sounded defensive.

268

"In murder it's always about the children. Even if they were only in the wrong place at the wrong time. Everyone feels things more intensely when kids are killed." After twenty-five years as a cop he'd seen a lot of evil but the death of children still filled him with outrage. It was an offence against nature. A line of poetry sprang into his mind and, for a ghastly, embarrassed moment, he thought he'd spoken the words out loud.

"All we've got to go on is this small rucksack and a football, sir."

Gill Martin didn't seem to have noticed anything odd, so he hadn't given himself away. Reading fine literature helped him to make some sort of sense of all the ugliness, but it must never intrude into his work. Private life should be kept private. He'd got his camouflage. Down the pub he'd listen to the football talk and maybe throw in the odd comment from the sports news he'd looked up for that purpose.

The contents of the rucksack had been laid out on a plastic sheet. Three cartons of orange juice, three packets of crisps, a tube of cough sweets and a small, spiky, blue, plastic oblong.

"What the hell's that?" said Tyler.

"A sticklebrick, sir… it's a kids' building toy."

He wondered if she'd got children. It could come in handy if she had. One of the strong points of his long-time DI was the knowledge and understanding Roy had earned by being a devoted husband, father and grandfather. Sometimes Tyler wondered what it would have been like to have kids. His ex-wife had loathed the thought of having children. Occasionally he'd regretted that, but he knew he'd have made a lousy father. He'd never let anything get in the way of his career.

"You got kids, Inspector?"

"No, but I was with a friend when she bought some sticklebricks for her grandson."

"I see." Perhaps that was as well. Whatever the politically correct propaganda claimed, it was still tough for a woman to get to the top of the police force when she was juggling job and family. "So we've got two kids who're school age here in the middle of Monday afternoon. What do you think they were they doing? Skiving?"

"Most kids who bunk off school head for the shops or the amusement arcade. Unless they were into drugs, glue sniffing or something."

"Maybe. Until the post-mortem it can't be ruled out. But the cough sweets could mean the kids have been off school with colds. If they were almost better, whoever's looking after them might have booted them out for a while."

"In that case someone will be missing them pretty soon, sir."

"Yeah but we can't wait for that. Get descriptions of the boys taken to all the local schools. Start with the nearest, St Ignatius, the private one just down the road. And, if anyone gets an ID, tell them to check if there are any other kids off school. Especially someone the teachers would expect to be with these two."

"The three drinks and packets of crisps? You think there was a third kid here?"

"What the hell do you think?"

He saw her face tighten into wariness and read her thoughts. She knew she'd screwed up and was waiting for him to give her grief. She should have guessed there were three kids from the moment she'd looked in the bag. There could be a kid out there in desperate need of help. If she'd deployed the search teams with that in mind they might be a lot further on. But what was done couldn't be altered by him yelling at his DI. It would do no good to undermine her confidence and, from what he'd seen, she'd done a reasonable job setting up, not easy when dealing with an unfamiliar team.

"I want this park searched quickly and thoroughly. And I want divers in that lake."

"Yes sir. We've already got people searching but I'll get more onto it, and I've requested divers as soon as possible." She hesitated, then asked, "Do you really think there's another victim?"

"I don't know." To Tyler, at this moment, every scenario seemed more evil than the last. "It's possible there's a child lying bleeding somewhere, unconscious or too scared to call out. But, of course, this third kid, if there is one, may not be a victim."

She stared at him. "You think a child could have done this?"

He shrugged. "In the US they've got kids as young as seven going out with guns to get even with a classmate who's pissed them off." He turned as the pathologist slipped quietly into the tent. "Afternoon Doctor."

"Good afternoon, Superintendent. If Scene of Crimes are ready I'd like to move the children as soon as possible."

"Of course." Tyler moved aside to allow the pathologist and her assistants access to the bodies. "Come on, Inspector, let's get out of here."

As they stepped out of the tent, the light made Tyler wince, although it was a cloudy October day. He wasn't fit to take on a case like this. He should have refused the Assistant Chief Constable's request to 'at least go down and take a look.' He'd taken a look and now he needed to go home.

They stripped off their scene of crimes' protective suits. They'd need to put on fresh suits before they entered the other crime scene to avoid cross-contamination.

"Give me a minute or two will you, Inspector? I've a call to make."

"Of course, sir." Gill Martin withdrew and headed across the park towards the other crime scene, where a second SOCO tent concealed death from public view.

Tyler dragged his mobile phone out of his jacket pocket. The display panel was unresponsive. It seemed the phone had completed the journey back in marginally worse condition than he had. He summoned a nearby constable. "Have you got a phone?"

"Yes sir." The young man handed him a police issue mobile and moved dutifully out of range.

Tyler tapped in the ACC's office number. "Sir, it's Tyler. I'm in Stone Park."

"Yes Kev? How bad is it?"

"Very bad. Someone else should deal with this."

"I'm sorry but I need our best SIO on this one. That's why I sent your team down there straight away."

Tyler felt no gratification at the compliment. Beneath the drag of jet lag he was aware of a deeper weariness, the on-going exhaustion of continually witnessing the results of violence and trying to deal with them.

"Please Kev. Otherwise I'll have to pass the case to DCI Aron. He's a very conscientious officer but…"

Tyler sighed. The ACC did not need to complete the sentence, they both knew Stephen Aron wasn't up to dealing with this.

"All right, sir."

"Thank you. Let me know if there's anything you need and keep me informed of developments."

"Yes sir." Tyler keyed off and handed the phone back to the constable.

"You're welcome to hang onto it if you need it, sir."

"Thanks."

"It was lucky I happened to spot you in the car park, sir."

Tyler wondered why everyone else's definition of luck didn't seem to tally with his own. If this young constable hadn't sprinted after him with the ACC's message, he'd have made it home and into bed, and nothing would have woken him.

The boy looked bloody young and too bloody eager. Saltern boasted as much violent crime as most other large towns in Southern England but Tyler was certain this youngster hadn't yet encountered a murdered child.

"This your first murder case?"

"Yes sir."

"Have you ever seen a dead body?"

"Yes sir, a few." For a moment the boy looked puzzled then comprehension dawned, "But they were accident victims. I guess that's different?"

"Yeah. It shouldn't be but somehow it is. What's your name?"

"Jones, sir. Liam Jones."

Tyler got out his wallet. "Right Jones, there's something I need you to do for me." The only hope he had of staying focused was a large coffee, strong and sweet.

After he'd dispatched PC Jones on his errand, Tyler took a few moments to collate information and study the layout of the park. So far he'd had no time to think things through. From the impatient looks Gill Martin was directing at him, he guessed she was waiting for him to head back to his office. That was the official role of senior cops, but it wasn't his way of doing things.

He noted the structure and position of the Children's Assault Course. On three sides, the playground was bordered by undergrowth and sheltering trees. This side of the park had two exits, one leading through allotments, the other onto a quiet, residential road. Three hundred yards away, over to the west, he could see the grey shimmer of the lake.

This park had been the scene of the first serious assault he'd investigated five years ago, when he'd returned to Saltern as SIO of a new handpicked Serious Crimes Team.

He strode across to the second crime scene, a formal garden bordered by a wide circle of seats. The paving slabs were creamy white, except where they were strewn with autumn leaves. A patch of brighter colour caught his gaze. Someone had lost a scarf. It was delicate, rainbow-beaded and woven in silver thread.

The vivid strands had filled with blood and, as Tyler looked, the outline of the scarf lost definition. Before his tired eyes the sparkling shapes transformed into a grotesque mosaic, the symbol of some primitive sacrifice.

About the Children will be out soon....